The Boy in the Black Suit

ALSO BY JASON REYNOLDS

All American Boys (with Brendan Kiely)

When I Was the Greatest

THE BOY IN THE BLACK SUIT

A
atheneum
A CAITLYN DLOUHY BOOK
NEW YORK LONDON TORONTO
SYDNEY NEW DELHI

JASON REYNOLDS

$\mathcal{A}$
atheneum

An imprint of Simon & Schuster Children's Publishing Division

1230 Avenue of the Americas, New York, New York 10020

ATHENEUM BOOKS FOR YOUNG READERS is a registered trademark of Simon & Schuster, Inc.

Atheneum logo is a trademark of Simon & Schuster, Inc.

For information about special discounts for bulk purchases, please contact Simon & Schuster Special Sales at 1-866-506-1949 or business@simonandschuster.com.

The Simon & Schuster Speakers Bureau can bring authors to your live event. For more information or to book an event, contact the Simon & Schuster Speakers Bureau at 1-866-248-3049 or visit our website at www.simonspeakers.com.

Also available in an Atheneum Books for Young Readers hardcover

The text for this book is set in Adobe Garamond.

Manufactured in the United States of America

First Atheneum Books for Young Readers paperback edition August 2016

10 9 8 7 6 5 4 3 2 1

The Library of Congress has cataloged the hardcover edition as follows:

Reynolds, Jason.

Boy in the black suit / Jason Reynolds. — First edition.

pages   cm

Summary: Soon after his mother's death, Matt takes a job at a funeral home in his tough Brooklyn neighborhood and, while attending and assisting with funerals, begins to accept her death and his responsibilities as a man.

ISBN 978-1-4424-5950-2 (hc)

ISBN 978-1-4424-5951-9 (pbk)

ISBN 978-1-4424-5952-6 (eBook)

[1. Funeral homes—Fiction. 2. Funeral rites and ceremonies—Fiction. 3. Grief—Fiction. 4. African Americans—Fiction. 5. Family life—New York (State)—Brooklyn—Fiction. 6. Brooklyn (New York, N.Y.)—Fiction.] I. Title.

PZ7.R33593Boy 2015

[Fic]—dc23   2014001493

FOR AUNT BUD
AND UNCLE CALVIN

AND FOR
WALTER DEAN MYERS.
THANK YOU, THANK YOU,
THANK YOU

Hey there, you, looking for a brighter season,
   need to lay your burden down.
Hey there, you, drowning in a helpless feeling,
   buried under deeper ground.

—LAURA MVULA, "SING TO THE MOON"

CHAPTER 1
EVERYTHING IS
BACKWARD

IT WAS THE FIRST DAY OF SCHOOL. ACTUALLY, IT WAS THE nineteenth day of school, but it was *my* first day, and all I could think about was how happy I was that I had already missed three weeks, and that this would be the last first day in this place I would ever have. Thank God. Don't get me wrong, I didn't hate school. I just wasn't really in the mood to be lugging books around, or learning stuff that didn't really matter to me, or even worse, being around people that I didn't really matter to. I know, I know— I sound like a prime candidate for black fingernails and emo poetry, but I guess what I'm really trying to say is that I just wasn't feeling too social. Scratch that—I wasn't feeling social at all. Lockers slamming, sneakers screeching and squeaking on the floor as every kind of teenager ran through the hallways laughing and shouting on their way to class—it was all like one big nail on an even bigger chalkboard. Everyone was zipping by, bumping me, as I sort of floated through the halls like some kind of zombie.

It was like I was living in a different world where everything was backward. Ms. Harris, the principal who normally spent most of her time hiding from students in her office, offered to actually *walk* me to my locker. Meanwhile, kids I was cool with—at least I thought I was cool with—like James Skinner, totally ignored me. See what I mean? Backward.

The last time I saw James was during the summer when our whole class had to meet up at the school to have our senior pictures taken. Me and James joked about how much we hated taking photos, and how our crazy moms were obsessed about the whole thing. I told him how my mother begged me to smile, but I knew I wouldn't. I couldn't. Not because I didn't want to, it's just that every time a camera was pointed at me, I never knew what to do with my face. Some people can smile on cue. You say "smile," and they go ear to ear, flashing every tooth in their mouth. And some people . . . can't. I was one of those. So, I knew in my senior pictures I would look just like I did in my junior, sophomore, and freshman pictures—like a robot. Except this time, it would be a robot face in a cap and gown, which is even worse.

The point is, I had just seen my so-called friend James—had just joked about this corny senior picture crap with him—and now he was acting like he didn't even know me. I guess that's what happens when people find out your mom just died. You become invisible. At least I did. To everybody. Well, almost everybody.

"Yo, Matt, I'm so sorry about your moms, man." Chris Hayes,

my best friend, slid up behind me while I tried to stuff myself into my locker. He was one of those guys who was supercool, crazy fly, and girls had a thing for his shaved head. He'd probably be voted "Best Dressed" or something dumb like that, and if he wanted to, he'd have a fair shot at prom king. And to top it all off, he was trying hard to be sympathetic to me, his pretty normal, now really sad homeboy. I appreciated it even though it did no good. But at least he had enough heart to come up to me and say something, instead of just avoiding me, like death was some kind of disease that anyone could catch just by speaking to me. Everybody else was either staring at me or trying way too hard to not look at me at all.

"Y'know . . . Mrs. Miller was like a second mom to me, and I'm so, so sorry I couldn't make the funeral," Chris went on.

Well, I'm sorry you couldn't make it either. I'm sorry I had to sit there in that church—which, by the way, had a broken air conditioner—sweating, watching all those people march down the aisle to look in my mother's casket and whisper to themselves all this mess about how much she looked like herself, even though she didn't. I'm sorry you weren't there to hear the lame choir drag out, song after song. I'm sorry you weren't there to see my dad try his best to be upbeat, cracking bad jokes in his speech, choking on his words. I'm sorry you weren't there to watch me totally lose it and explode into tears. I'm sorry you weren't there for me, but it doesn't matter, because even if you were, you wouldn't be able to feel what I feel. Nobody can. Even the preacher said so.

That's what I *wanted* to say, but I didn't because Chris didn't deserve all that. I knew he would've been there if he could've. But he just couldn't do it. I get that. So I turned around to look at him and said, "It's all good, man." I swallowed hard and reached out for a five, holding back my tears. *Do. not. cry. Not in school.*

Chris grabbed my hand and pulled me close for a man-hug. And right at that moment, with perfect high-school timing, Shawn Bowman ran up behind Chris, slapped him on the ass, and rambled off some dumb joke, calling us gay or whatever. And of course, after Shawn said that, the girl he was with—Michelle something—smacked him on the arm and sucked her teeth. She yanked Shawn close and whispered in his ear, and I could tell she told him my mom had just died because his face went from blue-black to—well, it stayed blue-black, but if he could've turned red he would've been a walking stop sign. Chris had turned around and glared at Shawn. He had his fists balled up and I could tell he was pissed.

"Asshole," Chris growled. Shawn just slinked away, embarrassed, which, judging by Chris's tone, was a good idea.

It was like all of sudden high school became . . . high school. A bunch of immature, irresponsible teens who felt invincible only because they'd never really been through nothing. The ones who had didn't act like everybody else. Like Shante Jansen. When she got pregnant our sophomore year, she changed big-time. That baby grew her up, and certain things about high school suddenly seemed a lot less important. She just wanted to do her work and go home. No time for the extra silliness. That's how I felt. Like all of a sudden I was way too old for high school, even though I really wasn't. Such a strange feeling.

JASON REYNOLDS

Luckily, I didn't have to be in school too long. Because I had done pretty good my freshman, sophomore, and junior years, I had a short schedule and could leave at noon everyday. Of course, I was a little behind, but Ms. Harris had all the teachers create make-up assignments for me so that I could catch up on the work I missed. I wasn't really worried too much though. School was always pretty easy for me. A lot easier than smiling, that's for sure.

The original plan was to go to school from eight forty-five to noon, then work at the bank from one to five thirty, as a part of the work-study program. I wasn't too gassed about working at a bank, just because it seemed like it would be boring as hell, sitting behind that thick glass counting other people's money all day. The paycheck, however, I was definitely excited about. But because I missed the first few weeks of school, I also missed the first few weeks of work, and the bank filled my spot with another student. So I was left without a job and nothing to do after class.

My father and I talked when I got word that my spot was being given away, and he told me not to worry about it, but that I should definitely try to find some work, especially since I was going to have so much time on my hands. When he said that, my mother hadn't passed yet. Now that she had, I *really* wanted to find a job, not just to keep busy, but also to try to help him out with the bills. And even though I considered myself to be pretty smart, I didn't have any work experience, at least not any that was on the books. Sweeping Ms. Jones's steps didn't really count.

So I did what anybody in my position would do. I tried to get a job at a fast-food joint. Cluck Bucket. The grimiest spot in the hood. But they were known for paying pretty good. At least more than most of the other fast-food spots. Everybody said it was because it was owned by some rich dude who felt like the least he could do was pay folks enough to survive, since he was practically killing the whole hood with the food. How could something that tastes so good be so bad for you?

I had eaten there tons of times. My mother would send me out to get chicken baskets on Friday nights. We cooked Monday through Thursday and then took the weekend off. Yes, *we* cooked. I was pretty much my mom's sous chef growing up, which is just a fancy way of saying I was her kitchen assistant. A little slicing, a little dicing. Some stirring, some sprinkling. What I'm getting at is, I'm kind of mean with the pot and pan. That's another reason why Cluck Bucket seemed like an easy choice for me. I can burn, and I like the food. Especially the biscuits. My mom always said they reminded her of real country biscuits. I never had a country biscuit, but Cluck Bucket's were incredible. As a matter of fact, Cluck Bucket's everything was pretty good, all the way down to the sweet tea.

"Can I help whoever's next in line?" the girl behind the register said with about as much enthusiasm as I had for anything right now—none. She wore a net on her head that made her hair look more like some kind of helmet, and a gold necklace was around her neck with a nameplate hanging from it. RENEE, it said in cursive.

I stepped forward, my sneakers making that weird sound you hear when something comes unstuck.

"Welcome to Cluck Bucket, would you like to try a combo, a special, the Cluck Deluxe, a shake, or a delicious treat from our list of desserts?" she rattled off while rolling her eyes and looking away.

"Are y'all hiring?" I asked, sort of quietly. I didn't care if anybody knew I was trying to get a job, but at the same time, I didn't want everybody in my business.

Renee looked at me for a second, sizing me up.

"Hold on," she said, annoyed. She turned around and yelled to the back, but it looked like she was yelling at the chicken stacked up in that big metal bed thing it sits in. "Clara. We hiring?"

Another woman appeared from behind the metal trays. Her shirt was white instead of purple like Renee's. She also had that hair thing around her head, but her hair was in braids and looked like snakes caught in a net.

"You looking for a job?" Clara said roughly.

"Yes."

She reached under the register and pulled out a piece of paper. An application.

"Fill this out over there." She pointed toward the tables closer to the door. "And bring it back up here when you done."

Clara then slapped a pen down on the counter and glared at me. "And don't steal my pen."

I sat down and started filling out the application, trying to block out the stale smell of old grease and the sounds of all the people coming in and out, yelling and cracking jokes, kids skipping school, construction workers on their lunch breaks, junkies begging for biscuits, and just about anybody else you could possibly imagine. The bell on the door kept jingling every time someone opened it, letting in the car horns and police sirens from outside. Noise from every damn where.

"What's good, Ma?" a young guy probably my age said to Renee. "You looking good with that thing on your head," he joked. His boys laughed.

I tried to see her reaction, but I couldn't because he was standing in front of her. But I could hear her.

"Yeah, whatever. What you want, man?"

The guy rocked left to right and adjusted the hat on his head, and his crotch.

"What's good with your number?" he said, slick.

"Nope. But how about some food," Renee said pretty flat. I'm sure she got this kind of crap all the time. Some fool crackin' slick in front of his friends. I always wondered if this kind of game worked. Like, does "What's good with your number" really bag the ladies? Doubt it.

"A'ight, a'ight, a'ight, whatever. Just let me get a Deluxe."

"No Deluxes. All out."

"Damn, a'ight. Well, let me get Five Cluck Strips."

"No strips."

"Come on, really?"

"Really."

"A'ight well, just give me a three-piece meal. I *know* you got chicken." The guy laughed and shook his head, disappointed.

At this point he moved to the side, just enough for me to see Renee. She turned around and looked at all the chicken in the hot bed. There must've been like sixty pieces in there. Then she turned back around to the dude.

"All out."

"What?"

"All out. No more chicken."

"It's chicken right there! What you talkin' about?"

"All out."

The boy stood there stunned.

Renee smirked and lifted her hands to her face, her fingers forming a pretend camera. She acted like she was taking a picture. "Snapshot!" she shouted. Then Renee looked at the make-believe camera as if she was checking the photo—guess it was an invisible digital—and teased, "Yikes, not your best face."

The dude's boys started laughing at him, and before he could say anything back, Renee said, "Next in line, please!"

Then he got all sensitive and cussed Renee up and down, throwing the typical "You ain't even that pretty anyway!" at her, bumping tables and chairs as he walked out. His boys trailed behind him like a litter of puppies. I looked down at my application as they were leaving. Guys like that always try to mess with somebody else to make them feel better, and I just wasn't in the mood.

Everyone else in line laughed, though. Especially when the next guy ordered fifty pieces of chicken and got every piece. Apparently, that's why she really couldn't sell that jerk the chicken. It was already spoken for.

"Thank you so much, love. I already have it squared with Clara," the man who ordered all the chicken said.

"No prob, Mr. Ray."

Mr. Ray? I looked up, and sure enough, it was Mr. Willie Ray standing there while Renee piled fried chicken into cardboard buckets.

Mr. Ray was a tall stick of a man who everyone in the neighborhood knew for two reasons. The first is, he was in the funeral business. A mortician. He owned Ray's Funeral Home after inheriting it from his father. It's weird to say, but most of the teenagers and old folks who've died around here have passed through Willie Ray's door.

The other thing everyone knows him for is, well, cancer. Mr. Ray beat it twice, and the only reason everybody knows that is because after he beat it the second time, he basically became, like, a Jehovah's Witness for cancer, knocking on doors and passing out pamphlets. He swears the only reason God spared his life twice is so that he could spread the word about the illness, as if nobody knew what it was. My mother used to always joke with him and say, "Willie, God saved you just so you could torture the hell outta the rest of us? That don't make no sense." He never got upset with her. He just used to laugh and shake his head while heading on to the next house.

"Mr. Ray?" I called out.

"Matthew, I didn't see you sitting there. How are you?" he said, walking toward me with his familiar limp.

"I'm okay." I stood and shook his hand. "What's with all the chicken?"

"Man, it's a funeral. Well, really it's a repast. They didn't have anyone to cater it, so they paid the funeral home extra for us to take care of the accommodations. So we always just come down here and get the chicken. It's easy and everybody likes it," he explained. "What you up to?"

"Just trying to get a job." I pointed to the application that I had literally only filled out my name on, so far.

"Where, here?"

"Yes sir."

Mr. Ray stood there for a second and gave me a once-over, as if he was upset that I was trying to work in Cluck Bucket. As far as I was concerned, it was an honest gig. I figured it was probably tough at times, but still, honest. Plus, I figured I could maybe learn what the secret to some of that fried deliciousness was so that I could take it back to my own kitchen. Maybe make those biscuits for me and my dad one day.

"Matthew, if you work here, you'll never be able to eat here again," he finally joked.

I didn't really think that was true. I mean, certain things you just never get tired of. Cluck Bucket, for me, was definitely one. That's like saying that if I would've gotten that job working at the bank, I would've eventually gotten sick of money. Yeah, right. Not that Mr. Ray was wrong. I just couldn't see it. But I didn't say nothing. Just shrugged.

"Listen. Your mother was a friend of mine. And your father still is. If you need a job, I'll pay you a couple of bucks to help me out down at the funeral home. I mean, I heard they pay pretty good in this crap shack, but I'm sure I can get close, and you won't have to come home smelling like deep-fried fat every night, or put up with these knuckleheads. What you think?" Mr. Ray inched his jacket sleeve up just enough to see his watch, which he twisted around so that the gold face was on the top of his wrist. "Unless," he said low, his eyes still on the time, "you got a thing for hairnets."

Funny. Real funny.

I thought for a moment. Mr. Ray was definitely a friend of my folks. He was the one who talked to my mother about the chemotherapy, and what that would be like. He said he didn't know much about breast cancer, but he did know that ice cream is the secret to feeling better when the treatment makes you feel sick. As a matter of fact, Mr. Ray was there the day my mom was taken to the hospital, the day she left home for good. He helped my father get her down the steps because she refused to let the EMT guys put her on a stretcher.

"I ain't no princess and I ain't no baby, so I don't need to be carried nowhere," she had snapped as Dad and Mr. Ray held her up by her arms and eased her down the stoop, one painful step at a time.

Dad cracked a joke about her being a queen. "Damn right!" she replied, and Mr. Ray was right there to cosign.

"The queen of your house, this block, Bed-Stuy—hell, Daisy, you the queen of all of Brooklyn!" Mr. Ray joked. "And guess what? Your throne will be right here waiting for you when you come home."

She never came home, but we appreciated Mr. Ray's positivity. He was always that way—a good guy. And even though I trusted him, did I really want to work at the funeral home with him? I mean, it wasn't him I was worried about. It was just the whole death thing, and the fact that I would have to be around sad people all the time. Losing my mom was already damn near too much for me to deal with, so being around a bunch of strangers dealing with the same crap just seemed like hell.

But the way Mr. Ray was talking, hell paid pretty good. And even though I didn't buy the whole "You wont be able to eat here" crap, I didn't want to risk it. But still, I didn't know if I could really do it. A funeral home?

"Thanks Mr. Ray," I said, tapping the ink pen on the application. "But I don't think I can do that. It's just . . . I just . . ." I struggled to explain why, but I could tell by the way he looked at me that I didn't really have to.

"No need to explain, son," he said, putting his hand up. "Trust me, I get it."

I looked down at the application, embarrassed. Even though Mr. Ray said he understood where I was coming from, I still felt a little stupid turning down his offer when the only other option was to work in a grimy chicken spot. But on the other hand, it just didn't seem like a good idea to take a job somewhere where I'd have to relive my mom's funeral everyday. Like being paid to replay the worst day of my life over and over again.

Mr. Ray put his hand on my shoulder. "Just let me know if you change your mind." I didn't look up. I just nodded and started filling out the address line, signing myself up for fry-duty. But it was either that or die-duty. Lose-lose.

As soon as Mr. Ray turned around to walk back toward the counter, the door swung open and a young girl came rushing in, her hand pressed tight to her mouth, her cheeks bulging from her face. And before she could get to the bathroom—hell, before she could even get all the way inside—she spewed red, lumpy slime all over the already sticky floor. It looked like that old-lady pudding. What's it called? Tapioca? Yeah. It was like tapioca. But red. And if there's one thing I just can't deal with, it's puke. Two things, really—tapioca and puke. I just can't. Everything about throw-up is gross. The way it looks, the way it smells, the way it sounds. All of it. Straight-up nasty. So when this girl came in chucking her lunch, I sprung from my chair and damn near jumped on Mr. Ray. I literally almost knocked him over.

"What the—" Mr. Ray whipped around after hearing the belching and hacking sound of spit-up, along with my chair sliding back from the under the table and my footsteps running up on him. "Clara!" he shouted. "Clara! You got a situation out here!"

I stood next to Mr. Ray, but faced the opposite way. I looked straight ahead at Renee and the other customers who were also grossed out, while Mr. Ray focused on the sick kid, who I could hear heaving.

Renee stretched her neck to see what was happening, and once she saw the mess, she just tightened her lips and shook her head. Like this was normal. "Clara, we need a clean-up," she said in a bored voice.

"Clara!" Mr. Ray barked again.

"I'm coming, I'm coming!" Clara yelped. She came through a

door on the side of the kitchen, rolling a yellow mop bucket. A guy followed behind her with what looked like a bag of sand and one of those big orange cones.

"Jesus," Clara said, passing me. I locked my eyes on the chicken. I couldn't stand to see the puke, because if I had seen it, they'd have had to clean up *two* tapiocas. "Put that stuff down and go get her some water," Clara said to the guy with the sand.

The dude ran back toward the kitchen and in a flash came back with a cup of water.

"Sit down," Clara said to the girl.

"I'm sorry. I'm so sorry," the girl cried over and over again, and I could tell she was lifting the cup to her mouth because her voice changed. "I'm so sorry. I just . . . couldn't make it to the bathroom." She sounded embarrassed, and to be honest, I was pretty embarrassed too. I mean, I was already feeling a way when I turned down the job Mr. Ray offered me, but now I was visibly scared of upchuck and I just knew the girl at the register was looking at me act like a pussy. So, yeah—pretty embarrassed.

"Next in line!" Renee called. Turns out she wasn't paying me no mind. She wasn't tripping about anything. For her this was just another day at the job. I didn't know how anyone could still have an appetite, especially since the whole place smelled like old, wet socks now, but people went on ordering.

Mr. Ray faced the front of the restaurant and put his arm around me. "All good, Matthew," he said. "Go ahead and finish up your application. Hell, they should hire you just for having to endure that!" He chuckled to himself and moved toward the register.

"Wait. Mr. Ray." I reached out and grabbed his arm. He turned back toward me. "Will I . . . uh . . . will I have to touch dead people?" Honest question.

He crossed his arms. "Do you want to?"

"No."

"Then, no."

I weighed my options. Funerals suck. The possibility of not being able to eat my favorite fast food, dealing with random crazies who come in and talk trash, and mopping up throw-up really, *really* sucks.

"Okay," I said to Mr. Ray.

"Okay?"

"Okay."

Mr. Ray smiled. "Okay," he said with a nod. "C'mon, you can start right now."

I followed him up to the register. I set Clara's pen on the counter while Mr. Ray reached in his suit jacket and pulled out a few cancer pamphlets and left them in front of Renee's register, like they were some kind of tip or something.

"Give these to your grandma," he said while we gathered up all the buckets of chicken.

"You got it," Renee said nicely as we headed toward the door. I held my breath as me and Mr. Ray tiptoed over the pile of sand that covered whatever was left of the vomit, leaving the application with only my name and half of my address on the table.

✕   ✕   ✕

"So, who's funeral is it up there?" I asked Mr. Ray as we laid the chicken out on platters. The repast (I actually didn't know that's what they're called, but it's the dinner after the funeral—the repast) was happening in the basement of the funeral home, and the actual service was going on upstairs. The only reason I knew that some funerals happen in the funeral home is because we used to always see people standing outside of Ray's dressed in all black, hugging, just like they do at funerals that happen at churches. The good thing about Ray's Funeral Home is, at least the AC worked.

"You know Rhonda Jameson?" Mr. Ray asked.

He placed a breast next to a leg.

"Ms. Jameson died?"

"No. Ms. Jameson is fine. Her father passed last week."

"Oh," I said. "Well, at least she had him for a long time."

"Yeah." Still, he shook his head. "But it never gets any easier."

Mr. Ray put these big, really nice bowls on the table and was scooping out spoonfuls of canned greens. I have to admit, the food area looked pretty good. He had tablecloths down and fake flowers on the tables (I hate real flowers, but I'll get to that), and had me set up the cushioned fold-up chairs instead of the regular, hard-butt ones.

After all the food was out and all the tables were set, there really wasn't much else to do, but I still didn't want to go home yet. At the same time I also hoped Mr. Ray didn't start digging into how I was feeling and all that. I mean, I know people mean well when they ask those kinds of questions, but at the end of the day, they are stupid questions. *How am I feeling? Well, let me think.*

My mother's funeral was a couple days ago, so I damn sure ain't happy.

Lucky for me, Mr. Ray didn't ask anything like that. He actually didn't say nothing about my mother at all. Instead he started talking about what he was like when he was my age.

"Man," Mr. Ray said with a sigh, "you better than I was. You responsible, y'know?" He leaned against the wall and crossed his ankles.

"I guess," I said, unsure of where this conversation was going.

"I mean, I wasn't thinking about no job or nothing like that. I was thinking about one thing only—skirts."

"You were thinking about wearing skirts?" I asked, shocked.

"No, man! I didn't mean"—his raspy voice sounded even more scratchy when he got excited—"I mean girls, man. Skirts. We were thinking about girls. Like your buddy, Chris."

Mr. Ray seemed disappointed that I didn't pick up on his old-school slang.

"Oh." I smirked. Chris *definitely* thought about girls. "Well, I think about them too. A lot. I just also think about other stuff, I guess." I didn't really see the big deal in that. Girls are great. But so is graduating from high school and leaving it behind. Forever. Seemed pretty basic to me.

"And that's why you're different. Man, me and my brother Robbie done wrecked many a car, taking our eyes off the road to check out some lady's hind-parts."

Hind-parts? I snickered and Mr. Ray started laughing too. He probably thought I was laughing at him and his brother, but what it really was, was the word *hind-parts*. Such an old-people word.

The whole time we talked I could hear the people upstairs moving around. I couldn't make out voices, but every footstep came through. I wondered what the people at Mr. Jameson's funeral were doing. If they were laughing or crying, or both. If someone was whispering stupid comments to the person next to them about how good Mr. Jameson looked dead. If Ms. Jameson was exploding. Like I did.

"Mr. Ray, can I ask you something?"

"Of course." I could tell he thought I was going to ask him something about girls by the way he crossed his legs the other way.

But I didn't.

"Can I go up there?"

"Where?" he asked, confused.

I pointed up. "Up there? To the funeral. Just for a second."

"Why?" He cocked his head slightly to the side.

I just shrugged. I couldn't tell him why because I'm not sure I really knew why at the time. I just all of a sudden wanted to. I *needed* to.

Mr. Ray looked at me for a few seconds, hard. Then he sucked his teeth. "Come here, Matthew," he said, taking off his suit jacket. "If you gonna go up there, be respectful." He held the coat open so I could slip my arms in. "And sit in the back."

THE FUNERAL OF CLARK "SPEED-O" JAMESON

Upstairs, the funeral home was pretty much the same as downstairs, except much darker and no tables. Just rows of padded fold-ups and a wooden podium in the front. The lights were dimmed, which was very different from the bright lights in the church at my mother's funeral. The darkness definitely made it seem more serious. Plus it hid you better in case you exploded.

Robbie Ray, Mr. Ray's younger brother, was the MC for the funeral, kind of like how the preacher is when you have one at a church. But Robbie Ray wasn't no preacher. As a matter of fact, he was pretty much still the same man who was crashing cars looking at "hind-parts" when he was younger, except now he was older. But he still looked young. Way younger than Mr. Ray. And he was always dressed like he was looking for a date. Tight suits with his shirt always unbuttoned down to the middle of his chest like we live on some island or something. He always wore gold watches, gold chains, had a gold slug in the front of his mouth, and wore a gold nugget ring on his pinky. My mother used to always clown him, saying he was stuck somewhere between 1970 and outer space.

"And now we're going to have a few words from some of Mr. Jameson's friends," Robbie said, his voice deep like a late-night radio show host's. Sometimes I thought he was making it that way on purpose, just to go with his whole style. But I could never tell for sure.

He moved his finger over the program to make sure he called the right name. "Mr. McCray?"

I slipped into a seat in the back like Mr. Ray told me. I felt a little silly, not because I was at a random funeral, but because my arms looked like tentacles in Mr. Ray's huge suit jacket. It fit me okay in the shoulders because Mr. Ray was skinny, but the sleeves were way too long. I kept pulling them up to my wrist, and tried to keep my fingers spread out so they wouldn't slide back down.

Next to me was an old lady dressed in a purple skirt and a black and purple polka-dot shirt. *Who said you had to wear all black to a funeral*, I thought as I looked down at my blue jeans and green and brown Nikes. I glanced over at her and nodded. She gave me an awkward look. At first I thought maybe she knew I didn't belong there. But then she kept wiggling her nose like she was going to sneeze, so I figured it was all the cologne coming from Mr. Ray's suit coat. I don't know what it is about old men and cologne. My mother used to say that when men get old they think anything that smells bad can kill germs better than soap and hot water, so they either bathe in liquor or cologne. I wanted to lean over to that old lady and tell her that I was sorry for the stench and that I hoped it didn't cause her more grief than she was already feeling. But I didn't. I just made whatever face I thought looked like it was saying I was sorry, and nodded my head to her.

"Afternoon, afternoon," a mumble came over the speakers. "I'm A. J. *McCrary*. Not McCray. *McCrary*." The old, bent-over man peered at Robbie Ray for messing up his name.

"Anyway, y'all know how Clark got the name Speed-O?" A. J. McCrary leaned on the podium and spoke into the mic. His face looked like leather, and his eyes were big and glassy. He only had white hair on the sides of his head, almost like he was wearing ear muffs made of pure cotton.

"Y'all wanna know?" he asked again, his voice pitchy and weird like all the teeth in his mouth were loose.

Some people in the crowd grunted, a few others shouted, "Tell it!"

"Oh, I'm a tell it," he said, adjusting the microphone.

"One time, a long time ago when we was kids, there used to be this old doughnut shop over on DeKalb all the cops used to hang at. So we outside of there, and Clark starts talking to me about the pig this and the pig that, and that he been reading black newspapers and checkin' what Malcolm X been saying up in Harlem. This was the sixties, so you know how it was. 'Fros, people changing their names and all that."

The older people in the crowd nodded their heads in agreement. I glanced over at the lady next to me and imagined her with an afro. Yikes.

"So Clark kicking all this revolution stuff, and I told him, 'Man you ain't 'bout nothin'. You just yappin' your trap. But you ain't gonna do a"—the old man caught himself about to cuss—"a daggone thing."

People started giggling.

"He said, 'Oh, yeah? Watch this.' Next thing I know this fool come running out the doughnut shop with one doughnut in his hand and one in his mouth, and a young white cop running behind him hollerin' 'bout his doughnut gettin' stolen. Can you imagine that? A cop yellin' out, 'Thief, thief!'"

Everybody started laughing at this crazy story. Even me.

"I didn't see him for a few days after that," Mr. McCrary continued, "but when I did, he told me he never got caught! And to prove it, he told me he had the other doughnut in his house for me. He said Brother Malcolm talked about whatever you do for yo'self, you do for your brother. So the other doughnut was mine. I couldn't believe it—one, because that's crazy; two, because he risked his life over some doughnuts; and three, because he actually outran the police! You know how fast you gotta be to get away from the cops . . . on foot? Pretty damn"—he caught himself again—"daggone fast! So I started calling him Speed-O, and it stuck."

He laughed and began coughing harshly into the mic, digging into his back pocket for a handkerchief to spit in. Robbie Ray reached out for him to help him to his seat, though Mr. McCrary didn't look like he was quite ready to sit down. But realizing that his time was up, he looked back into the crowd and pressed his lips to the mic as if he was kissing it.

"We'll miss him, and many blessings to his family. Thank you," he added quickly, his voice now way too loud, popping through the speakers.

Everybody shook their heads, confirming that Mr. Jameson was that kind of guy.

Robbie Ray came bopping back up to the mic to introduce the next speaker. I kept feeling something sticking me in my chest, so I reached my hand into the jacket to see what kept poking me. Of course, not thinking, I pulled out what had to be at least ten cancer pamphlets. For a moment I forgot whose jacket I had on. The lady next to me shot her eyes over at me. I just made the weird robot face I make when I'm taking pictures—big eyes, tight lips— and tried to stuff the pamphlets back in the pocket as quickly as possible. Especially since I didn't know what Mr. Jameson died of. Might've been cancer. That would've been awkward.

"Mr. Wallace," Robbie said next in his weird, fake sexy voice.

A giant rose from the second row. Seriously, the biggest man I've ever seen in real life. His head was the size of a basketball, and his back was like a king-size mattress. Except made of bricks.

"Good afternoon," the giant said.

I tried not to laugh, but I couldn't believe what I was hearing. This humongous monster of a man had the voice of a six-year-old. High, squeaky. Like, cute. I could hear that weird sound when you try to hold in a laugh, but a little bit leaks out—like a mouth fart—happening all over the church. People were trying not to crack up, but his voice made it *so* hard.

"Um, my name is Mouse," he said, leaning down to get to the microphone. His hands, the size of oven mittens, were gripping the sides of the wooden podium. He could've ripped it apart like nothing if he wanted to.

"And Speed-O trained me when I first got the job with the trucking company. We worked together for a long time. Had a lot of fun. A lot of laughs." Mouse smiled, flashing a big gap in his two front teeth, as if he was suddenly reminiscing in his mind about some of those moments.

"Anybody who knew Speed-O knows he loved to tell stories, and the crazy thing was, you never knew if the stories were true or not. You knew he wasn't no liar, at least he ain't seem like one. But some of the stories were just so ridiculous." Mouse laughed a silly laugh. It sounded like a never-ending hiccup.

"Like this one time, we riding through Arizona on a five-day delivery. I think it was August—the heat was kicking something terrible. Brooklyn summer ain't got nothing on Arizona." He pretended to wipe sweat from his face. "So we pull up to this gas station, some random spot off the map. And Speed-O get to talking about how the last time he had been down in Arizona he stopped at that exact same gas station, and that it was so hot last time that he seen a horse leaning up against the ice chest—you know those old ice chests that sit outside of some stores? One of them. He said the horse was leaning with all four of his legs crossed at the ankle and was panting like a dog. All four legs! Then he said that somebody slipped a cigarette in the horse's mouth to smoke because the dang horse looked so stressed out by the heat."

The room broke out in laughter.

"Shoot, so I asked him," Mouse continued. "I said, 'Speed-O, you sure the heat just wasn't getting to you, and you was seeing things?' You know what he said? He said, 'Nope. I know it was real, because I was the one who lit the horse's cigarette!'"

The room erupted again. People squealed, rocking back and forth, wiping tears from their eyes. I mean, not only was the story hilarious, but the fact that the huge guy telling it sounded like a little kid made it even better. I looked over at the old lady next to me and she was chuckling. She glanced at me and saw that I was laughing too, and nodded. Everyone was nudging each other and I could tell that some of the other folks in the room had heard that story before. And in a weird way, I kind of felt like I knew Mr. Jameson, at least for that moment.

"He was so serious. He never ever said he was kidding or even cracked a smile. He just told the story while lighting a smoke and unwrapping a honey bun, which was his favorite road snack. He was a good friend. I'm gonna miss him a lot, but I'm glad I got to know him."

Mouse maneuvered his way back to his seat, bumping just about everything and everyone. While most people were still laughing, Ms. Jameson stepped up to the mic.

"My name is Rhonda Jameson." She stood there a moment and waited for the crowd to quiet down. "Clark, or Speed-O as most of you knew him, was—is my father."

Ms. Jameson looked tired, but was still upbeat. It definitely seemed to be a pretty cool funeral from what I could tell. Nothing like my mom's.

"I just want to say thank you to everyone for coming out. My father would be so thrilled to know that you came to say your final good-byes." And just like that, her eyes started to swell and fill with tears.

"I'm not gonna cry," she whispered to herself, taking deep breaths. "He would've wanted you to know that he did everything his way. He was honest, his way." Everyone laughed lowly as Ms. Jameson shot a wink to Mouse, who flashed his gappy grin. "He was loyal, his way." Now she nodded to Mr. McCrary.

"But most importantly, he loved, his way," she said, her face starting to melt as the water rose up in her eyes. "He loved . . . ," she started, but couldn't get it out. The breakdown was coming, and there was no stopping it.

I sat in my seat, suddenly anxious. My stomach started to feel weird, and strangely I felt a little desperate to see what was going to happen next. Would she cry? Would she run out? Would she pass out? It wasn't like I was going to be happy to see Ms. Jameson, a lady I had known most of my life from the neighborhood, sad. But I wanted to see if I could tell if she was feeling what I had been feeling.

"He loved . . ." Her voice fluttered. "I'm sorry. I just . . . I just . . ." She turned away from the mic and looked to her left as if she was looking for someone to help her, but no one was there. She started shaking and biting her bottom lip hard enough to draw blood. A few people in the crowd shouted, "It's okay!" But it really wasn't. I knew that and she knew that, more than anyone else in the room. Robbie Ray came over to help her, and he held her close while she stumbled and wept through the rest of her speech. After that—and this may sound weird—I felt satisfied.

I didn't stay for the repast, which would pretty much become tradition. Funerals only. Nothing else. I gave Mr. Ray back his funky coat, and told him that I needed to head home.

"Homework?" he asked, like an old man.

"Yeah, unfortunately," I lied. I didn't have any homework. I just didn't want to be around when people started introducing themselves and talking about how they knew Mr. Jameson. It would've been pretty awkward if his loved ones found out that I actually never met the guy. That we never shared a joke or advice or nothing like that. That I was just kind of hanging out watching the funeral like it was a pickup game at the park, or some kind of reality TV show. *Crashing Caskets*.

"Yeah, you a different one, a'ight. Nothing like how me and Robbie was," Mr. Ray said again, slipping his arm back into his suit jacket. "You go 'head on. We'll meet back here tomorrow after school is through."

I nodded. "I'll be here."

CHAPTER 2
HEAD TO FOOT

IT'S SO WEIRD HOW A PERSON CAN BE A NORMAL PART OF your everyday life, and then just disappear. And when they do, you realize that some of those everyday things go with them. Like the smell of food cooking. Or the sound of Rick James, Frankie Beverly, or the Isley Brothers playing as background music in our house. The kettle, whistling. Water running in the kitchen sink. She was always at the kitchen sink, my mom, doing a two-step or something. Her voice, and her voices.

My mother had a thing for accents. She learned a bunch when she was in acting school way before I was born, which is how she met my father. Well, sort of. She moved to Harlem from South Carolina to be an actress, and he moved up here from Baltimore to do the same thing. Only difference is, she went to acting school, and he "went with his gut," as he puts it. While they both waited for their big breaks, they worked in a soul food restaurant. Dad was a dishwasher, and Mom was a waitress, where she tried out her crazy accents on random customers. She said it was always funny when people would get confused, hearing a little country mixed in with Russian (especially coming from a black girl). The French one was my favorite—it was the one she did the most. *Oui, oui,* never again. Only *au revoir.*

Now the house was totally silent. And it had no smell. It was empty, and for the first time it actually felt that way. Stale. Old, but I guess new at the same time. My first thought as I walked in was to call out for her like I normally did when I got home. But I caught myself. Instead I just sat at the kitchen table and looked around at all the things that I was used to, that now suddenly seemed so strange.

The sink. There were no dishes in it. No pots, no pans. The clock radio flashed 4:04 p.m. in green digital numbers. A photo was taped to the wall just above the faucet of my mother and father when they were much younger, holding my hand on the boardwalk at Coney Island. They looked happy. I looked miserable. I don't even remember taking that picture. It was my first trip to the beach. My mother always teased me about how I didn't understand what sand was, and how I was afraid to let it touch my feet. So I cried most of the trip. The photo had started to change colors, especially at the corners, which were fading into a weird brown, probably because of all the steam coming from the sink over the years. I never really cared too much about that picture, but all of a sudden it seemed special. Us as a family.

I glanced at the old cooking notebook my mom made for me sandwiched between the can of sugar and the can of flour on the counter. It was where my mother wrote easy recipes for me to make. It was like her way of passing the cooking torch so that I could do my thing in the kitchen without having to open up one of those lame, thick, usually way too girly cookbooks. I grabbed it and sat back at the kitchen table. Written on the blue, nasty-stained cover was THE SECRET TO GETTING GIRLS, FOR MATTY, in my mother's loopy cursive. That was our joke, that cooking is what girls really like. Her telling me that definitely made me feel better about being a dude and knowing what a whisk and a colander are. That's for damn sure.

I had tried to open it a few days before, but couldn't do it. Figured I'd give it another shot. I cracked it open, smack dab in the middle.

THE OMG OMELETTE FOR MATTY (THANKS FOR TEACHING ME "OMG")

Closed it. Immediately. Even though I was starving and that omelette—the OMG Omelette—would've hit the spot, I couldn't do it. Her writing, I could hear her voice . . . *NO!*

I slid the notebook to the other side of the table like it was possessed, leaned back in my chair, and yanked the refrigerator door open. Bread. Butter. Half carton of eggs. Milk. Half an onion turning brown. Two Chinese food cartons, one with bits of fried rice stuck to the sides, a white plastic fork sprouting from the top, and the other with some sort of sauce caked around the rim. That's pretty much what me and Dad had been eating. Takeout.

Obviously. Seeing as though I couldn't even keep the notebook open for ten damn seconds.

I grabbed the Styrofoam container with the sauce. Shrimp and Broccoli. I sniffed it. *Ugh!* Chinese leftovers were *not* on the menu for tonight's dinner. Not unless I wanted the next funeral I went to to be my own.

Still, instead of just whipping up something quick (we always at least had pasta in the house, and I didn't need to check the notebook to boil water), off to the bodega I went with two dollars crumpled in my pocket. I figured I could talk Jimmy into letting me walk with a sandwich, and getting the extra dollar to him later. Jimmy was the guy who owned the bodega. He was probably in his forties and was from Pakistan, even though everyone in the hood thought it was funny to just say he was from Iraq. The only reason I knew he was from Pakistan is because I asked. My mother made me. "Don't be ignorant," she used to say. I also know his real name is not Jimmy, but Ahmed, which he also told me. He's a good guy, but he's crazy. One time some dude came in there and tried to steal. Jimmy pulled the biggest knife I ever seen—I mean, like a machete—from behind the register and started banging the blade on the counter. He started screaming something about this being his neighborhood too. Everybody in there was scared. The guy who was trying to steal just put the chips back and apologized. Jimmy told everybody in the store that day to never, ever try to steal from him and that if you're short, just say you're short, and he'll try to work with you. He then said that if he catches anyone stealing, he'll leave their fingers on the bodega floor for the cat to nibble on. Gross. But nobody tries to take anything anymore so I guess he proved his point.

I stepped into the store and was greeted by the rank smell of cat litter and cooked cold-cut meat.

"A little bit of mayo. Just a little bit," a young guy said to Mike the sandwich maker, whose name also wasn't Mike, but Tahir. "Y'all be gettin' mad heavy-handed on the mayo. And put sweet peppers on there for me, my dude."

Jimmy sat behind the counter, divvying out loosie cigarettes, matchbooks, blunt cigars, lotto tickets, and dime candy.

"Matty, what's good, baby?" he said in his weird, mixed-up, Arabic–New York accent.

"I'm good," I said, walking up to the counter.

Jimmy leaned over a little. "Yo, I heard about Mrs. Miller. Sorry 'bout that, fam. How y'all holdin' up?" he whispered, trying to be respectful.

"We good," I said, short, and looked away. I just didn't really want to go into all that standing in the middle of the bodega. I didn't even know how he knew. I take that back; yes I did. People come in the bodega running their mouths all the time. It was the only place outside of church you could find out anything and everything about the hood, even though most of it was made up. I kind of wanted to know what he had heard. Like, what were people saying she died from? Knowing this neighborhood, people were probably saying it was a drug overdose, because that's always what people say. "Yeah, she used to get high. That's why she was always so funny," they were probably saying. So I didn't even bother to ask. Didn't matter what they thought.

I slid my wrinkled dollars up on the counter almost as if it were a secret note I was passing in class.

"What you need, man?" Jimmy asked, adjusting his Nets cap.

"I need a sandwich. I'm short a single, but I'll get it to you tomorrow," I said softly.

Without even thinking about it, Jimmy took the two bucks and threw them in the register. And then he yelled something in Arabic to Mike, who stood behind the meat cutter holding a turkey breast in his arms like a football. Mike said something back. It all sounded like a whole bunch of throat clearing, but I was used to it.

"Matty, you know you family, and I know you or your pops is good for it. Matter fact, take two. One for Mr. Miller." Jimmy smiled and held out his fist for a pound.

I walked over to Mike. He just nodded, which was his way of saying, *Can I take your order?*

"Let me get honey-glazed on a roll. Lettuce, tomato, mayo, provolone, sweet peppers, oil and vinegar, black pepper, meat and cheese, hot," I rattled off like naming brothers and sisters I don't have. I've been ordering the same sandwich since I was a kid. It's the way my dad orders. "Two of those, please."

"Three," a voice came from behind me. "Make that three of those, Mike. Cheddar though, not provolone. Don't nobody want all that fancy cheese."

Mike shook his head and smirked.

I turned around, already knowing who I'd see.

"Wassup, Chris."

"What's good, Matt." We slapped hands. "What's goin' on?"

I've known Chris pretty much my whole life. He lived in the apartment building at the end of the block, and let me tell you, living in a brownstone and living in an apartment building are very different. In a brownstone you either own the whole house like us, or the floors are split between two other families—three, max. But in an apartment building, it's like twenty families. Sometimes more. So it's always a bunch of mess going on. That's how it was in Chris's building. A bunch of mess. Everybody around here called it the crazy building. There's always a gang of dudes posted up outside all night, talking trash, and pushing packs of whatever to whoever. Nobody even parks their car in front of that building, scared that when they come to get in it in the morning, it'll be sitting on blocks. And that was probably the truth.

"Chillin'," I said. "Just grabbing dinner."

Mike gave Jimmy my sandwiches, and Jimmy, like always, licked his finger and pulled a paper bag from underneath the counter. He took the bag and flung it in the air, almost as if he was swatting at a fly, just to open the bag up. Of course he could've just slipped his finger in the bag and opened it that way, but Jimmy likes to be cool. The popping sound the bag made made Chris jump a little.

"Yo, Matt, wait for me," Chris said, putting a soda on the counter and slapping a five-dollar bill down. "I'll walk with you."

My house came way before his, so we stopped and sat on the stoop for a little while. I won't lie, it was cool to have someone around. It had been a minute since I had hung out with anyone—since when my mother transferred to the hospice wing of the hospital. Me and Dad spent most of our time with her, opening the get-well-soon cards and propping them up on the side table by her bed. Dad would always ask if she wanted him to read them to her, but she always said no. Of course he read them out loud anyway. I think he just wanted to believe she would actually get well. Besides the cards, there was a ton of flowers and balloons that came in everyday, from neighbors and friends. Mom hated the balloons. She said they freaked her out at night.

"Sometimes I wake up with one of these stupid balloons bopping me in the face, and be ready to crap myself in here," she said, snorting a little from her own joke.

I, on the other hand, hated the flowers. I mean, they're just stupid. What's the point of getting somebody you care for something they can't do anything with but look at for a few days until it dies. Just seems cruel. But my mom, she loved them. The day she passed, she gave away all the flowers to the nurses, except one bouquet. She said something about them taking up too much space, and that she wanted to give them all a gift for putting up with her anyway, which I'm sure they all deserved, because Daisy Miller was definitely a trip. She told me and Dad to take the last bunch, as well as all the cards. I tried to tell her that we didn't need them and that she should keep them for herself, but Dad gave me that look that means, *Just shut up and listen.* So I gathered all the cards and notes, and Dad took the flowers. We both thought it was strange. Not her wanting to get rid of the cards—she couldn't care less about them—but definitely her giving away the flowers, or as she called them, her "lovelies." But we didn't question it. We just did what she asked us to do, and ultimately found out the reason why later that night.

My father got the call around four in the morning. I wasn't asleep, and neither was he. He'd been down in the kitchen, pouring shot after shot of cognac since around midnight. He'd pulled the bottle out of the cabinet and set it on the table when we first got home, but he didn't drink any. Even though my mother would have a drink every now and then, I had never seen my pops take even a sip. But I could tell he was thinking about it. And I couldn't blame him. He just flipped from card to card, reading the get-well messages out loud to me like bedtime stories. At one point I thought he was going to offer me a drink, y'know, as some kind of father-son bonding thing, but he didn't. He just let the bottle sit there like it was a third person in the room. I stared at the flowers and thought about just trashing them since they'd be dead by the morning anyway. Pointless.

I knew Dad would be upset about it, but I just couldn't keep my mouth shut. "We really keeping these?" I asked, snatching a petal off. Dad kept reading through the cards. "Dad? We might as well just get rid of them. It's not like Mom's gonna care. Shoot, they're gonna die anyway."

He paused for a second. Then, like I hadn't said a word, he continued with the corny poems with lines like "back on your feet" and "love is the best medicine."

I left the flowers alone.

Eventually, I dozed off at the table and woke up again and he was *still* reading. I got up and headed to bed, kissing him on his head. When I got halfway up the steps, I finally heard the liquor pouring. Then my father hissing as he swallowed the first shot. Then, pouring again.

Hours later, when the phone rang, I didn't hear anything my dad said. But as soon as I'd heard it ring, I knew. A few minutes after the call I heard him slowly coming up the steps. Then, there was a knock at my door.

"Come in," I mumbled.

When he opened it, I was already dressed. And from what I could tell, we were both already numb.

"So what's been going on?" Chris asked about a millisecond before stuffing almost half of his sandwich in his mouth. Strings of shredded lettuce hung from his lips; he pushed the stragglers in with his thumb.

"Not much, man, just came from work."

"Work? You working? Where?" Chris sounded surprised.

"Took a gig after school at Ray's, just helping out with little stuff, y'know? For work study, and for some extra cash for the house and stuff," I explained. "Can't put it all on Dad," I added, still unwrapping my sandwich.

"Ray's, like the funeral place?"

"Yeah."

"Huh," Chris said, while cramming the other half of the

sandwich into his face. Watching him eat, all I could think about is how my mother would always get on him about inhaling his food like this. "It ain't gonna run away from you, Christopher," she'd tease while plucking the back of his head. I thought about plucking him myself.

"You gotta touch dead people?" he said. I could tell this was something he really wanted to know, but after he said it, he instantly got weird because he'd said "dead people," and now my mom was one. But it didn't bother me. "I mean, I mean," he fumbled, "you have to, uh, uh . . ." It was like he was choking on air.

"Yep. Gotta touch dead people," I said, putting my hand on his shoulder and squeezing a little.

"Come on, man!" he shouted, bits of food flying from his mouth.

I laughed. "I'm just playing, man. I ain't touch no dead people, and Mr. Ray told me I don't have to. I just help out with setting up chairs and stuff like that."

"Oh." He balled up his sandwich paper and shot it like a basketball at the trash cans sitting in front of my house. Way off.

I could tell he was itching to get his hands on my sandwich paper to try again, but I took my time eating mine. I told him how I felt about school now, and how everybody had been treating me weird—James Skinner, and even some of the teachers. He explained that a lot of people wanted to say something to me, or act like everything was cool, but they were scared because they didn't want to make me upset. Everybody thought they were going to say the wrong thing. I told him that I was fine, even though I really wasn't. And I told him that out of everybody, I needed him to hold me down and treat me normal just because we had so much history.

"Treat you normal?" he asked, just to make sure he heard me correctly.

"Yep."

"Like usual?"

"Yep. Like usual."

"Oh, okay." He smiled in a sneaky way, flashing his crooked bottom row. "If that's the case, then who that other sandwich for?" he said, eyeballing the paper bag. "Matter fact, how 'bout you whip up some of that Matt Miller magic sauce to go with it. What's the special ingredient again?"

"Garlic powder."

The sauce Chris was talking about was something my mother taught me to make a long time ago. It was in the notebook but it didn't really have a cool title. She said I had to name it myself, so in the book it just says BLANK SAUCE. It's a sauce that pretty much goes with everything. Burgers, chicken, and even bodega sandwiches. It's just ketchup, mustard, honey, brown sugar, and garlic powder, which really kicks up the flavor of anything you're making in the kitchen. I was going to try to get Cluck Bucket to pick it up if I would've taken a job there. Maybe give it some kind of catchy, corny name like All Sauce. That could work.

"Yeah, garlic powder." Chris nodded, anticipating my answer.

"No."

"Come on, man. I thought you said we were going to be normal?"

"We are, but I ain't in the mood to cook nothing."

"Ain't nobody ask you to cook. Just make sauce!" Chris pressed. Then, realizing that I was annoyed, he chilled out. "Okay, okay. Squash the sauce. Just let me have the sandwich."

I laughed and shoved Chris in the shoulder. I guess it *would* be normal for him to eat his food and mine. The boy was a machine when it came to food.

"No! It's for my dad, man."

"Man, he don't want it," Chris argued.

I laughed again, thinking at first this was more trying-to-get-the-sandwich business. But something in his voice caught my attention.

"Because I just seen your father right before I stopped in the bodega. He's over on Albany, standing outside the liquor store with that fool Cork."

Cork was the youngest Ray brother. He was the brother who they let help out whenever he was around, which was almost never, mainly because he was always staggering up and down the street with a wet spot in the front of his pants. To say it plainly, dude was a straight-up drunk. I don't know what his real name is, but everybody calls him Cork because he drinks a whole lot of wine, and because his face looks like a cork with all the holes in it, which my mother said comes from too much liquor. I knew that if my father was hanging out with him, nothing good was happening.

"Well, I'm still gonna save it for him," I said, now a little mad.

We sat for a while longer watching ladies push carts filled with groceries and laundry, and kids bopping down the sidewalk talking loud, kicking whatever wasn't nailed down, until suddenly the streetlights started to buzz and flicker.

"Man, I'm gonna go 'head home," Chris said. "You know I don't play with the night."

Chris almost never stayed out past dark. Even though he was old enough to hang out later, he still went in when the streetlights came on, just like when we were kids. Not because he had to, but because when it got dark, the stoop in front of his building became a base for those dudes I talked about before, who loved to give anyone and everyone a hard time. Just like those losers in Cluck Bucket—looking for a target, somebody to mess with.

There was this time when me and Chris were like seven, and my folks were trying to have some alone time for Valentine's Day. Chris's mother said she'd babysit me. My dad walked me down there, and when we got to the building, all the guys stood out front, purposely blocking the door.

"Excuse me," my father said to the one standing directly in the way.

No response. Just flat out ignored him.

"Excuse me!" This time my father said it louder and got real close to the guy—the dude was just a teenager, but when you're seven, teens seem way older and much bigger. The kid had no choice but to move or my father was going to, as he put it, "bring Baltimore out on his ass."

Though everyone was always afraid of what was happening outside of Chris's building, that night me and Chris learned that maybe we oughta be scared of what goes on *inside*, too. That was also the night, by the way, that Chris and I went from good friends to best friends. Here's what happened. Chris and I were lying in the bed laughing like crazy. We were lying head to foot, like we always did, but that night Chris's feet smelled like he'd been soaking them in toilet water. They were so bad we couldn't stop laughing about it, fake gagging and pretending we were going to puke up his mom's way-too-tomatoey spaghetti. (Now that I think about it, it just needed some garlic powder.)

Despite covering my face to protect it from Chris's toxic toes, and laughing like a maniac, I heard something—a bunch of noise suddenly coming from outside. But not outside the building, just outside Chris's apartment door. In the hallway. A couple was arguing. The man was doing most of the yelling, even though we couldn't really make out anything he was saying.

Chris and I stopped joking and lay still, listening through the walls. I really wanted to get up and peek out the front door to see if I could hear better or even see something. I don't know why. I guess I was just nosy, especially since this kind of drama never really went on in my house, where nobody lived but me and my parents. But in Chris's building there were tons of families, and most he didn't even know. He knew the lady across the hall, Ms. Rogers; the old man next door, on the left, with the barking dog and the weed habit, Mr. Staton; and the girl on the right, Nicole, who at the time was probably twenty-two or twenty-three, and was me and Chris's first fake wife. But those are the only people he really knew, for the most part, in the whole building.

The shouting went on, and I couldn't stop myself. I sat up.

"What you doin'?" Chris whispered.

"Goin' to see what's happening."

Chris's eyes went wide. "Are you crazy? My mother will kill us. You know her rules."

I did know the rules. Ms. Hayes ran them down to me every time I came over.

> <u>Rule 1</u>: All empty food containers, like Chinese food, or even empty McDonald's bags, have to be put either in the microwave or in the refrigerator until we take the trash out in the morning. Do NOT put it in the trash, because even if it's just crumbs left, mice will get in there.

> <u>Rule 2</u>: We can't both wash up at night. One of us has to wash up at night, and one of us has to wash up in the morning, to make sure she gets to have some hot water too. I didn't really understand this one, but I guess there was only enough hot water for two people in the apartment, not three. Chris and I would do rock-paper-scissors to see who got to wash up at night. He was easy to beat because he was one of those people who always picked rock. But I should've let him win that night, so his feet wouldn't have smelled so bad.

<u>And Rule 3</u>: If you hear any noises outside of the apartment, whether in the hallway or on the street, do NOT try to see what it is. Just pretend like you don't hear anything.

"Come on, man. She 'sleep," I now said. "We'll just take a peek and then we'll come right back in here. We'll just crack the door."

Chris took a deep breath. I could tell he was mad about me even trying to get him to break his mom's rules, but I really wanted to see what the fuss was about.

Finally, he huffed, "Man, you gonna get us in so much trouble." And he was right. If we got in trouble, we were definitely going to be punished for it. My mother gave Ms. Hayes the green light to pop me if she needed to, and Ms. Hayes was the kind of woman who would do it. "Let's just make it quick," he said, sliding out of bed.

We tiptoed out into the hallway. Chris put his ear to his mother's door. Snoring. I knew she was 'sleep. We crept into the living room trying our best to avoid every creak in the floor. Ms. Hayes kept their house super clean, so we didn't have to worry about tripping over nothing. We could hear the voices much clearer in the living room. The man was saying something about how he loved her and how could she have done this to him. All of his words were long, like he was halfway singing, so we knew he was drunk. And the lady was pretty much screaming, "It's over! It's over!" and kept telling him to go home. I couldn't really tell, but it seemed like maybe the man came to wish her Happy Valentine's

Day, but they were already broken up and she had a date with someone else. That was the scenario I made up in my head, at least.

Chris turned the bolt lock slowly, making sure it didn't click loud. Then, he turned the knob. My heart started pounding, mainly because I didn't want us to open the door and have his mom wake up from all the hollering.

But it was too late. Chris was opening the door, and as soon as a thin strip of light from the hall came shining through the opening, the loudest sound I had ever heard in my entire life came rushing toward us, making both of us shout out and slam the door. Then came the screams of the woman, and the drunk man in the hallway now mumbling something about him being sorry and that he didn't mean it. Chris's face seemed like it had turned blue. Mine felt like it looked the same way.

"What the hell?" Ms. Hayes came rushing from her bedroom, her hair pinned and wrapped in a blue scarf with flowers on it. Somehow I remember that. She flipped on every light in the apartment in what seemed like two seconds.

I knew we were about to get a whole lot of the "rough side of a belt," as my mother always said, but I couldn't even worry about that.

Ms. Hayes looked upset, but then she took one look at our faces and came rushing over. She wrapped us in her arms, her pink robe like a cocoon for us to feel safe in.

"What happened?" she asked. But neither of us could answer.

Ms. Hayes was now on her knees, breathing hard, and the sleep on her breath stung my nostrils.

"What happened?" she asked again.

"The . . . the . . . the . . . ," Chris tried to explain, tears rising in his eyes. "The man, the man outside . . ." he stuttered. That's all he could get out. His mother cracked the door, peeked out, then slammed it shut, quickly. She cussed to herself.

"You boys get on away from the door," she said, pushing us back. "Matter fact, go back to your room and stay there, you hear me? Stay there!" she added in a shout. *No problem*, I thought. I wouldn't have minded if we had to stay in that room for the rest of our lives, the way I was feeling.

We got back in the bed. Head to foot. I didn't care about Chris's stinky feet anymore, and our friendship was pretty much sealed, forever. We just laid there wide awake, listening to the neighbors in the hallway, the police officers and their fuzzy walkie-talkies asking questions (but nobody saw nothing), the ambulance sirens, the screams of what sounded like a little girl, and Mr. Staton's dog, barking all night long.

CHAPTER 3
THE BLACK SUIT

"Dear Mama." That was my bedtime song after my mom died. It was like Tupac was singing—well, rapping—some kind of ghetto lullaby to me. I laid on my back with my earbuds in and that song on repeat, staring up into the darkness, imagining there was no ceiling, or roof, or clouds, until there really was no ceiling or walls, and I was no longer in my small bedroom, but instead in some strange dream. The kind where you swear it's real because everything looks real, and feels real, and you don't even remember ever falling asleep.

In the dream I was at a church, the same church my mom's funeral was in, except this time the air conditioner was cranking. The same people were there. The greasy preacher. Ms. Wallace, my mom's co-worker. The same usher women with their ashy-looking stockings and white shoes. But my mother wasn't in the casket.

Instead she was sitting on my left, with her arm around me and her face smushed against mine. In the dream, even though the casket was empty, everyone was crying. The preacher was crying. The family friends and neighborhood folks were crying. Everybody. And I'm not talking a little whimper. I'm talking an ugly, snotty, loud sob. A painful cry, like the one I had. And while all the weeping was going on, my mother and I just sat in the pew smiling, until everything faded to black, and sleep faded back into awake.

I laid there for a second confused and a little pissed that the dream was a dream. It seemed so real that I could even feel the AC blowing in the church. At least I thought I could. I rolled over to see what time it was. Four in the morning. Tupac had probably said *Mama made miracles every Thanksgiving* at least a hundred times, and my father was just getting home.

Normally, I wouldn't have heard him come in over the music, but he didn't tiptoe up the steps and slip into his bedroom like I would've done if I stayed out way later than usual. Nope. Dad made it clear he was home by making a whole bunch of noise.

A loud thump. Then, the sound of glass breaking followed by my father howling like a sad dog.

"Dad?" I called from the top of the steps.

"Matt," he said, surprised. "I'm fine, I'm fine. Go back to bed."

His words were slurring. I ran down the steps to find him on one knee, holding on to the kitchen counter, trying to pull himself up. His face looked like he was terrified, as if he were gripping the edge of a cliff or something. On the kitchen floor was a soggy paper bag, soaked with what was obviously cognac. The bottle had broken and glass had torn through the bag and cut his hand. Liquor and blood, everywhere. It was all on the doors of the cabinets and was dripping in the sink as my father struggled to get back on his feet.

"Dad!" I shouted. "What happened?"

In my mind, I already knew what happened. After Chris told me he saw him hanging with Cork, at first I wanted to jump down his throat and tell him he didn't know what he was talking about. But that wouldn't have been right. Chris wasn't no liar. Even if he wanted to lie, he couldn't. Plus, I had a feeling it was true. My dad had definitely been drinking more and more since the night my mother died. But hanging with Cork? That was definitely a move in the wrong direction. I knew where he was. I knew what was going on, but I still asked anyway. Maybe I was hoping I was wrong.

"I'm fine, Matt. I'm fine," he repeated in that voice people talk in whenever they're trying to convince someone that they're not drunk. Cork always sounds like that, and it never fools anybody. "I just slipped, that's all." He was still struggling to stand. His feet kept sliding around like our kitchen floor was icy. Recognizing that standing just wasn't going to happen, I grabbed a chair from the kitchen table and pulled it over to him.

"Here. Sit," I said, frustrated.

"Shit, I cut my hand," he groaned, plopping down on the chair. He squeezed his hands together to put pressure on the cut. Blood dripped from between his palms as if he were crushing cherries. As my dad rocked back and forth in pain, I grabbed a dish towel from under the sink.

"Let me see," I said, kneeling down, holding the rag out.

Dad unclenched his hands. Red. I wrapped the cut hand in the towel, and told him to keep it tight. I could smell the liquor coming through his skin; with every grunt, his stale breath slapped me. He looked at me, his eyes glassy and lost like I was some stranger helping him out, instead of his son.

"Better?" I asked.

I knew it wasn't better, but it's one of those questions he had asked *me* a hundred times when I was growing up. It's like a reflex. When I fell off my bike and scraped my arms all up, he slapped Band-Aids on them and said, "Better?" When I got in my first and only fight—got the crap beat out of me in middle school—he put some ointment on my lip and said, "Better?" And it was never better. I mean, it was eventually, but never when he asked. But for some reason, whenever he asked, "Better?" I always felt like I had to say yes.

My father grunted in reply. It was like he suddenly had no words left, like his tongue was dead. Then, he grunted again, and out of nowhere a spreading wet spot appeared on his pants, and the cognac, now mixed with the smell of his piss, floated through the air.

Seeing him that way automatically made me think about how he must've been all the time, back when he first started dating my mom. She used to always talk about how when she met him at the restaurant, he was a part-time dishwasher and a full-time drunk.

"Baby, the bottom of the bottle was your daddy's second home," she'd say, shaking her head. Then she'd always add, "And if I didn't stop him, he would've made that second home his grave."

Even though she loved him (whenever he wasn't wasted), she told him that she wouldn't marry him unless he gave it up. So he did. He gave it up for twenty whole years. But now . . . now, without Mom . . . he just . . . damn. It's like he fell apart. At the same time, I kinda understood. And literally, by the time I stood back up, he was already 'sleep, slumped in the chair, snoring. And I looked at him like he was my kid—like we had switched places and this was his first night getting wasted and I was suppose to yell or punish him or tell him how irresponsible he was. Again . . . backward. And I couldn't do none of that. Because he wasn't my son. He was my father. All I could do was pray to God that he would get a handle on it.

The next morning was weird for a few reasons. The first was, I decided to put on a suit. The same one I wore to my mom's funeral. The only one I had. I figured since I was now working at a funeral home, a suit would be a better look than jeans and Nikes. Yeah, I knew that it would draw attention that I really didn't want at school, but I figured a few hours of immature giggles were better than having to put on Mr. Ray's jacket that smelled like old man. At least my suit fit. And it smelled like me, which smells like nothing. Not to mention, I didn't look too bad in it, though I must admit it always took me a few tries to get the tie right. The first two times it always ended up a tiny, little, jacked-up knot. Then I remember to loop it twice, and it's good.

The second thing that was weird about the morning was my

dad. I didn't come downstairs and find him with his forehead slammed against the kitchen table, drool oozing from his mouth like slime, which is definitely what I was expecting. Instead, I came downstairs to a clean kitchen. No glass, no blood stains on the floor, not even a whiff of leftover funk. My father stood at the stove sipping from his usual mug, the smell of burned coffee and almost-burned toast in the air. (He can't cook a lick. Can't even make toast!) His right hand—the cut one—was neatly bandaged and he held the coffee cup in his left, which was funny because he's right-handed and was clearly having a hard time getting the mug to his lips. But that seemed to be the only thing he was having a hard time with.

"Morning, Matt," he said, like nothing had happened a few hours before. Then he looked me up and down. "What's with the suit?"

"Doing some work for Mr. Ray after school," I explained, but for some reason I felt like it went in one ear and out the other. It was like he wanted to know why I had on the suit I wore to Mom's funeral, but he didn't *really* want to know. He also was standing at the sink, and didn't notice that the picture of us at the beach was gone. I had taken it to my room the night before.

He shrugged and went back to his toast and coffee.

"Want breakfast?" he said, plain.

I stood there for a second and examined him. He was in his raggedy gray sweatpants, his belly poking out as usual. This had become his uniform since he had decided to take some time off from fixing up houses—stripping floors, dry wall, the whole nine. Now his day job was pretending nothing was wrong. But he couldn't fool me. He wasn't okay.

"Naw, I don't want to be late," I said, still feeling uncomfortable about last night and wanting to get out of Bizzaro World as fast as possible. Even school would be less strange than the kitchen I spent the last seventeen years in.

My father smirked. "Hey, it's your funeral." He's said that line tons of times, but on this day it stung, and even pissed me off a little since I was literally just babysitting him a few hours before. I wanted to say back, *and it was almost yours last night.*

"Yeah," I said, throwing my backpack over my shoulder, suddenly wondering if I should go back on my promise to myself about not saying anything.

I turned toward the front door, but then he began scratching scratching scratching his butter knife against his toast, the sound making me cringe inside. It was like the screeching sound the train makes when it pulls into the station. It pushed me over the edge. I had to say something. Maybe not everything, but something.

"Dad?" I turned around to face him.

"Yep?"

I thought for a moment.

"Last night . . . ," I started. He instantly stopped scratching at the toast, but he didn't look at me. He just looked down at the half-black, half-brown bread. But I couldn't do it. I couldn't zing him like I wanted to—and trust me, I *really* wanted to—only because, well, we were both messed up, hurting, and it would've just been a wack thing to do. Just . . . mean. So I flipped the script and continued with, "You weren't here when I got here, and I wasn't sure if you ate or not, so I bought a sandwich for you. It's in the fridge. You don't have to eat burnt toast."

He took a deep breath, obviously happy I didn't say what he thought I was going to say.

"Oh." He exhaled, looking at me, finally showing some signs of embarrassment. "Thanks."

Uh-huh, I thought to myself.

It was another one of Brooklyn's crappy fall days, where the clouds make nine in the morning look like six in the evening, but the rain just won't come down. Instead there's a constant mist like someone or something is continuously spitting on you. Gross. And to top it all off, I had on the most uncomfortable shoes in the world—stiff, clunky dress shoes, cutting into my ankles, forcing me to walk like my butt hurt.

"Man, you should've just left without me," I told Chris, as I waddled up to the bus stop. He stood there with a gigantic umbrella, way too big for such puny raindrops.

"You said to treat you like normal," he said, shrugging his shoulders. "This is normal."

I laughed and nodded to him.

"But this big-ass umbrella ain't," I joked.

"Neither is that monkey suit you got on," he gave it back.

I laughed again. "It's for my job. Remember? At the funeral home. Where I touch dead people," I said, pretending like I was going to touch him. "And anyway, I don't even know why you talking. You probably don't even have a suit. Probably can't even tie a tie."

"You right. I don't have a suit. But what I *do* have is an umbrella." He pulled the large umbrella farther down over him.

The funniest thing was when the bus came and Chris tried to close the umbrella up. He couldn't get it to snap and lock in place, and it kept flying open every time he tried to step into the bus. He kept cussing and trying and cussing and trying until finally I just turned around and did it for him. People on the bus sniggered. Even the driver. I could tell Chris was embarrassed, but even he knew it was funny.

School went its usual way. I bumped around from locker to classroom, dodging varsity jackets, chicks with fresh doobie wraps peering into cheap, stick-on locker mirrors, making fish faces while applying lip gloss, gossip hanging above our heads like cigarette smoke. I was sure my name was somewhere in it, especially since I was shuffling around in an all-black suit, looking like some kind of secret agent with bad feet. My classmates probably just thought the suit was some sort of grieving thing. Like I was making some kind of point, which I'm sure they all thought was weird. But I didn't really care because, like I said, high school seemed like nothing to me now.

I sat in Mr. Grovener's class and listened to him read Old English stories, where the way they talked was weirder than Shakespeare's language, and I faded in and out of writing notes and scribbling squiggly lines in the margins. All I could really think about was the day before. Not just my dad, but also Mr. Jameson's funeral. The old man and the big, squeaky-voiced dude telling those crazy stories. The laughing and joking. And of course, I also thought about when Ms. Jameson got up to speak. I sat in class and replayed in my mind, over and over again, that watery look in her eyes, the weird thought of her face fighting itself to smile, and the strange satisfaction I got watching it all go down. I felt bad about it, but I also felt good about it. Maybe misery really does love company. My mother used to always say that, but I had never really thought about it before.

She also used to say a watched clock don't tick, and I was definitely watching the clock. Every second seeming like a minute keeping me trapped in this lame prison of cool kids and square pizza. I didn't care about Canterbury, or whatever Grovener was yapping about. All I cared about was breaking free and going to the funeral home to help Mr. Ray.

And sitting in on another funeral.

CHAPTER 4
NINETEEN

M<small>R</small>. R<small>AY</small> <small>WAS STANDING OUTSIDE THE FUNERAL HOME SIPPING</small> coffee from a bodega cup when I got there. For the most part, my suit was still in pretty good shape. No stains, all tucked in, and only wrinkled on the shoulders because of my backpack straps. And y'know, I felt different in a suit. I felt like I was really going to work to do something important. Little did I know, I was.

"Look at you, slick. Sharper than a ice pick, ain't ya?" he said, extending his hand to me.

"Hey, Mr. Ray," I said, a little embarrassed. I met his hand with mine.

"What made you wanna put on your spiffs?" he joked, turning the blue paper cup up to take one last gulp of coffee.

"Just felt like it, I guess," I said. I couldn't exactly tell him that it dawned on me that the suit would make it easier for me to sit

JASON REYNOLDS

in on more funerals because, well, anyone in a black suit could fit right in to any funeral, no problem.

He looked at me for a second. "Well, you look good, son. Now if you can get all your little knotty-head buddies 'round here to put on some decent clothes and pick their pants up off their asses, we'll really be in business. Pants so low, they gotta walk like cowboys. Like they rode here from the Bronx on a horse."

I snickered. I couldn't help it, that was a good one, plus it reminded me of something my mother used to say. She used to call the boys from the neighborhood ghetto penguins because of the way they waddled.

"They ain't my buddies," I told him. The whole pants-sagging thing was never really my style. Just seems weird to have your whole butt showing like that.

Mr. Ray nodded. "I know, Matt," he said, tossing his cup in the trash.

He looked over my shoulder at a car pulling up behind me. I turned and there was a black Cadillac easing up almost to the bumper of Mr. Ray's car. It had dark windows and a neon pink paper hanging from the rearview mirror. I recognized the driver. Robbie Ray. I could almost smell the hair grease; his oversize dark sunglasses made him look like some kind of bug. There was a man in the passenger seat, but I didn't know him.

"But seriously, son, all jokes aside, I'm glad you wore a suit today, because I need you."

"For what?" I said, edgylike because all I could think about was how I said I didn't want to touch no dead bodies.

"You know what a pallbearer is?"

"Naw." Never heard of it.

Behind me, the pop and squeal of one of the car doors opening.

"Any sign of Cork, Willie?" Robbie Ray asked from the car.

Mr. Ray looked at his brother and twisted his mouth up in a sarcastic way, making it clear that Robbie's question was a dumb one.

"Well, what about the kid? He gon' do it?" Robbie Ray asked, his voice concerned and impatient.

Since I was the only kid around, I figured he was talking about me. I also didn't know what "it" was, but sort of put two and two together and guessed it had something to do with whatever a pallbearer was.

Mr. Ray narrowed his eyes at his brother. "Gimme a second," he said to Robbie in a serious tone.

Robbie Ray nodded his head all nervous, and ducked back down into the black car.

"Sorry 'bout that, Matthew," Mr. Ray said, tapping a box of cigarettes against his palm. "But like I was saying, pallbearers are the guys who, pretty much, carry the casket."

I just gaped at him as my heart dropped to my knees.

He continued. "I mean, sometimes family members do it, but a lot of the times the funeral home does it. Usually we have enough guys, but nobody can find Cork."

Yeah, because he's probably out getting my father smashed, I thought.

"So," Mr. Ray said and sighed, "you're pretty much all we got."

I didn't know what to say. I couldn't say no. I mean, I could have, but then I might not have been able to go to the funeral, which was the whole point of me wearing a suit. But I wasn't sure I wanted to say yes either. I had never carried a casket. What if it was too heavy? What if it smelled weird . . . like dead people or something? Were there special ways to do it? Would I be able to learn how to do it on the car ride over? What if I dropped it? All these things were flashing through my head as Mr. Ray waited for an answer. I could feel wet nastiness start to develop under my arms as my nerves kicked into superdrive.

"So, whatcha think?" he asked, doing a manly version of the whole puppy-dog thing.

I just nodded my head. *Damn!*

"You know where you going?" Mr. Ray said. He was talking to his brother on his phone, but using a headset like the ones they use when they take orders at Cluck Bucket. I thought about maybe suggesting earbuds, but Mr. Ray seemed too old school to switch up.

"No, Robbie. You gotta start paying attention, man. *Monroe* and Stuyvesant. Not Madison. *Monroe*," he said, frustrated. He shook his head and mumbled something to himself. I looked out the window at my neighborhood as the guy on the radio complained about the New York Giants.

Staring at stoop after stoop, I thought about my mother. I can't really say what I was thinking about exactly. Just everything. Just her. It's crazy to believe you can always put into words what you think of when you think of a person who's gone, mainly because a lot of times it's not about specific things. Sometimes you just think about how that person made you feel. That's what I was daydreaming about. The way she made me feel. Like I was the luckiest kid in the world. Like I couldn't lose. Like I was somebody important.

Mr. Ray didn't say much on the way, but I could tell he kept glancing over at me. I knew he knew where my head was, because right when I could feel the tears creeping up, he put his hand on my shoulder.

"Hey man, you a'ight?" he asked, his eyes off the road.

I cleared my throat. "Yep. I'm fine," I said, trying to sound normal.

"You—" and before he could say "sure," he shouted, "Shit!" and slammed on the brakes. Red light. He almost ran into the back of Robbie's car.

A loud thump came from behind us. I figured we must've been rear-ended, but we weren't. Mr. Ray reached his hand up to the window directly behind our seat and slid it open. It's funny, I didn't even realize there was a window, completely blacked out, right behind my head. It was sort of like how cabs have that window separating the front seat and the backseat, except in Mr. Ray's car, it was tinted.

Mr. Ray peered into the back of the car. I turned my head to see what was back there that caused that thump and practically choked when I saw it. The casket. I thought the casket was in Robbie's car since he was leading the way. Even though I tried not to look totally bugged out, I couldn't help it. It's just what happens

when I'm nervous. Robot face. But can you blame me? A freakin'
casket was right behind my head!

"Hey, it's okay, man," Mr. Ray said, stretching his neck to see
the traffic light ahead of us. "This passenger can't feel a thing," he
joked. I forced a smile.

"Yeah, I guess," I replied, fixing my gaze back toward the
window.

The light turned green, and we were on our way to the church
again. I could feel fear boiling inside me. I tried to calm down.
I thought to myself, *Mr. Ray is right, the person in that casket can't
feel nothing. So it won't be the end of the world if my hand slips and
I drop it. No biggie, I'll just say "do-over" and pick it right back up.
Nobody will even care, right?* Then I caught a glimpse of myself in
the side-view mirror, and it was me who looked dead.

THE FUNERAL OF NANCY KNIGHT

"You know her? I mean, you knew her?" I said awkwardly to Robbie.
I'm no master of small talk or nothing, but I had enough home
training to know that you at least try to spark a conversation with
people you're working with.

Mr. Ray had run into the church to talk to the pastor about
bringing the casket in, and Robbie didn't seem like he was in
the mood for chitchat. At least not with me. I figured that was
probably because he was embarrassed about Mr. Ray barking at
him in the car with me sitting right there. I guess I could understand that.

"Nope," he said, swinging the back door of Mr. Ray's trunk open. Looking in that trunk was like looking down a hallway. Robbie ran his hand along the casket like he was stroking the face of some pretty woman.

"Ooh wee! Yo, Benny, we got steel and eighteens on this one!" he shouted like he was talking about a car. Benny was a regular-size, medium-skinned guy, with a thick black beard that looked like carpet covering the whole bottom half of his face. He sat on the passenger side of Robbie's car with the door open, one leg in and one leg out, puffing a cigarette.

"Oh yeah?" Benny said. He got out of the car and closed the door, took one more pull from the cigarette, burning it down to the yellow part, then plucked it into the street. "What's your guess?"

"Hmmm," Robbie hummed. "I'm going with business woman?"

"Man, please. Business woman? Getting buried around here? Doubt it."

"What you mean? You don't think folks from around here can be business people?"

I was confused about what was going on.

"Man, you know what I'm saying. It just ain't likely Ms. Knight, or whatever her name is, or was, or whatever, was some banker down on Wall Street. You know it. I know it. Shit, even little man knows it." He chin pointed at me.

"Well, her casket says different."

"Man, that casket could've been paid for by anybody. Hell, even *your* broke ass probably gonna have a good casket just 'cause your family in the business." Benny stung Robbie with that one, but before Robbie could snap back, Mr. Ray came out of the church with two other guys also dressed in black suits.

"A'ight, I got a few of the brothers from the church to help us out. That makes six of us. Three on each side. Put young blood in the middle. Should be smooth."

Benny and Robbie straightened up and stopped talking about the cost of Ms. Knight's casket. Mr. Ray got respect. I liked that.

Robbie, Benny, and I got on one side with me in the middle, and Mr. Ray and the other two guys took the other side. Before I knew it, the casket was coming out of the car, and I was holding tight to the steel rails that ran along the sides of it. My hands were slick with sweat, and all I could do was pray that I didn't drop this dead lady's expensive casket. I imagined some old woman telling my mother on me up in heaven, shaking her head and wagging her finger.

Up the steps. One step at a time. Mr. Ray called out each move like a captain in the army. The other four guys grunted with every step, which made me think I wasn't really carrying much weight. But I wasn't about to let go and find out.

Once we got inside the church it was easy. We hauled the casket down the aisle toward the altar. A big wooden cross hung high up on the back wall, surrounded by the usual, big stained-glass windows.

"Okay, gents. Lift on three," Mr. Ray ordered. "One, two, up."

We hoisted the casket onto what looked like a big table.

"Jesus, this thing is heavy," Mr. Ray moaned, using his hand-kerchief to wipe smudges off the pearl box.

"Yeah, it's got copper and eighteen gauge," Robbie said, stepping back into the aisle to make sure it was centered on the big table. "Expensive."

Mr. Ray shot him a look. "Don't start." He turned to me and spoke softly. "These fools always trying to guess what kind of money folks got based on their caskets."

I wanted to ask if my mother's casket was heavy. But it probably wasn't.

"Mainly, 'cause they ignorant," he added while unlocking the first half of the casket.

I took a step back, realizing that he was going to open it up. I wasn't really afraid of seeing anything, mainly because I had seen my mother in one, but I wasn't sure who this old lady, Ms. Knight, was, or what she was going to look like. I imagined she would be wrinkly, but pretty in a rich old-lady kind of way. Pearls or diamond earrings. A ring. A fancy dress. Like she was taking a nap before dinner at an expensive restaurant in Manhattan. Something like that.

Mr. Ray clicked the last lock, and lifted the lid of the casket. I took a peek and was so surprised by what she looked like. Ms. Knight wasn't old at all. As a matter of fact, she was young.

"Sad," Mr. Ray said to me. "Gone too soon."

I stared at her face, smooth and round. No wrinkles. Small diamond studs in her ears. A silver necklace around her neck with a little heart charm on it.

"How old was she?" I asked.

"Nineteen."

JASON REYNOLDS

Nineteen! Two years older than me. I gulped.

"What happened to her?"

"Her mother said it was an asthma attack."

"Asthma? How could she die of an asthma attack? I mean, I just never heard of nobody actually dying from that. Like, you just do a few squeezes of your inhaler and you're fine," I said. Asthma? Nobody dies from asthma!

"Yeah, I know. The thing is, no one knew she had asthma. Not even her. So," Mr. Ray said and shrugged, "no inhaler." Mr. Ray stared down at the teenager. Then he patted me on the shoulder. "Help me bring in the flowers."

The funeral was way different than Mr. Jameson's. It was packed with tons of teenagers. Some I recognized from the neighborhood, but most I had never seen before. I sat in the back as they came rolling in in jeans and sneakers. Some wore T-shirts with Nancy's face printed on the front. A lot of the girls came in with their hands covering their mouths, and a lot of the guys would take off their hats, but wouldn't take off their sunglasses. And even though I thought that was a little rude, I got it.

I stood in the back with Mr. Ray, Robbie, and Benny and watched as everyone did the funeral march, the same kind they did at my mom's funeral, when they would look at the body and say some crap about how she looked like herself. But the way the teenagers looked at Nancy was different from the way the old ladies looked at my mother. The young people just looked surprised. Surprised that their homegirl was gone. That all of a sudden they would never talk to Nancy on the phone again. Or in class. Just like that, it was over. I got that, too.

There was no choir, thank God. Just a skinny girl with braids who got up and blew the roof off the church. She sang "His Eye Is on the Sparrow," and when I say she sang it, I mean she *sang* it. She dug deep and belted out notes strong enough to reach Nancy, I swear. Tears streamed down her face, and even though I couldn't see anybody else's face, really, I could tell a lot of people were crying by the way folks were thumbing the corners of their eyes. I paid close attention to Nancy's mother, a pretty, dark-skinned woman, sitting up front in all black. She had dreadlocks wound up in a bun, and she rocked back and forth while another woman wrapped her arm around her and fanned her with one of the church fans.

I looked at the program. Next was the obituary.

The preacher stepped up to the microphone. I'm not sure if he had on a sharp suit, or just jeans and a T-shirt, because he wore a long burgundy robe like the ones you wear when you graduate from high school. I was looking forward to wearing that same kind of robe soon. He had a baby face, but I could tell he was way older than he looked by the creases in his forehead. He stood at the mic for a moment, and then began to read the obituary off the program.

It was pretty short, I guess because Nancy's life was only nineteen years long. She barely had time to do anything. I thought about how if I died, my obituary would only be a few sentences.

Matthew Miller was the son of Daisy Miller and Jackson Miller.

JASON REYNOLDS

His best friend was Chris Hayes. He couldn't land a date to save his life. So he died. The end. Oh, and there would probably be a picture of me on the front of the program. One of my senior pictures. Robot face number twelve.

The pastor read. Nancy was the oldest of two. She graduated from Brooklyn Tech with honors. Her favorite subject was English. She loved poetry and music, especially R&B, but her favorite thing to do was run track. She got a full scholarship to the University of Maryland to run and did really well her freshman year, winning her first race a few days before she died. Or, as the pastor read off the program, "before God called his angel back home." The preacher at my mom's funeral said something like that too. I guess that's better than saying "died." But it still means the same thing. It doesn't really matter what you call it. It still sucks.

I thought about Nancy. She was a runner. A winner. She was good at school and at sports, which almost never happens. And judging from all of the teenagers jammed in this church like kids stuffed in a camp van, all on top of each other, sitting in the aisles, standing along the back and side walls, she also was pretty popular. Nancy must've been a cool chick. But even though she could run, she couldn't run fast enough to beat death.

I also couldn't help but think about her mother, in the front row, heaving and rocking, and occasionally lifting her hands as if begging God for some kind of help. I now knew what it was like to lose a mother, but I don't know how my mother would've felt if she lost me. She used to always say whenever we'd hear about some kid dying in the street, "Parents ain't supposed to bury their kids. It just ain't right." I knew, and not just because she told me a trillion times, that she loved me like crazy, and that she would've been shattered just like Nancy's mom, begging for God to take her instead, crying, screaming for me to have a second shot at life. There wouldn't have been a joke in the world funny enough to help her laugh through it. There wouldn't have been a joke in the world funny anymore, period.

So I felt for Ms. Knight. Ms. Knight didn't look like she had a whole lot of money, so I could only imagine how much she spent on that heavy casket. But to her, I bet it was worth it. My mom would've done the same thing.

Nancy's sister was called up to the podium after the pastor was done with his words. She looked about sixteen and I could tell she was cute, even though black lines streamed down her face from all of the tears mixing with her makeup. Her hair was cut short in a little bush, almost perfectly round, and she stood at the microphone holding a piece of paper, shaking with nerves. Her name was Alicia.

"This"—she started, her voice vibrating like her hands—"this is a poem for Nancy."

Alicia put one hand on her chest and took a deep breath.

"Nancy
Remember when we would run
and see who could beat the moon.
Remember when we laughed
and cracked jokes all afternoon.

Remember when Ma made a cake
and we fought over the spoon.
Remember on your birthday
when I popped the best balloon.
Remember staying up all night
singing our favorite tune."

She paused and said, "'Can't Take My Eyes Off of You,' by
Lauryn Hill."

Her mother, now sitting up straight, nodded. Even though I
couldn't see her face, I could tell her mom was sort of smiling.

Alicia went back to the poem.

"Remember staying up all night
singing our favorite tune.
Remember snowball fights in January
and water fights in June.
I never thought—"

She stopped again, her hands trembling even more, her throat
swallowing what we all knew was a lump of emotions.

Alicia looked up at the crowd, then at her mother, then at her
sister Nancy, lying there peacefully. I could feel the churning in
my stomach. That feeling. The same one I had the day before at
Mr. Jameson's funeral.

Alicia continued. "I never thought you'd be gone so soon."
Her voice gave way to the tears, as they rolled down her chocolate

cheeks. She folded the paper into a small square and slipped it into the casket on her way back to her seat, where her mother wrapped her up in all the love she had left. Like the preacher at my mother's service told me, no one could feel the pain like I could. And I knew watching Alicia and Ms. Knight that the same went for them—no one in that church was hurting as much as they were. And again, I was satisfied.

Mr. Ray started walking toward me, signaling for me to follow. Benny, Robbie, and the other two guys fell in line behind us as we started down the aisle toward the casket. The pastor was giving his final prayer, and the young girl who sang the first song had come back to the microphone to close the funeral with another selection, this time something upbeat that people could sing along to: "This Little Light of Mine."

I took my place between Benny and Robbie again. But now I wasn't as nervous as we all grabbed the metal bar. I turned my head toward where Ms. Knight and her daughter were sitting. They were both singing and wiping a last few tears from their faces. I caught eyes with the both of them and smiled. Ms. Knight smiled back. Then, Robbie elbowed me in the arm. It was time to go. On Mr. Ray's cue, we lifted and turned, and slowly marched Nancy with all her friends and family behind us singing, into the sunlight. *Let it shine, let it shine, let it shine.*

CHAPTER 5
WHEN IT RAINS . . .

"'SUP MAN?" CHRIS WAS WALKING UP THE BLOCK TOWARD ME, his giant umbrella now being used as a cane to put some extra cool in his bop. It looked ridiculous, him walking like some pot-belly pimp. Like Robbie Ray. Chris's backpack, loose, stuffed with books, sagged down to his butt.

"Chillin'," I said. "Just seeing what you was up to."

"Yeah, but ain't something wrong? Because you was blowing me up like something was wrong."

"Man, I ain't blow you up!"

"You was blowing me up, Matt!" Chris pulled out his cell phone and counted out all the text messages I sent him. Nine. I *was* blowing him up. But it was because I was feeling weird. I left the church right after we put Nancy's casket in the back of the hearse. Instead of hopping in and riding in the parade to the gravesite, I decided to just walk home. Mr. Ray understood, and gave me thirty bucks for the day, and thirty for the day before. Not bad.

As I'd walked home, I'd started thinking about life, and friends, and how things had just been crazy with Mom being gone, and everything being flipped upside down, and how this just wasn't the way things were supposed to be. It was all supposed to be smooth. The most uncomfortable thing I was ever planning to experience was picture day. That's it. Now here I was, by myself, coming back from being a pallbearer at a funeral of a girl around my age who had no idea she was going to go. And to make it worse—oh man, here it is—I liked being at the funeral! Yeah. Weird. But it was like, I felt better there than anywhere else since my mom died. Stuff like that can make you feel crazy, and I just wanted to be around a friend. So, yes, I blew Chris up.

"Man, whatever," I said to him now. "Look, I got some money. You trying to get something to eat?"

I flashed the cash. Tens and twenties. My mother would've tripped if she knew I was showing off like that. Chris tripped too. His eyes bugged out.

"Man, where you get that from?" he said, as if he expected me to say I was pushing drugs or something, even though he knew me well enough to know that I got it in some legit way. I just wasn't that type of dude.

"Work, fool," I said, folding the bills in half. "So we eating, or what?"

"Still not cooking?" Chris asked.

"Forget it, you don't wanna eat." I stuffed the wad back into my pocket.

"I didn't say that! I'm just not used to you not whipping stuff up in the kitchen. You the only dude I know who knows how to burn." Chris swung his umbrella at something I didn't see.

"I'm just not in the mood," I said, pushing the sleeves of my suit jacket up. That thing was getting hot. "Y'know, that was something me and Mom used to do. Our thing."

Chris looked down, now tapping the stupid umbrella on the sidewalk as if he were smashing an ant. "I got you. It's cool," he said, looking up. "So, where we going?"

I thought for a moment. Chris rubbed his baldy like he was trying to shine it, which he usually did when he was thinking, too. But we both knew what the answer was. It was what it always was. Cluck Bucket.

We started up the block, our cement world of trash cans blown into the street, stray cats begging, stoop sitters dressed in fresh sneakers smoking blunts in broad daylight, old ladies sweeping the sidewalk, tired nine-to-fivers walking slowly on the final stretch before home. The buses, and cabs, and bicycles, and skateboards. The shop owners hollering out their two-for-one deals. The little girls singing, the older boys laughing, the babies crying, and the two of us moving through it all.

"Hold up," I said, patting my pockets as we got to the corner where the bodega is. "I gotta stop in here right quick. I owe Jimmy some cash."

"Good to know you'll pay your debts when you get rich," Chris said, laughing.

I pushed the door open. The cat jumped from on top of the soups over to the paper towels.

"Jimmy, how much is two D batteries?" a woman dressed in business clothes and sneakers asked.

"Two-fitty."

"Two-fifty! That's ridiculous. For two damn batteries. A'ight, well forget the batteries. Just give me two Wheel of Fortune scratch-offs." She tapped the thick plastic case to make sure he knew which scratch-offs she wanted.

"Five dollars."

"Five dollars! Jimmy, these are two-fifty a piece now too?"

Jimmy noticed me come in.

"Matty, what's good, my man?"

The lady slapped a five-dollar bill down and slid it across the counter. Whatever she needed those batteries for wasn't as important as her trying to win more money. Maybe to buy more batteries. Or more scratch-offs.

"Jimmy, wassup. Just wanted to come give you what I owe you," I said, reaching down into my pocket.

"Naw, it's good man," Jimmy said. "Your pops came in here and took care of it earlier."

"Really?" I was confused. "Was he with somebody?"

Jimmy gave the sneaker lady her two scratch-offs.

"Yeah, man. It was weird. He bought a few beers and some loosies for that drunk that always hangs on Albany. The one with all the nasty holes in his face."

My stomach tightened up.

"Around what time?"

"I don't know. A little before ten," he said shaking his head. "That's how I knew he was copping for that drunk dude, because Mr. Miller don't seem like he drink in the morning."

Jimmy was right, my father didn't seem like the type. He was always so on point. So together. But he also always had his wife around to keep him that way. I thought about my prayer—that he would get a handle on this whole drinking thing. Guess God or whoever is up there didn't hear me.

"A'ight man, later."

I flung the door open.

"Yo, nice suit, Matty!" he called after me in his throaty accent.

Outside, Chris was leaning up against the wall playing a game on his cell phone.

"You ready?" I said.

"Yo, what's the most you ever got"—he paused—"on Temple Run?" he asked without looking up, his fingers flying across the screen of his phone. His umbrella hung from his wrist.

I didn't answer.

Now he looked up.

"What's wrong with you? Jimmy charge you interest?" Chris smiled. Then, when I didn't answer, he shut the game down and slipped the phone in his pocket.

"What?" he asked again.

"I ain't have to pay him. He said my dad came in earlier and took care of it."

"So. What's wrong with that?"

"Jimmy said Dad was with Cork."

Chris frowned, but he didn't say anything and neither did I.

We walked a few more blocks. The silence was thick between us. At Albany I thought about heading down the block to check on my father. But I didn't want to do that with Chris with me. I mean, all right, I felt embarrassed enough—I didn't want Chris to see my old man not being the Mr. Miller he knew growing up. I didn't want to see it either. My mom always said you can't run from reality. But I wanted to. Man, I wanted to.

Chris decided to break the awkward silence.

"How was work, suit boy?" He dragged the tip of the umbrella over a drain. It rang out like a church bell.

I thought for a moment about how the only things I had to talk about was my dad tripping, or how I spent the day at some teenage girl's funeral. Maybe Mr. Ray and Robbie had it right when they were my age. I should've been thinking about girls. About skirts, as Mr. Ray called them. And maybe they were right about me. Maybe I was different, different in a weird way.

Chris was waiting for an answer though, so I said, "Cool." That was dumb. I caught myself. "Well, not really. But you know what I mean. I went to a funeral and had to carry a casket."

"What?"

"Yeah, man, I was one of the guys who had to carry the casket. A pallbearer. Crazy."

"Sounds like it."

"And the wild part was, the funeral was for a girl only a little bit older than us."

Chris looked over at me. His eyes were wondering why she died.

I explained. "Died of asthma. She didn't even know she had it."

Chris shook his head. I could tell he was thinking something, but just didn't know how to say it.

"What?"

"Nothing. I just don't know how you can just . . . go to funerals every day? Like it's nothing?"

I thought for a moment.

"They won't be every day, man. Plus, you don't make money like this at Cluck Bucket," I joked, pulling the wad of cash from my pocket again.

Of course, I couldn't tell him the truth. The truth that I was having a hard time telling myself. I *liked* the funerals. And in thinking about how I couldn't tell Chris that, I started thinking about why I was actually so into them in the first place. I wasn't just being a creep. Well, I sorta was, but it wasn't for no reason. I know that now. I liked watching other people deal with the loss of someone, not because I enjoyed seeing them in pain, but because, somehow, it made me feel better knowing that my pain isn't only mine. That my life isn't the only one that's missing something it will never have back. See? Reasons. I couldn't explain that to Chris. I mean, he didn't have a father, but he never had one. It's not like having one and then losing him. At least I don't think it is. And his mom was fine, so he wouldn't understand. But Ms. Jameson . . . she understood. And Ms. Knight did too.

"Yeah, and you won't keep money like that if you keep treating me to food!" Chris popped me back into reality. And the guy was right. At Cluck Bucket he ordered a Cluck Deluxe, which was basically a huge chicken sandwich on a hero, with mayo, lettuce, tomato, onion rings, some kind of special sauce, and pickles on it, with a large fry and a large chocolate shake. Then he asked me if he could get a banana pudding, too. All I got was a three-piece, dark, and a biscuit. His: $8.50. Mine: $3.35.

And guess who took our order?

"Your total is eleven eighty-five," Renee said, turning around to scoop the fries. She looked just like she had the first time I saw her, wearing that ridiculous net on her head, and that greasy purple shirt. She looked funny, but she probably thought I did too, with the suit on. At least she looked silly in a cute way. I thought about saying something to her. Maybe mentioning how the way she embarrassed that dude that day was hilarious. I don't know, just something to spark conversation. But now that I was right in front of her, that seemed like a stupid idea. My mother used to say to simply start with "Hello, how are you?" but my mom ain't grow up in this neighborhood. She grew up in the South where everybody's nice. But, who knows? Maybe it would work.

Just say it. Hello, how are you? Say it. It was on the tip of my tongue. *Just. Say. It.*

Nothing.

"Eleven eighty-five," she repeated, now holding her hand out.

I didn't say a word. I just pulled out my wad of money, like I was some kind of hustler—not a good look—and paid.

We walked back to our block, stuffed. Chris looked ridiculous as he tried to get the last bit of chocolate shake up through the straw. His face was all sucked in and his eyes looked like they were going to pop out of his head. He made drinking a milkshake look painful. I saved some chicken for my father—the breast, and half the biscuit. I didn't have much of an appetite anyway, and figured that he would need to put some food in his stomach whenever he got in. I was pissed at him, but what can I say, he's my dad.

In front of my house I asked Chris what he thought of Renee. "Who?"

"Renee, man. The girl who took our order."

"You know her?"

"No, not yet. But I want to know her."

"So you stalking her." He grinned.

"No, man," I said, frustrated. "Look, I just wanna know what you think of her."

"Oh." He thought it over for a second. "She a'ight."

"A'ight?" I asked, shocked. To me she was way better than a'ight. Chris replied with a shrug. Damn.

I wanted to ask what he thought I should do to get her, but the conversation pretty much ended because the sudden sound of sirens on another block drowned out everything we were saying. Plus, the rain that started the day off came back to end it, dripping softly at first but picking up speed. And to top it all off, the street lights started to glow, so Chris popped his gigantic umbrella open—like a parachute—and called it a night.

Inside, I dropped my backpack at the door. Then, I picked it back up and plopped it down on one of the kitchen chairs, worried that if I left it by the door, Dad would come stumbling in, trip over it, and we'd have a repeat of the night before. I set the Cluck Bucket box on the counter, the grease seeping through, making the bottom of the box soggy. I washed my hands. Then, as carefully as possible, I took my suit coat off and inspected it. It was the only one I had and I was wearing it a lot now because of this new job, which, come to think of it, was really more like a weird new hobby. Working funerals, crashing funerals. Same thing.

No dirt on the collar. No stains. No snags. And only a few wrinkles up on the shoulders. I took the jacket into the living room and laid it lightly across the arm of the couch, a big burgundy thing my mother used to call "the spaceship" when I was kid. I slipped off my slacks, which was much easier than pulling off jeans, and laid them on the other arm of the couch. Then, just like when I was a kid, I flopped down on the spaceship, except now I was really hoping it would take me away. I sunk into the cushions, took a deep breath, and listened to my empty house, wearing nothing but underwear and socks. It was noisier than you'd think an empty house would be. The sink was dripping. The fridge was buzzing. Things cracking and creaking as, like my mother used to say, the house settled. The rain came down hard, sounded like television static. And the sirens still wailed. So annoying. But the noise I wanted to hear—the sound of someone else—wasn't there.

I reached for the remote. I wasn't about to go all sensitive and whatnot. *Click.* News. *Click.* Basketball game. *Wish I was more into sports. Click.* Cop show. *Click.* News. *Click.* Reality TV. One of those shows where the rich parents try to plan their daughter's sixteenth birthday. This girl was telling her mother that she wanted to take a private jet from Los Angeles to New York with all of her friends, party on the jet, then, when they got to New York, have dinner with Jay-Z and Beyoncé. Wow. My sixteenth birthday I had dinner with my folks at the restaurant they met at. Well, it's not the exact same restaurant anymore—no soul food—but it was good. I remember Mom did her French accent the whole time as a joke, and when she ordered a side of French fries, gave the young waitress a whole story about how French fries were created in France by her great-great-grandfather. The poor waitress asked for her autograph and everything, and probably still tells that story to customers. Ouch. While all that's going on, Dad inspected every fork, knife, plate, and glass, since he used to be a dishwasher in that place. Nothing was clean enough.

"Everything is spotty and streaky, Daisy. They can't even wash dishes right no more."

"Ohhhh, calm down." She blew him a kiss across the table. "Not everyone can bust a sud like you." She winked at me.

"It's machines. Machines can't do everything. They can't replace elbow grease," my dad said, his elbows on the table.

"I know, babe. Why don't you go on back there and show them how it's done. That way you can feel better about it, and we won't have to pay for this meal." She laughed. We all did. Happy sixteenth birthday.

✖ ✖ ✖

I settled into the old couch and figured this show would at least be entertaining, because as far as I was concerned, it was the furthest thing from reality. At least, my reality. And that's what I needed, a spaceship and a TV to take me away. And they did just that. Next thing I know, I woke up with a string of drool connected from the corner of my mouth down to my chest, and some other show was on. I didn't even know I had fallen asleep. The last thing I remembered was the young girl throwing a fit because the mother refused to let her get breast implants for the party. Yikes.

I turned the TV off. The sink was still dripping. The fridge was still buzzing. The house was still settling. The rain was still pouring. But the sirens were gone. At least there was that.

Even though the DVD player flashed 9:26 across the screen, I decided to go to bed. I was exhausted. It's not like I'd done a bunch of work, or anything like that, but I think my mind was just tired and ready to shut down for the night.

I climbed into bed, pulled the covers up to my chin, and thought for a moment about Nancy. Then about the way her mother heaved and cried. Her sister's poem. Nancy and her sister having snowball fights. Or water fights in the summer. Was Nancy's boyfriend there at the funeral? What did that feel like for him? Maybe what it felt like for Dad. Maybe Nancy's boyfriend is somewhere getting drunk right now too.

Then I put it all out of my mind and reached for my earbuds. Tupac. "Dear Mama." *And there's no way I can pay ya back, but my plan is to show ya that I understand. You are appreciated.* Halfway through the song I blinked—at least it felt like a blink—and when

I opened my eyes, I was back in the church. Back with the old ladies, the white stockings, the white shoes, the fans, sitting next to my mother at her own funeral again. The casket was empty like it was before. She was sitting next to me, with her arm around me again, hugging me tight. I wasn't crying and neither was she, but she was holding me so close. Everyone else was mourning. Ms. Jameson was there, and Nancy's mother, and Alicia, her sister. But my father wasn't there this time. I wondered where he was. Did he choose not to come to his wife's funeral? He wouldn't do that.

A knock came from the back of the church. A bang. Someone was pounding on the door. That had to be him. But the ushers wouldn't let him in. He banged again.

I stood up. "Let him in!" I shouted at the top of my lungs.

They didn't move. The pounding continued. Louder. Louder.

"Let him in!" I shouted again, now stepping into the aisle. "Let him in!" I started walking toward the door. The pounding. Harder. Harder.

Pounding. I woke up. Pounding. Someone was banging on the door downstairs. Banging and banging and banging. I popped up in the bed, realizing the dream was over and I was back to my life. The earbuds had fallen out of my ears and Tupac was whispering. My heart felt like it was trying to break free from my chest.

More banging. I jumped out of bed and ran down the steps, ready to let my father in. *He must've left his keys. Or he lost them. Yeah, he probably lost them. He's banging so hard because he's drunk. Probably already pissed himself. Here we go again.*

I looked through the peephole. A dark figure stood at the door.

No, two dark figures, one slumped behind the first guy. A shadow, long and thin, like death itself with its awkward assistant, trying to bang my door down. And neither figure was my dad.

"Matthew!" a voice yelled from the other side of the door. "Matthew!"

I cracked the door. The rain, thick sheets of it, was still coming down. I could barely keep my eyes open it was pouring so hard, bouncing off everything, splashing me in the face.

"Matthew, it's me! Mr. Ray!"

Mr. Ray? What was he doing here? I know he didn't come by to talk about work. Not in this weather. That could've waited until tomorrow. Or he could've just called. And who was the other guy? Then I thought about how my mother had been begging my dad to put a light out there. This could've gone smoother if I could see.

"Mr. Ray?" I stepped back from the door. And there I was . . . in my underwear. Didn't think to put on pants because I thought it was my father at the door.

Mr. Ray pushed the door open and sloshed his way inside, the man behind him still hidden. It was almost as if the guy was purposely trying to hide from me.

"Matthew," Mr. Ray said, sliding the wet hat from his head. "I'm sorry for popping up on you like this. I tried calling, but the phone rang and rang."

Tupac, the rain, everything was so loud.

Mr. Ray stepped to the side and yanked Quasimodo from behind him. The man lifted his head. You know when a person has a unique feature on their face, it's always the first thing you see. Like if someone has a mole or a birthmark or scar on their face, that's always what your eyes go to. This person had a special thing. Well, maybe not special, but something you'd always recognize. Holes. Like tiny spoons had dug tiny spoonfuls out of his cheeks. Cork.

"But listen, we gotta get you to the hospital," Mr. Ray said, straight to the point.

"What?"

"Your father. He's in the hospital . . ." Mr. Ray paused, his face dripping, his eyes sad. "He's been hit by a car."

I felt like I suddenly couldn't breathe. My eyes started to blur. I was having another one of those moments, just like when I walked into my parents' room months ago and saw them sitting on the bed, holding each other, my mother trying to keep it together, asking me about those stupid senior pictures right before she told me she had breast cancer. I remember asking God to not let it be what I thought—knew—it was. And here I was again, asking for the same thing. *Not again, God. Not again.*

"Is he okay? Is he hurt?" I pleaded, my voice high and shaky.

"I don't know, but we have to go," Mr. Ray replied. He looked at me with the same face he gives people who've come to him for funeral service. The "sorry for your loss" face.

I don't even remember getting dressed. I just remember, in a flash, being in Mr. Ray's big black car. Cork sat behind me. The leather made a weird sound, almost like a fart, every time he shifted positions. The smell of damp, and liquor, sifted through the space left between the three of us.

Cork still hadn't said a thing.

Mr. Ray adjusted the rearview mirror.

"Y'know, he was with your father today," Mr. Ray continued, "and Matthew, it really doesn't matter what they were doing, but—" He stopped. And looked at his younger brother, through the mirror.

"You know what, *you* should tell him," Mr. Ray said to Cork, his voice suddenly steely.

I stared straight ahead as the rain pounded down onto the windshield, the wipers working double-time.

"He was jus tryin' get home," Cork said softly. His words slurred, his voice made the hairs stand up on the back of my neck. "It started ta rain, and he just, wuh gonna try to make it home before it gah bad."

I twisted my mouth up to hold in my anger. And my fear. You would think that after your new drinking buddy got hit by a car, you would sober up.

"Tell him what happened, Cork," Mr. Ray demanded.

It was no use. Cork was fading in and out.

"Cork!" Mr. Ray barked.

"Mr. Ray, can you just tell me. Please," I said, my voice cracking. "I need to know what happened to my dad." The tears were making their way up.

Mr. Ray sighed, clearly disappointed and embarrassed by his brother.

"He was trying to come home. At least that's what Cork said. He said they were hanging out over on Albany, and the rain started. So Jackson left. But when he got to the corner of Fulton and Albany, he lost his balance and stumbled out into the street. Gypsy cab got him."

My eyes started to sting.

"He was drunk," I said.

"Now, we don't know that, Matthew," Mr. Ray said quickly.

"No, I wasn't asking. I was telling you, Mr. Ray. He was drunk."

I don't know why I said it, but I did. Because I knew it was true.

CHAPTER 6
BROKEN AND
BONDED

Beeping. Buzzing. Electronic doors clicking, sliding open. The smell of dirty and clean, mixed up together. The hospital was the same as it was when my mother was there. Nothing had changed about it except for the person I was there to see.

Cork sat down in the waiting room, his body almost melting into the chair. That was probably the safest place for him. Somewhere he could just go to sleep. Mr. Ray walked me to the front desk and pretty much did all the talking.

"Excuse me, ma'am, we're here to see Jackson Miller," he said to the lady behind the desk.

She began typing, squinting at the computer screen.

"Looks like he's still in Emergency," she said to the monitor.

It felt like I could feel the blood moving through my body, in my hands, my legs, my chest, my stomach. I don't even know if there are veins in my stomach, but it sure felt like there were. And I was having a bad case of bubble-guts, so the blood in there must've been boiling. Usually people say their minds run a mile a minute when these things happen, but mine wasn't running at all. It was standing still. I was only thinking one thing. *God, please don't let my dad die.* That's all.

"Ma'am, this is his son," Mr. Ray said softly. "We just need to know something. Please," he begged.

The lady at the desk looked up at me. Her eyes were bright even though I could tell she was tired. She looked sorry for me.

"Hold on," she said, picking up the phone. She dialed a few numbers. Mr. Ray patted me on the back and nodded. His face didn't look too worried, but the way he balled his hat up let me know he was definitely nervous. A man like Mr. Ray doesn't ball his hat up, ever.

The lady behind the desk asked whoever was on the other end of the phone about my father, and wondered if there was any word. She explained that I, his son, was there.

"Uh-huh. Uh-huh. Okay," she said, then hung up. Then she closed-mouth smiled. "Someone will be out in a second."

The doctor came through the big double doors in the typical doctor getup. Greenish blue pajamas and that thing on his head that looked like the hat that ninjas wear. He also wore a mask, but it was pulled down under his mouth, so he could talk.

"Here for Mr. Miller?" the doctor asked, his face pale.

"Yes, I'm Willie Ray, and this is Mr. Miller's son, Matthew."

"Dr. Winston."

Mr. Ray shook his hand, and then I did. The doctor squeezed tight.

"Well, Matthew, your father is going to be okay."

I exhaled. It felt like I had been holding my breath since we left the house. "But," Dr. Winston continued, "he's banged up pretty bad."

I just nodded. At least I think I nodded. I wasn't really sure, but I know I moved my head.

"The car was going pretty fast and caught him from the side. He has multiple fractures in both legs, a few cracked ribs, and a hairline fracture in his jaw from hitting the windshield. The legs, they'll need surgery. But rods and pins'll have him up walking again, eventually. But the good thing is, his spine is fine, and his brain is fine too, which is really what matters most."

Mr. Ray clapped me on the back—good bad news is better than bad bad news.

"Well, that's good news, Doc," Mr. Ray said. "That's good news."

"Damn right it is," the doctor said.

I don't know why, but I liked the fact that he said damn. It made me feel comfortable. Like somebody I already knew. Like someone who actually cared about my dad.

"Now, he's got a long night ahead of him. More tests to make sure the ribs haven't punctured anything, and that the broken bones in his legs haven't lacerated any blood vessels, and then straight to the OR we go. So unfortunately, you won't be able to see him till the morning." That was fine with me. As long as I knew he wasn't going to die, I was okay.

"Is there a Mrs. Miller?" the doctor asked. Came out of left field and caught me right in the gut. I guess it made sense to ask, but I wasn't ready for it. I cleared my throat to answer, but got stuck.

"No," Mr. Ray chimed in and bailed me out. "But I'll be here." He clapped my back again.

Dr. Winston never missed a beat. "Perfect. Like I said, you can see him in the morning. He'll probably do a few weeks here, and if all goes well, we'll move him next door to the rehab center to start teaching him to walk again. Sound like a plan?"

I nodded as the doctor shook our hands again and walked back through the big double doors.

3:00 a.m. Back at home. Back upstairs. Back in bed. But not back to sleep. Instead, I sat there thinking about how quickly things change. How quickly life changes. I was just pissed at Dad the night before—hell, I was pissed at him earlier that day—and now all I could do is think about hugging him and telling him that I loved him, and that I needed him. It's strange to think about. How that could've been it. He could've died. Only a month after my mom. And even though he didn't—die, that is—I still felt so alone. Even though Mr. Ray was helping out, and Chris was cool, I still felt like I went from a not-so-fancy version of the Cosbys to a one-man family. Like that movie with Tom Hanks stuck on an island—I felt like him, far away from everything, calling out in the dark, the waves splashing up on me, the deep water waiting to swallow me up.

I don't remember falling asleep and I don't really remember waking up. It was like I just closed my eyes for a few minutes and then opened them when my cellphone started vibrating on top of my dresser. But I didn't feel rested, or awake. It was six thirty and Mr. Ray said to be outside at seven so that we could make it to the hospital right when visiting hours started.

In a haze I washed up, put on my white dress shirt, buttoned it bottom-up, and slung my black tie around my neck. I tied it once, the wrong way as usual, then tied it again. Downstairs I slipped on my slacks, then wiggled my foot into the stiff black dress shoes. The heel was always the hardest part. Lastly, the most important piece—the jacket.

In the kitchen I picked my backpack up, slipping one arm through one of the straps and bounced it up on my shoulder. Then, I thought about it. Was I really going to go to school today? What if Dad needed me to stay at the hospital? What if something went wrong in the surgery? They probably would've called me, but still . . . what if? Did I really want to sit there listening to Mr. Grovenor explain for the twentieth time what fabliaux were? *Fa-blah*. With everything that was going on? I don't think so. I dropped the bag back on the chair and headed for the front door.

Mr. Ray was already sitting out on his stoop reading the paper. His dark slacks were raised high above his ankles. His hat, a different one, but the same style, hid his fuzzy hair. When he heard my door close, he looked up. Then, he rolled the newspaper up into a tight paper pipe, grabbed the brown bag next to him, and stood.

"Good morning," he called out.

I trotted down the steps and met him at his car.

"Morning," I said. Just "morning." There was nothing good about it.

"Breakfast?" Mr. Ray said, as he opened the paper bag.

"No thanks."

"Yep. Breakfast," he repeated, making it clear that this wasn't an option. He reached down into the bag and pulled out two bagels, one for me, one for him.

"Hope you like cream cheese," he said, handing me a bagel, still warm. "They always pile it on at the bodega." He shook his head at the cream cheese overload and reached back into the bag.

"Here," he said, handing me a cup of coffee without looking. "Light and sweet."

I didn't drink coffee. When I was around seven, I once took a sip of my father's. It was terrible, like drinking smoke. I decided right then and there that juice would be my choice of breakfast drink. But I couldn't turn down the coffee, and knew that even if I tried, Mr. Ray would've insisted and probably said something like "Today you become a man," or some mess like that. I probably would've taken anything he offered me. Even a cigarette.

We got to the hospital at seven thirty on the dot. Mr. Ray was always crazy about being on time, but I guess when you do his kind of work, you really can't afford to not be. Don't want the dead people showing up late to their own funerals. My head was buzzing from the coffee—not spinning, just kind of jumping around. It felt weird but I guess that was the point of coffee. To get the brain jumping around. Mr. Ray checked his face in the flip-down mirror and wiped away a smear of cream cheese caught in the corner of his mouth.

"Before we go in," he said seriously. He flipped the mirror back up and continued. "I need to tell you that I, uh . . ." Mr. Ray looked straight ahead for a few seconds before finally facing me. I could see his jaw flexing, as if he was chewing on his words. "I, uh . . . I'm sorry, Matthew. For all this."

"You didn't do nothing," I said.

"I know, but . . ." He started swinging his head side to side, like he was working kinks out of his neck. "But this is my brother's fault. And I feel responsible."

"Mr. Ray—" I started, but he cut me off.

"Just listen, son," he said sharp. "My brother, he . . . he always . . ." Mr. Ray pressed his lips tight, obviously frustrated that he couldn't get it out. Then he started again. "I just want you to know that from here on out, I'm gonna look after you. While your old man is getting himself together, I got you." He patted his chest.

"Mr. Ray, really I—"

"Eh, eh, eh," he interrupted again, shaking his head. "I feel like it's my duty. And I owe it to your folks. Hell, I owe it to you."

This time I decided not to even try to respond. I just nodded.

"Okay," he said, switching back to a lighter tone. "Ready?"

Tubes and wires everywhere. My father laid in the bed with both of his legs strapped up in some weird contraption, already with thick white casts on them. His face was badly bruised and swollen, leaving purple splotches around his eyes and on one whole side of his face.

"Good news," Dr. Winston said, still there, just as upbeat as he was in the middle of the night. "The internal fixation surgery was a success. He's got a few extra screws in him, to bond the bones, and we're still going to monitor his legs closely, especially the inflammation, but so far so good. Bad news is, he won't be able to speak," Dr. Winston said. "At least not yet. We also had to immobilize his jaw so that the fracture would heal, so it's wired shut."

I came close to my dad, looking at him top to bottom, bottom to top. A tube in his arm. A tube down his throat. I wanted to hug him but I knew I couldn't. I just stood there staring at him while he slept, feeling pretty damn helpless.

"He's also going to be out for a while. We got him pretty doped up for the pain," Dr. Winston said. "But judging from the surgery and all the test results, it's looking like he's going to be fine. It's gonna take some time, though. I can't stress that enough."

I nodded without looking at the doctor. I couldn't stop staring at my dad lying there stiff, broken. I didn't know if I should be angry with him for doing this to me—to himself—or if I should feel sad. Or even happy, just knowing that he would survive, and recover. I didn't know what to feel, and that frustrated me. My eyes started to twitch and burn, and the water came streaming down my face. I wiped the tears quickly, but they kept coming. Mr. Ray must've noticed me crying, because he asked the doctor if he could step out with him for a second to talk about rehab stuff.

When they left, I pulled a chair up beside the bed and sat down. And for the first time since Mom's funeral, I let it out.

On the way back to the neighborhood Mr. Ray and I didn't talk too much. He turned the radio on and hummed to old songs from the seventies, snapping his fingers, and sometimes even singing some of the words. His voice wasn't too bad. Raspy, but not bad.

"Want me to drop you off at school?" he said, turning the radio down a little.

I didn't know what to say. I didn't want to lie to him and tell him yeah, and then cut school, but I also didn't want to tell him the truth, that I didn't want to go. Especially since he always said I was different from how he was, growing up. I could tell Mr. Ray looked at me as a good kid, not a dude who skipped school. And that was true. I never cut school, but today I just needed a break.

"Um," I grunted.

Mr. Ray tucked his lips into his mouth like a man with no teeth and tried to hold in his laughter. "I'm kidding, son," he said, now flashing a cocky grin. "I know you ain't going to no damn school. You ain't even got your books with you."

I looked at him, surprised and relieved.

"It's cool. You're smart enough to make it up," he said confidently. "But you got your suit on, so I see you're ready for work."

"Yeah."

"Well, ain't no work to do today, son, so you all dressed up with nowhere to go." Mr. Ray slid open the ashtray under the radio. He wiggled his finger inside of it and pulled out a small key. "But I wanna show you something."

He turned the radio back up and jerked his head back and forth, singing. Marvin Gaye, my mom's favorite, was playing. "Inner City Blues."

I had never actually been inside Mr. Ray's house. I mean, I had been in his *funeral* home, but never his *home* home, even though he lived right across the street from me. When we got to the top of his stoop, which felt like it took forever because of his limp, he jammed a key into the wooden door. Then he jooked it around a little until it turned and clicked.

"This bad boy got a trick to it," he explained. "I was gonna buy a new door when this lock started sticking, but then I thought, nope, I'll keep it how it is." He pushed against the old wooden door until it popped open.

I didn't really know what to expect from Mr. Ray's house. I mean, I didn't really think much about it as a kid. I never wondered what it was like because he seemed like just a regular guy, sitting outside with his newspaper, coffee, and his cigarettes, watching the neighborhood live, prepared to do his job whenever a piece of it died. Other than that, he handed out cancer pamphlets and minded his own business. So I figured his house probably looked a lot like mine. Why wouldn't it?

But I was wrong. Mr. Ray's house wasn't normal at all. Not to me. Don't get me wrong, it wasn't creepy or nothing like that. As a matter of fact, it was incredible. Something straight off MTV. Leather couches and big flat-screen TVs hanging from the walls next to art in fancy frames, which seemed weird because he didn't seem like the TV type, or the art type. Everything was leather and wood, and not that regular wood you see in most people's homes—that light wood. Nope, he had dark wood everywhere, wood the color of me. I could just tell it cost a lot. I had no idea funeral homes made so much money. I don't think I ever even thought about Mr. Ray getting paid. But he was living a sweet life and nobody in our neighborhood would ever be able to tell, judging from the outside of the place. I mean, he had to wiggle his key just to open the front door! And then it hit me why he didn't have that janky door replaced. If he kept the old raggedy one he had, no one would ever suspect how dope his house was on the inside. Smart move.

"You want something?" he said, slipping his arm out of his coat. "Some water? Coffee?"

I tried to not stare at all the awesome stuff he had everywhere.

"I'm good, thanks."

"I'll put on a pot of coffee anyway," he said, heading around the corner to what I guessed was the kitchen.

"Come on in here," he called.

The kitchen was all marble and stainless steel. No dishes in the sink. No crumbs. Nothing like my kitchen. Chris's kitchen was like my kitchen. Every kitchen I had ever been in was pretty much like my kitchen. Except this one.

Mr. Ray poured us huge cups of coffee, mine light and sweet, his black. My coffee high from earlier had worn off, finally, and here I was about to bring it right back. I don't get why people drink this crap.

Mr. Ray stood at the counter and took a sip, a slurp. He seemed to be studying me, reading me. Then out of nowhere he just blurted, "You know, I meant what I said earlier."

"I know."

Mr. Ray nodded and took another sip of his coffee. It seemed like there was something else he wanted to tell me. I was hoping it wasn't another apology. Didn't need another one of those, especially since I didn't blame him for nothing. But I appreciated it. After a few more awkward sips and swallows he finally said, "Come with me."

He led me through the kitchen, back into the living room, to a door on the far side of the room. He dug into his pocket and pulled out the small key he took from the ashtray in his car. He slipped it into the doorknob and jiggled it around just like he did the front door. He looked back at me, smiled, and shrugged.

The door opened. Darkness.

"No one has seen what I'm about to show you. Not even my brothers," he said, running his hand along the wall, trying to find the light switch.

"What is it?" I asked, holding the mug up to my mouth and blowing on the hot coffee.

Mr. Ray slipped the key back into his pocket.

"How come kids today gotta know everything? Nothing can be a mystery or an adventure anymore. Takes the excitement out of life."

I slurped the coffee. It burned my tongue.

"I'm just asking," I said.

Mr. Ray sighed and mumbled as if he wasn't talking to me, even though he was. "Guess it's better than being a sheep and just going wherever people tell you. Lord knows we don't need no more of them." Then he spoke louder. "You know what a vault is?"

"Like the kind they got in banks?" My voice went from high-school Matt to middle-school Matt.

"Yeah."

"You got a vault down there? Like, full of money?" Now it was at elementary-school Matt.

Mr. Ray almost spat coffee everywhere.

"Not exactly," he said. "But my basement is like my vault." He turned and started heading down the steps. "I can't really explain it, son. Just come on."

The wooden stairs felt flimsy under my feet. There was no railing, and I wondered how Mr. Ray would be able to keep coming down here, to this secret lair, when he was older, especially since he was already limping. As we got closer to the bottom of the steps, the light, though still dim, got a little brighter, and I could see that the room, this dungeon—the vault—was overloaded with photos taped to the walls like posters in a teenage girl's bedroom. Photos of ball players, newspaper stories, old and dry, some even framed. Smaller pictures, some Polaroids of a woman, her skin dark and smooth, her teeth bright white. She smiled big in all of them, so natural, like she was actually happy to have her picture taken.

There was a table in the middle of the floor, under a lightbulb that hung from a wire. Mr. Ray pulled an extra chair up as I stared at all the oldness. I looked closely at one news article about a high-school ball player who scored eighty-five points in a game.

"You know what that is?" Mr. Ray said, sitting down on one of the fold-up chairs.

I leaned forward, read, then gaped. "Is this about you?" I turned to look at him, then turned back at the brownish gray paper stuck to the wall.

"Do it say my name?" Mr. Ray joked. "If so, then I guess it's about me."

"This says you scored eighty-five points?" I'm not a big sports dude but I know enough to know eighty-five points is a lot of damn points. "I didn't know you played high-school ball."

Mr. Ray nodded.

"And college," he said, pointing to some other cut-outs on the wall. "Syracuse."

I moved down the wall to see some of the college clippings.

RAY AT THE BUZZER FOR THE WIN!

RAY OF LIGHT, WHY WILLIAM RAY RULES THE COURT

RAY ALL THE WAY! SYRACUSE SOPHOMORE'S GOT WHAT IT TAKES

"This is amazing. I mean, you were amazing!" I said, boosted. He'd been *so good*!

Mr. Ray rubbed his head. "Yeah." He smirked, then pointed. "Read that one over there."

In the corner there was another clipping, this one from the *New York Times*. It was pinned to the wall by itself. Nothing around it. Front page of the sports section. It read in big black bold letters:

WILLIAM RAY, BROKEN KNEE; SHINING STAR'S SEASON OVER

"What they shoulda wrote was 'Career Over,'" Mr. Ray said. "Y'know, I was slated to go top ten in the draft." He leaned back in his chair. "But the knee never healed. They never do."

I walked back over to the table and set my coffee down.

"Oh man, you must've been pissed! I mean, so close, and then something fluke happens and ruins everything. All that money." I shook my head.

Mr. Ray laughed. "All that money. And yeah, son, I was pretty damn pissed. Martin Gandrey's big ass fell on me and ruined my ball career." He took his hands down from his head and tapped on the table like he was playing the piano. "But I was okay, after a while, because I had her."

He was looking over my shoulder at the wall. The other pictures. The ones of the pretty dark-skinned lady, cheesing for the camera.

"Who's that?"

"Ella," Mr. Ray said, his eyes still focusing on her pictures. "Ella Dansfield. Man. I used to get lost in that smile."

I turned to look at the pictures again. She did have an amazing smile. Seemed like all her teeth were showing, but not in a weird way.

"Yeah. Ella." He sighed.

"Was that your girlfriend?"

"*Girlfriend?* Ha! Son, a man my age don't keep pictures of his teenage *girlfriend* up on his walls. What that look like?"

I didn't really think about it that way, but I guess that would be strange.

"Ella was my wife. I met her in college, and we were engaged before I even graduated. Before I broke my knee. And after I broke it, I started learning the funeral business under my old man and was able to provide a good life for us. I missed basketball, but as long as I had her, I was fine."

"I didn't even know you had a wife. Never seen her."

"That's 'cause she's gone, and I ain't got the heart to wear the ring no more."

"She left?" I frowned.

"No. See, we had this thing. Once a week we would have date night at one of the restaurants around here. Because I was always working so hard at the funeral home, she usually just met me at work, and then we'd go on to get something to eat. One day, December seventeenth, 1975, a bitter cold night after a day of rain, she left the house to come meet me. I guess there was black ice or something on the stoop. She slipped, hit her head, and was gone before anyone could even get to her. Twenty-nine years old."

I checked his eyes. No water. But I was feeling crazy inside, like I was going to cry at any moment. I could tell he still felt the burn, but it didn't make him as emotional anymore. I wondered how long it took him to get to that point, and how long it was gonna take me.

"I'm so sorry." I didn't know what else to say.

"Oh man, please. It's been over thirty years. I was a goddamn mess then, which is when I started this room, this shrine of all the fucked-up things that happened to me. I used to sleep down here, on that couch, around all my sadness. But I always kept upstairs all clean and new because I didn't want nobody to know about this—to even suspect it—my pain room. My vault. Not even my brothers," he explained. "But now . . . *you* know."

I did my best to maintain composure and just take it all in. Here was this man, a man I always saw as the dude who beat cancer twice, the old guy across the street who ran the neighborhood. But I didn't know he used to be a ball player and a husband, and lost both his wife and career for absolutely no reason. A man who used to sleep in his basement surrounded by images of who he used to be, his life suddenly changed forever. I looked at him sitting there across from me, and suddenly imagined him crying his way through his twenties, and probably most of his thirties. I can't even believe he's still here, alive. And not nuts. And cancer too? Clearly, Mr. Ray was a man made of steel, and I had had no idea.

"But why are you showing *me*?" I wasn't sure if I should ask that, but I really wanted to know. Of all the people to show this, he chose me. What for?

"I don't know. I guess I've been waiting to show someone who would . . . get it," Mr. Ray said. "And, well . . ." He didn't finish his sentence. He just took the last few gulps of his coffee, a little trickling down his chin, black like oil. He wiped it with the back of his hand and stared into the cup like it was a crystal ball.

I didn't say anything. I just kind of watched him take a few more moments down memory lane, back when he could make the game-winning three-pointer, then kiss his girl after he came from the locker room. Days long gone.

"You play chess?" Mr. Ray suddenly snapped out of it and set his mug down. Seemed like such a random question. *Chess? Right now? In this dungeon?*

"A little. I mean, I can play, but I'm not like a master or nothing like that," I fumbled. Truth is, I just wasn't very good. But I knew some guys who were super good. Like three-move-checkmate good. Funny enough, Chris was one of them. It was a way he kind of got through a lot of things. Smacking heads in chess. And in the hood, if you can play chess, you get some respect.

"Good, 'cause I don't wanna play," he said, relieved. Like I was going to ask him to play. "It's an overrated game that people, especially New Yorkers, think is the friggin' holy grail of games. Like you can learn all there is to know about life by playing chess. A bunch of bull." He shook his head.

People did make it seem like chess was a game about life and that you have to always think out your next three moves and the moves of your opponent in order to win . . . at life. I always thought it was wild to see dudes you knew were hustlers playing chess for hours. Junkies come cop dope from them right in the middle of the game. Crazy. But Chris used to always tell me that drug dealers played to keep their minds sharp. To always know their next move and the move after that. I guess most of them weren't too good at chess, because they still got caught.

"What about I-DEE-clare War?" Mr. Ray leaned forward and rested his arms on the old table. He looked me dead in the eye.

"What about it?" I leaned back a little.

"You play?"

"When I was, like, six." I laughed.

Mr. Ray didn't laugh. At all. Not even a smile.

"Let's play," he said, sliding his chair back from the table and reaching for a deck of cards on the shelf behind him. "This is a real game."

Mr. Ray slid the cards out of their soggy box and attempted to shuffle them, but the cards were so old they kept sticking together. So he just laid them all on the table and mixed them up like a child would do before playing Go Fish.

"This is really the holy grail of games," he said, dealing the cards one by one. "The game of life."

"You think so?"

"I know so." He lifted his eyes from the cards and gave me a five-second stare down. "See, in chess, you plan everything. You strategize and all that. And even though we like to believe life goes that way, let me tell you, son, it don't." He waved his hands around as if to say, *Look at this room. This is proof that life don't always go as planned.* But I didn't need to look at his walls to know that. All I had to do was look at my father. Or sit in my empty house at night. I was definitely with Mr. Ray on this one.

"But this game here, I-DEE-clare War, is how life really goes down." Finally done dealing, he picked up his stack and held it in his hand, face down. Then, he flipped the first card.

"I flip a card, then you flip a card," he explained, and waited for me to turn my first card. A six. His was a ten. "Sometimes I win"—he raked the cards off to the side, close to him—"and some-times I lose." He flipped another card. An eight. This time I turned a queen and beat him.

"And sometimes," he continued while flipping another one, "I can lose and lose and lose and I don't know why. But there's nothing I can do but just keep flipping the cards. Eventually, I'll win again. As long as you got cards to keep turning, you're fine. Now, *that's* life," he said, pushing another hand I won over to me.

CHAPTER 7
AGAINST THE RULES

AFTER ME AND MR. RAY'S DUNGEON ADVENTURE, THINGS kind of smoothed out for a while. Well, maybe not smoothed out, but at least there were no more surprises. And that was a good thing. Me feeling crazy about my mom dying was still there, bugging me the most at night when I was in bed, and Tupac probably wasn't helping, but even the pain was just becoming a part of me. The dreams of my mother sitting with me at her own funeral kept coming every night on schedule, and y'know, I started to look forward to them. It was like our time together for a few hours that felt only like a few minutes, making me happy to see her, but leaving me disappointed to wake up to an empty house in the morning. But at least I was sleeping through the night. And at least, when I woke up, I knew why my father wasn't home, and it wasn't because he was dead too.

Mr. Ray, who became like a big brother to me—well, maybe more like an uncle—was worried about me staying in the house by myself. But I assured him that I was fine. I mean, it's not like I was a kid. Not to mention, I was at school for the first part of every day, and with him for most of the rest of the day, so I was actually only alone in the house at night. And all I would do is look through my mom's old cookbooks—not that I was cooking anything—and try my best to go to sleep.

Mr. Ray took me to see my father every Monday, Wednesday, and Friday before school. While I went in to see my broken-up pop, Mr. Ray usually stayed out in the lobby and talked to the receptionist who'd helped us the first night. Looked like Mr. Ray hadn't lost all his cool yet, and that lady was getting a healthy dose three times a week.

The first two weeks of Dad being in the hospital were the roughest, mostly because his mouth was wired shut, and there was a skinny tube shoved down his throat, which I learned was how they were feeding him since he couldn't chew. You ever seen liquid food pumped through a tube, straight down a man's throat into his belly? Not cool.

They also were giving him less pain medication, so at least he was able to keep his eyes open long enough to know I was there. I remember the third morning I showed up, it was the first time he was all there and not doped up on medicine—he looked at me and squeezed his eyes into little slits as if he was trying to make sure it was really me, standing there. I was dressed in my funeral suit. All black. I could tell he was confused.

"No, you ain't dead yet," I said. "This ain't your funeral."

He grunted and I could see his stomach bouncing a little under the white sheet from him wanting to laugh but trying not to because of his broken ribs. He couldn't smile, but I could tell by the look in his eyes he was happy to see me. And probably happier that I wasn't the grim reaper.

By the third week they had transferred him to the rehabilitation center next door, which was good. Even though recovery was going to take some time, it was better than sitting in that hospital. Nobody likes hospitals. He probably would've been in rehab sooner if it wasn't for all the other injuries. They finally pulled that hose out of his throat so he was able to talk again. So glad I wasn't there to see that. Gross. It wasn't perfect, but it was good enough.

"Man, it was terrible," he said, his voice hoarse and muffled. "I mean, I really thought it was gonna choke me to death before they got it out." He used the back of his tongue to scratch the inside of his throat, ribbitting like a frog.

Whenever I would go see him, he spent most of the time asking me questions. It felt like he missed a lot of my life, even though it had only been about three weeks since he'd been out getting wasted every night with Cork. The first thing he wanted to know was what was up with the suit.

"It's for work. Remember I told you I'm working for Mr. Ray? Ray's Funeral Home?"

My father bugged his eyes out. "I don't remember you telling me that." Of course he didn't. The morning I told him he was too busy pretending he wasn't hungover. He looked skeptical. "Well, how is it? I mean, you gotta touch dead people?"

I thought of doing to him what I did to Chris when he asked that question, but my father might've flinched and thrown all his broken bones out of whack even more.

"Naw, man. I just help out with the stuff like flowers, and ushering, making sure the cars are clean"—yes, Mr. Ray had me washing the hearses—"and stuff like that. Sometimes I have to be a pallbearer, too."

My father tried to shift around in bed, squinting his eyes closed in pain at the effort. His legs, still in their big white casts, looked like two albino elephant legs. When he finally got comfortable, he asked, "Well, do you like it?"

"It's cool."

"Is it paying?"

"Yeah."

My dad nodded. "Well then, you like it."

Yeah. I liked it. Man, I *loved* it. And I would've still done it even if Mr. Ray didn't pay me the thirty bucks. But I couldn't tell my dad that. I couldn't tell him that school was boring and pretty much a big blur every day, where I daydreamed about dead people and their brokenhearted family members most of the morning, and was still managing to pass with nothing lower than a B. No way would he have understood that. No one would've.

Working at the funeral home was the best thing I had going for me. It was my golden ticket, almost like a VIP pass to any funeral I wanted to go to. Each one was different. Different people, different places. But the one thing that was always the same was how the closest person to whoever the funeral was for reacted. Day after day, week after week, funeral after funeral, I searched for that person—almost always sitting in the front—and watched them deal. Saw them rock back and forth, the sound of their hearts breaking, weeping, sobbing, all in the pitch of pain. Desperately begging for help in a room full of uncomfortable people who want to be helpful, but just don't know how. Because they can't help. Nothing helps. I knew that. Every time I saw them, the closest ones, bent over in tears, it felt like a warm rain came down inside me. Even though I knew that I couldn't help them and they couldn't help me, just knowing that we were all struggling with this thing . . . *that* helped.

And you wouldn't believe how many different kinds of funerals there are. Hood funerals, like Dante Brown's, where all of his friends showed up in all red, and dropped red bandanas, big heavy gold chains that looked fake, and crew pictures in his casket. It's weird to know when people have guns in church. Makes it hard to close your eyes when it's time to pray. The Bloods stood all along the back wall of Cornerstone Baptist. Each one wore sunglasses, tattoos peeking from under the collars of their T-shirts, permanent frowns on their faces. I stood along the side wall. I mean, I didn't think anything would happen to me if I stood in the back with them, but I wasn't going to take any chances. Plus, the side wall gave a better view of Dante's mother and girlfriend, sitting in the first pew, holding each other face-to-face, their tears mixing. The sound of them crying and shushing the cries of Dante's newborn baby boy at the same time is one I'll never forget.

Or the funeral of Marie Rogers, a happy funeral. Marie passed away in her sleep three days after her hundredth birthday. She was a New York City school teacher for forty years, and after she retired, decided to travel the world with her husband. Then, once Donald died, she decided to become a painter, and had a pretty good career the last thirty years of her life, as an artist. So her funeral was pretty cool. A lot of people got up to say how she influenced them. Even some of her old students, who were now almost eighty years old. That was wild. To hear an eighty-year-old talk about how he had been affected by this woman seventy years ago was amazing. She outlived all of her family, including her only child, Bernard, who didn't have any kids himself. So as you can imagine, the church wasn't too full.

Of all the people who got up to talk about Mrs. Rogers, there was one person who got up there and then couldn't say anything, who just couldn't get the words out—Mrs. Rogers's helper. Her name was Ola. And Ola, out of everyone who was there, was the only person crying. She had spent the last ten years with Mrs. Rogers, looking after her, talking to her, driving her around. She was the closest to her. And though this wasn't a sad funeral, what Ola was feeling, nobody else could.

And, yeah, there were funny funerals. The funniest was Glendale Price's. Mr. Ray told me that Mr. Price was a friend of his from way back. He said my mom might've even known him, because he was an actor who mainly did theater work on Broadway, and had gone to the same school as my mother when she was chasing her acting dream. Mr. Ray said Mr. Price was pretty successful, but refused to leave the hood. He said Mr. Price used to always say, "I was born here, and I'm gonna be buried here."

He had lung cancer, something else Mr. Ray made it a point to say.

"Yeah, he was my buddy. He'd invite me and Ella to his shows—this is before he was doing Broadway—and we'd all go out afterward and run through a pack of smokes like it was nothing." Mr. Ray half-smiled and half-frowned, probably thinking about his own cigarette habit that he couldn't kick, even after cancer. Twice.

Mr. Ray went on to tell me that when Mr. Price found out his lung cancer was terminal, he started working on what he thought would be his best role ever. To play himself, at his own funeral. The only catch was, he only wanted the play to be seen *at* his own funeral.

I'll tell you, it was like no other funeral I had ever been to. People filed in and were handed a program as they took seats. On the cover there was a picture of Mr. Price, and it read: THE FUNERAL OF GLENDALE PRICE, A COMEDY. The program listed a cast of characters, and of course when it got to his name it said, GLENDALE PRICE, AS HIMSELF.

So you'd think it'd be all sad, especially since they left the casket open the whole time, but actually the play was pretty funny. It was about this guy, Glendale, who spent his whole life playing different characters on stage, and how when he died, all those characters showed up at his funeral to talk trash about him. It was like one of those roast things celebrities have, but better. It was like clowning on the block. The only character I recognized was Hamlet, who went off on Mr. Price in Shakespearean talk. Hilarious. Mr. Grovenor probably would've loved it.

Everyone was laughing, holding their guts and their sides as these actors gave Mr. Price his final wish, and acted out his funeral play, a comedy, at his funeral. At the end of it all his wife got up to speak. Her smile was big and you could tell that she had had quite a laugh herself.

"And the award for best actor goes to," she called out, then she looked down at the casket, "Glendale Price!" Everyone laughed and stood and clapped for Mr. Price, lying there stiff as a board in his burial box. There was no smile on his face. No final bow. Nothing. Mrs. Price's smile faded a little. Just a little. Most people probably didn't catch it because they were too busy clapping. But I caught it. She never broke down, but that split second when the truth of the matter flashed across her face was all I needed to know it was there.

Besides the happy, sad, and funny funerals, there were the super quick in-and-out funerals, or as Robbie Ray called them, drive-bys. There was also what they called "reunerals"—funerals where people showed up who the rest of the family hadn't seen in years. A reunion. And not only did long-lost members of the family show up, but they usually turned the whole service out with screaming and hollering. One time I even saw a woman try to climb in the casket with the dead person. One of her family members damn near had to put her in a headlock to get her to sit down.

Mr. Ray said it's always when people die that we start thinking about the wrong things we did to them, and that reunerals were the funerals where the guilty came to apologize.

Then there were the disorganized funerals. These were the worst, only because they usually lasted the longest for no reason at all. Nobody ever knows who's supposed to read the obituary. The little girl they chose to read the scripture can't read. The old choir members are having a hard time remembering what song to sing. Nobody knows who the pallbearers are. Just a mess. During these funerals Mr. Ray would usually just take charge and get it done. No matter how crazy or boring the funeral was, it didn't matter. As long as I could spot the person hurting the most, I could feel the warm buzz filling me up inside, like a hit to a junkie. And to be honest, I didn't feel like such a creep about it all like I did when I first started sitting in. Don't get me wrong, I still knew it was weird, but as long as I got out of there before the repast—as long as I could disappear before anyone started asking questions— I was cool. No repasts. Ever. That was the rule.

But of course, like all rules, there was one time—and one time only—that I broke it. November twenty-fourth. Two days before Thanksgiving, three months after my mother's death, and two months after my father's accident. I went to the rehab place to see him early that morning. His jaw was all back to normal by then, the wires out, his ribs were healed, and the casts were off, but the leg exercises they had him doing—the ones I saw—looked painful as hell. He basically had to learn how to walk again. Dr. Winston was there as usual, even though he wasn't the rehab doctor. The rehab doctor was Dr. Fisher, who wasn't really as funny as Dr. Winston, but she was nice. Dr. Winston was just there to make sure everything was going smooth—and to crack some early-morning jokes.

"Okay, Mr. Miller, we gotta work out these legs. But listen here"—Dr. Winston leaned in a little—"today it's not gonna just be machines. Today we're going to actually get you upright, and I'm not gonna lie, it's gonna hurt like hell. And to top it off, you're going to have on a hospital gown, which means your ass is gonna be out. And I say this to add, don't cry. No one wants to see a grown man with his ass out, crying like a baby. Trust me." Dr. Winston smiled.

"No, *you* listen, Doc," my dad said, joining in on the joke. "I'm gonna cry if I feel like it. And if anybody got a problem with that, well, my ass will already be out for them to kiss." Then my father glanced at Dr. Fisher, who just stood there looking at them both like they were two teenage boys. "Not you, Dr. Fisher," he said, smiling.

Then Dr. Winston burst into laughter, shaking my father's hand. And I realized that my dad sounded like himself again. He sounded like Daisy Miller's husband.

Once we left, Mr. Ray told me he was having a hard time building up the courage to ask the receptionist lady—her name was Melissa—out on a date. See, even though my dad was transferred to the rehab, Mr. Ray would still pop by the main hospital part to see her while he waited for me.

"I just can't seem to do it," he said, palming the steering wheel.

"If this was twenty years ago, I'd a already married her." He gave the poor steering wheel a pound. Mr. Ray had no problems opening the door, but he just couldn't close it, as my dad would say. This was the one area Mr. Ray's too-smooth brother, Robbie, had over him.

"What you scared of? She sure likes talking to you," I said. Not that I had any good advice to give. Talking to girls wasn't that easy for me either, and now I told myself that if I saw Renee again, I would take a shot. It might be a bad shot, but still a shot. But Mr. Ray was . . . Mr. Ray. The man. He had money, a job, and was the nicest guy in the world if you asked me, or anyone else in my neighborhood.

"Scared?" His face suddenly tightened up. "How long has it been since I been talking to her up there?"

I ran through the dates in my mind.

"About two months."

Mr. Ray looked at me, surprised at how fast two months went. He slammed his hand down on the steering wheel again.

"A'ight, I'm gonna do it. Soon. I got to. This is crazy." Then, like usual, he turned the radio up and headed toward my school.

"So who we got today?" I asked Mr. Ray, casually. I always liked to know ahead of time whose funeral it was, just because every now and then it was somebody I knew. And if it was, then I could relax a little because it was easy to fit in to a funeral of a person I actually knew, and then I didn't feel like as much of a weirdo.

Mr. Ray turned the music down. "A woman named Gwendolyn Brown. You know her?"

Gwendolyn Brown. Gwendolyn Brown. I thought for a second to see if the name rang a bell. "Nope. Didn't know her."

"I did. She was a good lady," Mr. Ray said. "Everything's pretty much taken care of. All you have to do is make sure the repast room is ready to go with food on the tables and all that. Oh, and of course you need to set up the flowers, which I know you *love* to do." He was used to me ranting about flowers, how they were a total waste of money and all that. "Other than that, you can"—he paused and flashed a slight grin—"y'know, do your thing."

I was pretty sure that the grin meant that he knew I had a thing for these funerals, but he would never say anything about it. He probably knew since the first time I asked to sit in on one. I wasn't sure if he understood it or not. But he didn't mind.

"What time?" I asked as he pulled in front of the school. I reached in the back and grabbed my backpack.

"Early. Church doors open at twelve thirty. Service starts at one."

"But I don't get out of here until noon," I explained, slipping out of the car. I grabbed my suit jacket off the back of the headrest. Mr. Ray taught me that. It keeps it from getting wrinkled.

"I know." He smiled. "That's why I'll be right here to pick you up. Twelve on the dot."

In New York it's pretty hard to see something you've never seen before. No one trips about anything because most of us have seen it all. But at noon, when that hearse pulled up outside and I went and got in, the fifty or so students who could leave early like me were definitely confused, and I knew there would be a new rumor boomeranging from lunch table to locker about how I ride around in death-mobiles.

"The hearse?" I asked, quickly ducking into the car. "You had to drive the hearse?"

"Well, how the hell else were we gonna get Ms. Brown here to her big event?" Mr. Ray laughed. "Now you're *really* the coolest kid in school."

Great. I had finally gotten people to stop staring at me for being the kid whose mom died, and then for being the boy in the black suit, and now I was the boy in the black suit whose mom died and who rides around in a hearse. Perfect. I was officially weirder than the goth kids. Even better, I was the kid the goth kids wanted to be.

"We got ten minutes to get to the church, so strap up," Mr. Ray said, mashing the gas pedal and whipping the car around the corner like it was a go-cart.

As we zoomed down Brooklyn streets, I looked out the window and stared at New York in the fall, the only time everybody realizes that there are way more trees in the city than we think. Normally you never pay attention to trees here, or even recognize them, but then November hits and every step you take, crispy leaves crunch under your feet, and you're forced to notice trees are clearly everywhere. But we never seem to see them. Maybe even they get drowned out by the madness.

When we pulled up to the church, the steps were covered

in brown and gold and red leaves that blew around in clusters.

"If it wasn't so windy, I'd ask you to sweep," Mr. Ray said, killing the engine. "But ain't no point."

Robbie Ray was already sitting on the top step, his gold chain gleaming in the sun, the blowing leaves slapping him in the face, driving him crazy.

"I kinda like the wind, actually."

I checked my cell phone. No missed calls, of course. 12:17.

Thirteen minutes. I had my instructions. Set up the repast room and take care of the flowers.

First the flowers. Usually they're sitting right in the front, five or six bouquets. But this lady, she had flowers galore! I mean, fifteen or sixteen bouquets of all these crazy-ass flowers I had never even seen before, in pots and vases just as wild looking as the plants. I didn't even know where I was going to put them all. I lugged each one up to the front and began putting them around the casket. By the time I was done, Ms. Brown looked like she was lying in a rainforest. And I looked like I had just run through one, I was sweating so bad. Some of those bouquets weighed a ton!

After that it was on to the easy stuff. Repast setup. I went to the basement of the church and laid all the cold food out on platters. The hot food, I had to put in pans that sit propped up on braces. They all come with these little cans, like jelly candles. I had to light the can-candles and put them under the pans of food to keep them hot. Nothing to it.

Next and last, tables and chairs. Mr. Ray said they were

expecting it to be a pretty big repast. Like fifty people. So I set up ten tables, five chairs each. While unfolding the brown chairs and sliding them under each table, I could hear the people start to come in upstairs. Someone started playing the organ, but I don't think it was a specific song. Just something to set the mood. Something sad, not like organs in churches can make another kind of sound other than a sad one.

I finished setting up, then tiptoed up the steps and slipped in to where the service was going on. It was a pretty good turnout. Almost full. Mixed crowd. Some old folks, some young folks, some middle folks. The usual funeral line was moving down the aisle, only a few people left to take one last look at Gwendolyn Brown. I took a seat in the last row of the church, and as soon as I sat down, someone was right there to hand me a program.

"Thanks," I mouthed to the old usher lady, her hair a weird purplish gray color.

She nodded with a tight face and quickly stepped back to her post along the wall like a soldier. Ushers had a way of being like that.

Gwendolyn Brown. The picture on the program was of a caramel woman with an afro, wearing an orange suit and big gold hoop earrings. I knew it must've been an old picture because she looked much younger than the woman in the casket. Plus, the afro and the orange suit. Seventies all the way.

The inside of the program was filled with other pictures. One with her playing cards with some other old people. One with her in the kitchen holding a spoon to her mouth, cheesing. Some of the photos were of her holding kids.

I skimmed through the obituary as the choir sang. She ran a homeless shelter for forty years. Loved playing cards and bingo. Never married. Survived by one granddaughter. Loved God. Loved music. Loved cooking. Loved flowers, obviously. And loved taking pictures.

I flipped the program over. One last picture took up the whole back of the program. It was her arm in arm with what I figured was the young granddaughter, but I couldn't really tell because the photo was so blurred, and basically looked like a thousand little colored squares.

"Ladies and gentlemen, family and friends, saints and sinners, old and young," the minister started. His voice vibrated, like he was singing, like he was some kind of bootleg Dr. King. "We are all here today to celebrate the home going of sister Gwendolyn Brown. We don't come in sadness. No, we come in joy, for sister Brown is finally at peace with the mighty King of Kings."

Blah, blah, blah. Heard it all before. I was used to almost every church funeral starting this way, and it killed me because I knew that the truth is that people *do* come in sadness. As a matter of fact, I don't think anyone comes in joy. It's a *funeral*.

The preacher continued explaining that it would be a short service because "it ain't no point sitting around pouting," and "sister Brown wouldn't want no whole lotta tears." He explained that the entire funeral would just be a few of Ms. Brown's favorite songs, and a few words from her granddaughter, Love.

"But with all things, we start with a prayer. Bow your heads and look to the Lord," the preacher said.

As he prayed, I thought for a moment about who in the world would name their daughter Love. I mean, black folks can get creative with names, but Love? Not that Love was a bad name, just different, I guess. I mean, don't get me wrong, it's better than my name, the most normal name of all time. Matthew Miller. Sounds like I was born to wear blue button-up shirts tucked into high-water khakis or something. But still . . . Love?

The singing went on for a while, one song after another. They were all upbeat, and, luckily, it was one of the few times a funeral actually had a good choir. I'm talking high notes, low notes, harmonies, solos. Before I knew it I was tapping my foot like everyone else, pretending to sing along to songs I didn't even know. I looked around at all the people clapping their hands and singing Gwendolyn Brown to heaven. Old ladies with their wigs wiggling around on their heads like live animals as they started really getting into the music. Some of them were even standing up, their big butts wobbling, and one was slapping a yellow tambourine against her hip.

This was going to be another happy funeral, and usually at happy funerals it was hard to find the person hurting the most. But I knew it wouldn't be too hard at this one because the preacher already said that the service would be carried out mostly by the granddaughter, Love, and I had already read in the obituary that this granddaughter was the closest family member left since Ms. Brown lost her daughter. So she was who I was looking for.

I tried stretching my neck to see if I could spot the granddaughter sitting in the usual spot, the front row, or as Robbie Ray called it, the good seats. I could see the back of the head of who I thought was her, but couldn't tell how she was feeling. With most people I could tell, even if I couldn't see their faces, just based on how they hung their heads. If the head was tilted up, that meant they were struggling and trying not to cry. If the head was down, they were already crying but still holding on, trying not to let anyone see them. If the head was down and the shoulders were bouncing—full-blown breakdown.

But with the granddaughter, she looked straight ahead and bobbed her head to the music, clapping and singing just like everybody else. None of the usual signs were there yet. At least that's what it looked like from the back.

After the final song the preacher returned to the microphone.

"God is good!" he called out.

"All the time!" the church said.

The preacher smiled and waved his finger. "No, y'all don't wanna send Sister Brown off the right way, 'cause if you did you'd act like it. I said, God is good!"

"All the time!" the church, now even more amped up, hollered. The old lady with the tambourine held it in the air and shook it.

The preacher nodded his head, satisfied by the response.

"All right, that's what I'm talking about." He looked over at Love. "You ready?"

She nodded.

"Like I told y'all at the start, we won't be here too long. Sister Brown's baby girl gonna come and say a few words, then we gonna pray, and sing it on out. Amen?"

"Amen!" the church rumbled.

He waved for Love to come to the microphone.

She walked up to the podium as calm and graceful as can be. But when she got there and lifted her head, I felt a lump in my throat, like I had swallowed a house. I straightened up and sat on the edge of my seat just to get a better look. I knew her. At first I wasn't sure, but as I stared a little longer, I definitely knew I knew her. It was Renee. From Cluck Bucket. Why was everyone calling her Love? Who was Love?

She looked way better at a funeral than she did at work. And then I tried to snap myself out of it, because it was crazy to be looking at a girl like that at her grandma's funeral. But still, she looked so different. She had her hair down and curled. And even though I was sitting in the back of the church, I could tell she had on a little bit of makeup, and for some reason I just knew she smelled good. *Snap out of it. Snap out of it.*

"Good afternoon, everyone," she said, her voice much sweeter than it had been when she took chicken orders.

"My name is Love Brown, but most of you here know me as Lovey. I don't really have a whole lot to say besides the fact that I loved my grams. She took care of me when my mom passed, and showed me how to be who I am today. How to be strong and independent when things get thick." She paused and smiled wide. "I'm sure we could all share some special times we had with her. But for me, our favorite thing was to take pictures. I remember when she first taught me how to use a camera. I was probably six! She would pose and I would snap, and she'd smile and poke her hip out like she was still young," she said with a touch of Brooklyn in her voice. People laughed a little bit. "I'll always remember that, and I'll always have those memories, and thankfully, those pictures to remind me. I'll miss her forever, even though I know I'll see her again." Here she stopped and started unfolding a piece of paper she had brought up with her. "And that's kinda what she wanted me to talk to y'all about, but I don't want to mess it up, so I'll just read what she asked me to." She smiled again, this time more nervously. "Grams was big on following directions, so let me do just that."

At this point the church was quiet. Not a sniffle, not a candy wrapper crackling, not a creak in the wooden church pews, nothing. I kept staring at Renee's—Love's—face, trying to find the weak point. The hard swallow, the drowning eyes, something that would give me the feeling I needed. Something that would tell me that there were explosions happening inside of her, and that she was one of us—a mourner. But this one wasn't coming as easy. I kept watching, waiting.

"It says . . ." She cleared her throat and looked down at the paper.

"Dear Sweethearts,

If you're hearing this, I've moved on. And if I'm lucky enough to have any one of you sad today, just know that it'll be okay. And that I'm okay. Better than okay.

Lovey will tell you that when her mom passed, the one word I would never let her say was death.

I wouldn't let her say it because I never believed in it. Dead means finished. Over. Done. That didn't describe her mother then, and it doesn't describe me now. I've just changed. Like changing clothes, when one outfit gets too old, gotta take it off and put on another. Or like changing jobs, once you've done all you can do, you get a new position. But to say I'm dead means that you'll never hear me, or feel me . . . but you will. I promise. Just because you won't see me for a while, doesn't mean I won't be there. I'll be there, with a new camera and a full roll of film snapping away."

Here the crowd laughed. I kept waiting for something to happen to Love. I kept staring, waiting for her to break, but she kept speaking, smoothly and confidently. A tear streamed down her face, but that wasn't enough. It was regular tears. Not like my tears.

"And when it's your turn to change"

—Love flipped the page and continued reading—

"to move on, I'll be here waiting for you, with a photo album, a cup of tea, and a hug like you never felt before. I love you all, especially my Lovey, and I'll see you all soon enough.

Yours, Gwen"

Love cleared her throat and calmly folded the paper back up.

"Thank you all so much for coming," she finished up, still no sign of a breakdown in her voice.

Every single person in the church stood and clapped for Love and for the words Ms. Brown wrote in that letter. I stood and half-clapped while watching her go from the podium to the arms of the preacher to the arms of some other old man, an older woman, and then back to her seat. I wondered what made her so strong. What made her so different. Maybe it was her grandma, Gwenolyn. Maybe Ms. Brown had been dying for a while and had time to prepare Love, and that's why she was taking it so well. I wasn't sure, but I knew this was the first funeral I had been to where I didn't find what I was looking for.

And maybe that's why I stayed after. Maybe I wanted to know what she knew that I didn't—that thing that was keeping her so cool. I mean, her grandma just died. And her mom was gone. And judging by the fact that there were no men sitting next to her in the pew, her dad wasn't around either. And no brothers and sisters. Pretty much everything I was living every day, except she was obviously doing it better than me. I bet she didn't go to sleep listening to Tupac every night. I had to know what the secret was.

Or maybe it wasn't even all that deep and I stayed just because I kind of had a thing for her, and today of all days, for some reason, I was feeling brave, or as my mother used to say, "froggy." Like the black suit was the cure to robot face. I mean, I did just tell myself that the next time I saw her I was going to make a move. But damn, the very next day? At her grandma's funeral?

Downstairs in the church, it seemed like everyone was talking all at once, their voices blending together to sound like a whole bunch of nothing. The plastic forks scratched against the Styrofoam plates, the fold-up chairs squeaked and honked as people scooched up to the tables. Family members stood in line with people who were obviously homeless and waited their turn to be served chicken, and green beans, mashed potatoes, and bread, by Love. The homeless folks dressed in their best, and either smelled like too much cologne or not enough deodorant, and the stench sort of snuck around enough for everyone to smell it, but not enough for anyone to care. The family dressed in the usual all black, the women with big hats, the men with shined shoes. But nobody made it seem weird that there were homeless people at the repast. Nobody frowned or made any slick comments. It was clear that this was the way Ms. Brown wanted it, and everybody understood and respected that. But I wasn't family or a homeless friend. I was just a kid . . . being creepy.

I stood in line behind one of the big hats and watched as the girl I knew as Renee, but whose real name was Love, dished out the food. Everyone had a little something to say, like "You did great," or "God bless you, sweetie," and the lady in front of me said, "You look so pretty."

She stole my line.

I was totally gonna use that.

Love did look pretty. She looked like Renee again, but without the hairnet. And with makeup on.

"White or dark?" she asked, looking me dead in the eye and not recognizing me.

"Um, white," I said.

She reached the metal tongs down into the pan and poked at a chicken breast.

"No wait, dark meat, please," I said, nervous.

She looked up at me, smiled, and shook her head. "You sure?"

I smirked. "Yeah." The nerves calmed a little.

She put the meat on my plate.

"Veggies?"

"Yes, please," I said, side-stepping. Too polite.

"Potatoes?"

"Sure." *That's better.*

She dug the spoon deep into the creamy potatoes and came up with a big scoop. She plopped it down, and the weight of the potatoes almost made me drop the plate. I fumbled it a little, and caught it before I had green bean juice all over my only suit. There's no coming back from that.

She tried to hold in her laughter, but couldn't, and pretty much spit all in the food, which then made me laugh.

"Do I know you?" she asked, shoving the spoon back into the potato pan.

"Uh, not really. I mean"—*Don't blow this, Matt*—"I mean, we met, once. Twice. Kinda."

Love looked confused.

"At Cluck Bucket," I reminded her. "I came in a few months ago trying to find a job."

She still looked confused. "Sorry, tons of people come in there looking for jobs. You know, the whole rumor about them paying well?" She rolled her eyes. "It ain't true."

"It's not? Dang. That's why I came in," I explained. "But remember there was a dude who was hitting on you, and you told him there was no chicken?"

"Ah." She smirked. "I remember that. These clowns think they can say whatever they want. I got his ass," she said, and then made a face like she was sorry for cussing in church. But we were down-stairs, so it couldn't have been as bad.

"And that girl came in, puking all over the place."

"Right." She stuck her tongue out and made a gag-face. "I remember you now. You came in again, another time too. Ordered a bunch of stuff for you and your homeboy."

"Yeah."

"Didn't look like you needed a job that day," Love said skepti-cally. She probably thought I was a hustler, pulling out that cash knot like that.

"Naw, it's not like that, I—"

"Hey, whatever you do is on you. None of my business," she cut me off, shrugging her shoulders. "But . . . uh . . . what are you doing here? How you know Grams?"

Uh-oh. My head started swimming as I thought through my options, and when I ran through them all, I realized there was no way I could win. If I lied and told her I knew her grandma because she took care of me when I was homeless, that wouldn't go over good. I mean, Love clearly didn't mind homeless folks, but I didn't know if she wanted to kick it with one (who she now thought might be a drug dealer as well). If I told her that I worked for the funeral home, then I would be dude who worked with dead people, which wouldn't be a bad thing—if I wasn't a teenager. Teenagers work at fast-food joints, not funeral homes. Maybe I could tell her I used to volunteer at the shelter with her grandma. But then I would still have to keep that lie going, and I just wasn't that great at stuff like that, especially with a girl.

I didn't know what to say.

"I uh . . ." I could feel my face start to stiffen up. Robot face was coming, and there was no stopping it. Then I felt a big hand on my shoulder.

"I didn't know you were still here, Matthew." Mr. Ray's raspy voice came sliding in between me and Love. "You're usually long gone by now." Then, realizing I was in the middle of a conversation, he looked at Love and said awkwardly, "Oh, excuse me for interrupting." *Wink.* "Take care of him, Love, he's one of mine. Best worker I got."

Then he looked back at me and bounced his eyebrows before walking away.

I dropped my head.

"You work for the funeral home?" she asked.

Busted.

"Yeah."

"So then what you doing eating my food? Ain't you still on the clock?"

I looked up and she was standing there with a fake attitude and a grin.

"Not really," I said. "You heard Mr. Ray. I'm usually gone by now."

She dropped her hand from her hip. "So what you stay for this time?" I could tell there was a little bit of flirt in her voice.

I grabbed a fork from the side of the table and put it in the mountain of mashed potatoes on my plate.

"Guess I was just hungry," I said, with a smile I hoped wasn't stupid looking.

I sat at an empty table and tore into my food, which by the way was pretty good. The chicken needed a little black pepper (or some of my All Sauce), and the potatoes a pinch of garlic powder, but all in all, not bad. I wondered if it was better than the food at my mom's funeral. I wasn't sure because I couldn't eat any of it. No appetite. But everybody else seemed to like it. Still, the food at Ms. Brown's funeral was definitely above average.

Every few bites I looked up and glanced at Love, still slapping food down on white, flimsy plates for all kinds of different people. She smiled and stretched her arms out to hug almost everyone from behind the food table. And whenever a few people would pass, she would shoot her eyes over at me really quick hoping I wouldn't see her looking. But I caught her every time, because I was looking at her, too.

After everyone had a plate, she came over to my table with a plate of her own.

"Anybody sitting here?" she asked, smiling because it was clear I was alone.

"Yep," I said, short, doing my best to return the flirt.

She set her plate on the table. "Well, they gonna have to find another seat."

Love looked so pretty, even though her forehead was shiny, glowing with sweat, from standing over the hot food for so long. Still, she looked awesome.

"So, Matthew," she said, scooping potatoes with a spoon, and eating a little at a time, like cheesecake.

"Matt," I said.

"Okay. So, Matt."

This was just like in the movies.

"So, Love."

"Lovey."

"Renee."

When I said that, her eyes shot up at me, but not in a flirty way at all. More like a surprised way. Like I said something wrong. Something I wasn't supposed to say.

"What?" she said.

"Renee. That's what I thought your name was, from when I saw you at Cluck Bucket those times."

"Why?"

I pointed to my chest. "The chain you had on."

Renee reached into the neck of her dress, and pulled the gold chain out. The nameplate hung from it. RENEE.

She held it up and looked at it for a second.

"My name is Love." She let the chain fall down to her chest. "Renee was my mom."

Ouch. Sometimes when you try to be too smooth, you really end up blowing it.

"I'm sorry. I didn't know," I said, sinking down into myself. I was so embarrassed, but even though I had made things a little uncomfortable, I still couldn't help but try to see Love break a little, at least at the mention of her mother. But she didn't even flinch.

"It's cool," she said, pinching the skin off a piece of chicken. "It was a long time ago."

"Never get's easier though." I knew I was going too far, but I couldn't help myself. It was like I had diarrhea of the mouth, as my mom used to say.

Love—Lovey—chewed the chicken and squinted as if she was thinking about what I had just said as well as trying to swallow her food before saying something back.

Then, she pointed her fork at me. "Not for people who don't want it to. But for me"—she stabbed a few green beans and lifted them to her mouth—"it definitely got easier."

CHAPTER 8
WIDE OPEN

"WAIT. LET ME GET THIS STRAIGHT. THE GIRL FROM CLUCK Bucket is your *girlfriend*?"

Chris took off his jacket and tossed it on the couch.

"Man, no, she's not my girlfriend. I just met her, forreal," I said, even though I couldn't stop myself from cheesing so hard it hurt. If only Lovey had been around when I was taking my senior pictures.

"Uh-huh," Chris said, looking at me. "You . . . you . . ." He paused. "You open." He busted out laughing and pointed at me like a kid. I wanted to tell him to grow up, but I couldn't front. He was right. I was open. From one conversation, wide open.

But it wasn't like a regular conversation. It was different. We talked about school, how she was in some special photography program at hers, and loved it, and was hoping to go to college to study photography, and then after college she wanted to just be a full-time camera clicker. But not like a paparazzi. Love said she wanted to be a photojournalist, and tell stories with pictures. I thought that was pretty cool.

I told her that I was finishing up this year too, and that I wasn't sure where I wanted to go to college. I mean, part of me wanted to get out of New York, go away somewhere different. Maybe Georgia where the weather's warmer. But another part of me didn't want to go too far and leave my father alone. I wanted to tell her all that, but I didn't because I knew it would make her ask questions about my folks, and I just wasn't ready for that. I mean, the conversation was flowing, but I was trying to keep it light.

Thankfully, she didn't ask anything that would force me to either lie or tell the truth that my mom had died. I knew her mom died too, but I didn't ask how because it didn't seem like she was offering all that up, which was cool. We were on the same page with that one. It was none of my business. But Lovey did talk about her grandma, Ms. Brown, telling me stories about how she raised her.

"Every holiday I had to visit and feed the homeless," she said.

I never really knew anyone who helped homeless people. I mean, I've seen someone give them some change on the train, but I was so used to ignoring them, or watching other kids laugh at them, that I never even thought about people really helping them. So I thought it was cool that Lovey was into that.

When the repast was over, and everyone had pretty much left, even Mr. Ray, I helped her pack the food up and waited with her outside for a cab. When the cab came we both got in with all the leftovers, some of which she gave to me.

"So, where you live?" I asked.

"Hmmm. I live alone now, and you seem nice but you could be a killer"—she joked, but was half-serious—"so how 'bout we drop you off first."

"But I also live alone and you might be a killer too," I said.

"Maybe," she replied. She tried to turn away and look out the window before I caught her smile.

As we pulled in front of my house, I reached up and gave the cabbie enough money for both of our rides, and the tip. Luckily, Mr. Ray paid me every day, so I could do that with no sweat and look pretty cool at the same time. Lovey seemed weird all of a sudden. Like, she got real tense right before I got out. I figured she was just nervous and didn't know if I was going to try anything, but it was way too soon for all that. I had just met her. She told me to put my number in her phone. I did, then just said, "Nice to meet you." It was all pretty awkward.

As I was getting out of the cab, Chris was walking down the block, coming from the store. I wanted to wait for him to get closer to the car just so he could see there was a girl in there, but he was taking too long, bopping down the street lazy and cool. It was still perfect timing, though, because I felt like I was walking on air and he was the only person I could really talk to about it.

✕   ✕   ✕

"But she definitely got something," I now told Chris as he flopped down on the burgundy spaceship couch. I loosened my tie and hung my jacket on the back of one of the kitchen chairs. Backpack, keys, money, cell phone, all on the kitchen table. Then, I put some of the food from the funeral in the microwave for Chris, which is always an extra reason for him to hang out.

"What you mean, she got something? Like a disease?"

"No, fool!" I snapped, already a little emotional about this girl. "Not a disease, just like a thing, man. It's hard to explain. Like, she's just so cool. She got like a *thing*, like a swag about her."

Chris nodded, trying to be serious. "What's her name, again?"

"Love."

So much for serious. Chris laughed. Hard.

"No joke, what's her name?"

"That *is* her name. Love. But people call her Lovey."

"But that's not what I remember you calling her when you asked me if I thought she was cute."

"I know. I thought her name was Renee, but I was wrong. It's Love."

"Oh. I thought you was trying to be all poetic and stuff." Chris frowned. I could tell he was thinking the same thing I was thinking when I first heard her name—who would name their child Love?

"Man, ain't nobody trying to be poetic," I informed him, taking a seat on the arm of the couch. "Plus, like I said, I don't even know her like that." I tried to play the whole thing off like I wasn't tripping about Love. But I was.

The microwave dinged. Chris literally jumped up, and when he saw me look at him like he was crazy, he tried to play it off and walk all smooth to the kitchen to get his food. He popped open the microwave door and a cloud of steam carrying the smell of reheated fried chicken came bursting out.

He took a deep breath. "Smells good, but let me see what this repath food taste like." He picked at the chicken.

"Repast."

"What?"

"Repast. Not repath," I explained, handing him a fork even though I knew he had no problem eating without one.

Chris picked up the hunk of meat and took a big bite right out the middle of it. It was hot, and he hung his mouth open like a panting mutt to cool it off. Then he grabbed his fork and ran it straight across his plate, making a valley in each mountain—the mountain of green beans, and the mountain of mashed potatoes—and took it straight to the face.

"Oh. Well, repast, repath, rerun, whatever they called, the food is slammin'," he growled with his mouth full of everything. "Your girlfriend cooked this? If she did, then now I get why you buggin'." Chris smiled, thankfully with his trap closed, all the food stuffed in his cheeks. "She cook better than you!"

"No, she didn't cook it, she's not my girlfriend, and"—I grabbed the garlic powder from the counter and sprinkled it on his potatoes—"it don't taste better than my food."

Chris took another spoonful of potatoes. His face let me know that now they tasted better.

"Okay, so maybe you're right about the food, but she's definitely your girlfriend."

"No, she's not.

"Not yet."

I didn't say anything back, just pretended I didn't hear him and let Chris go on inhaling his food like a human vacuum. But I couldn't help but think about the possibilities of him being right. I mean, Chris had more experience with girls than I did. He used to kick it with Shannon Reeves, a certified winner. Shannon was so fly, all the older dudes would try to get at her until they found out she was only sixteen. And even then, some of them still tried to get at her. He also used to kick it with Lauren Morris and Danni Stevens at the same time. Danni was kind of geeky, but in a cute way. And Lauren was a cheerleader at our school, so she had that whole thing going on. Long hair, pretty smile, in shape, all cheery, all the time. The two girls knew about each other, because Chris was up front and told them the truth. Crazy thing is, they didn't even care.

Guys always wondered how Chris was doing it—how he was getting all the ladies. But I knew exactly what it was. He was nice. He was honest. He was always dressed in the latest, which was a major plus. He was hilarious. And the key to it all was the fact that he was a mama's boy. I was too, but it was different. My mom had my dad to make her blush and feel all fuzzy. Chris's mom had nobody but him. His pops wasn't around and she never had a boyfriend (said she wouldn't date until Chris went to college), so he spent a lot of time figuring out what made his mother smile.

What made her feel special. And that pretty much made him the smoothest dude I knew. So, for that reason, I had to listen to him whenever it came to understanding girls.

"I mean, just tell me the truth," he said, now taking a sip of juice. "You like her?"

"Yeah."

"She like you?"

"I don't know."

"Did she flirt?"

"I think so, but she's hard to read."

"Did she look at you when she flirted?"

I thought about the car ride, and how she looked away.

"Naw, I don't think so. She kept looking out the window," I explained.

Chris leaned back in the chair like a proud father who just watched his child figure out how times tables work. But instead of times tables, I was figuring out females, and Chris was loving every minute of it.

"What?"

"C'mon, Matt. You the smartest dude I know. And the dumbest." He laughed.

"What, so if she looks away, then that automatically means she likes me?"

Before Chris could give me some slick answer, my phone started buzzing, vibrating the whole table. The noise shocked me. I reached down to see what it was.

I TEXT MESSAGE

"It's her," I said, way too excited. I tried to catch myself but it was too late.

The text said: *Hey. It's Lovey. Busy?*

I put the phone back on the table so Chris could see it. He read it, a cocky grin spreading across his face.

"Told ya."

CHAPTER 9
IN LOVING MEMORY

Can I ask u something?

By now I had pretty much pushed Chris out the door. He tried to be funny and finish his food slowly—something that I'm sure took every ounce of will power he had—but I leaned over and coughed right on his plate, a stupid immature move I learned from twelve years of New York City public school.

"Not cool," Chris said, heading toward the door. "You lucky you my best friend, and I understand you in love, and it's making you a little crazy and—"

"Yeah, yeah, yeah," I said, opening the door. "I'll just holla at you tomorrow."

✘   ✘   ✘

I laid down on the couch, trying to keep myself as calm as possible while talking—well, texting—Lovey. We had been texting for exactly thirteen minutes, asking random questions, trying to figure out if we knew any of the same people, or if we liked the same kind of music—the usual interview process you go through when you're trying to get the job as boyfriend. Of course we talked about where our families were from. It's a thing you sort of have to discuss in New York, because everybody's family is from somewhere that ain't America, like Jamaica, or Haiti, or Trinidad, which is where her grandma was from. That's if you black. Unless you're me. My folks were from Baltimore and South Carolina. So curry wasn't a big part of our meals, but I could tell you what crab cake and barbecue are supposed to taste like.

Can I ask u something? I read her latest text again.

I responded, a little nervous, just because whenever someone asks if they can ask you something, there's always a sucker punch in the nuts right behind it.

Yep . . . ???

When we were in the cab, and u said u live alone, is that true?

Lol yea

Oh . . . why? I mean not to be all in your biz, just sayin' I don't know nobody else our age who live alone

Dang. Nosy!! Lol

Whatever. You don't have to tell me :-/

Of course I had tell her. Well, I didn't have to, but for some reason I wanted to. It was one more thing we had in common.

It's cool I'll tell u . . . my mom passed a few months ago. Breast cancer. And my pops . . . car accident, but he alive. Recovering.

:(*I'm sorry.*

Don't be. I'm cool. ;)

I propped my head up on the armrest to get more comfortable. I felt like I was doing a good job talking to Lovey. Like, I knew I was being honest and just being myself, but without all the awkwardness I usually have around girls. Probably because we were texting, and texting is way different from really talking to someone. Texting *My mom passed away*, and saying it out loud, are two very different things. I mean, I could say it and not break down, but I would definitely feel more of a sting and probably get all robot faced. But texting it, I didn't feel much of anything, and I liked that. It was the first time I could mention her death and not feel like I was dying too.

I waited for the next message and daydreamed about what Lovey was doing, even though she had already told me she wasn't doing anything, which means she was probably watching TV. Nobody really does nothing. She was probably lying on the couch, just like I was lying on mine, her cell phone next to her head so she could read the messages without having to pick the phone up. I imagined she had on sweats and a T-shirt, and had her hair wrapped in a silk scarf, like my mother used to do before she went to bed. Clearly, I don't have a very sexy imagination, but there was something about her that made it okay to imagine her in baggy pants, a faded family reunion T, and her hair pinned and wrapped. She was that fly.

My phone buzzed. 1 TEXT MESSAGE.

Next question. Ready?

Lol ok

What u doin for thanksgiving?

Probably finishing the rest of these leftovers u gave me. U?

Same thing. Lol.

I didn't say nothing back. I just waited, hoping the conversation wouldn't end here and that the phone would buzz one more time. *Come on. One more time.*

Buzz. 1 TEXT MESSAGE.

So maybe we could eat old chicken together?

Only if we pretend it's turkey ;)

I was *so* much smoother on text message.

Lol. Fine. But we gotta meet at my house.

Why not my house?

You know . . . the killer thing? :)

Smh.

The next morning, sunbeams shined brightly into the living room, almost forcing me to open my eyes. It's amazing how you know when a room has light in it, even when you have your eyes closed. Light always wins. I was buried deep in the couch cushions, lying in a position that wasn't uncomfortable at all, until I woke up.

First thing first. I reached for my cell phone. Every muscle in my body cracked. Neck, back, legs, fingers, popping and snapping, reminding me of why I should never fall asleep on the couch. It was like I got thirty years older overnight.

I ran my hand along the floor until I found my phone.

3 NEW TEXT MESSAGES

The first message said, *So it's a date* :)

Then ten minutes later, *Hello???? U sleep???*

Ten minutes after that, *Goodnight smh lol*

I read them and just like that, I was young again. I laid there for a minute with the phone flat on my chest. A date. Matty Miller, the boy in the black suit . . . had a date. *Hope you're watching, Mom.*

I can admit it, school that day was way better than it had been since it started, but nothing was really different about it. The guys were still being stupid, slapping books out of people's hands and running through the halls dodging teachers. And the girls were still checking the reflection of their faces in their cell phone screens, powdering their cheeks, and buttering their lips. Gotta make sure you look good . . . when you gossip. Class was still ass, but I didn't care, because I felt ten feet tall. It was like all of a sudden I had a force field around me—nothing could phase me. The black suit seemed like it was just a really smooth outfit, not a work uniform. Not a funeral suit. Like it made me even cooler. I was untouchable because I had a date, and the one person I wanted to tell more than anyone was standing at my locker when I got there.

"Wassup," Chris said, leaning against the locker next to mine.

"Wassup," I said, cool, turning the lock left, then right.

I could tell Chris was waiting for me to spill it, and I wanted to, but I didn't want him to think I was pressed to just run to him and tell him everything. So I just started putting my books away like nothing was going on. The whole time, my heart was high-fiving my brain, and I literally felt like at any second I could sprout wings.

"Come on, Matt," he said, flat.

"What?"

"Matt."

"What?" I said again, staring into my locker. I cracked a slight smile. I couldn't help it.

"What happened?"

I pulled *The Canterbury Tales* from my locker and dropped it in my backpack. Even that boring-ass book couldn't ruin my mood. Then I slammed the locker door. Chris stood there staring me down.

"Come on, Chris. You of all people should know, real dudes don't run their mouths. I don't kiss and tell." I totally do kiss and tell, just not in the first twenty seconds of talking to my boy.

"Oh, I see," Chris said, crossing his arms. "Only thing is, you ain't kiss her yet, fool!" He laughed. "Plus, I know you want to tell me, Matt. Stop frontin'."

He got me.

"Seriously, it ain't really nothing." I looked over my shoulder as if what I was about to say was a secret. "We just gonna spend Thanksgiving together. Alone."

I had to throw the "alone" in there, just for Chris. I mean, it was true, but I said it because I knew it would definitely add some gas to the story, which is what we both wanted. The way I see it, it's not really gossip if I'm talking about myself.

Chris's eyebrows went way up and he extended his hand to me. I grabbed it, and we did a grown man shake before going off to class. I definitely deserved one, I thought, and bopped to Grovenor's room like a prom king in the making.

There was one other person I wanted to tell about Lovey. Mr. Ray. I know I said I don't kiss and tell but I had to tell Chris because he was Chris—my dude. And I had to tell Mr. Ray because he was my . . . old dude. So old that I knew he wouldn't gossip. Who was he gonna tell? One of his superchatty casket dwellers? Right. Anyway, after school, I caught the bus to the funeral home. I knew there wasn't any funerals going on that day, but I still showed up ready to work, just in case something popped up. Plus, whenever we didn't have a funeral, Mr. Ray would always find some work for me to do, which was really just a reason to pay me.

When I got close to the funeral home, I noticed Robbie was sitting on the stoop, trying to light a cigarette. Every time he flicked the lighter his gold rings blinged in the sun.

"I'll be damned, young blood, you right on time," he muttered, the unlit cigarette dangling from his mouth. "Willie said you'd be here at twelve thirty, and"—he checked his watch—"it's twelve twenty-nine." Robbie cupped his hands around the cig to try and light it again without the wind blowing out the flame.

"Wassup, Robbie," I said, sort of wondering what he was getting at.

Robbie flicked the lighter a few more times, turning his body away from the breeze, until finally the tip of the cigarette turned red. He inhaled slowly, then blew the smoke up into the air as cool as anybody could. He reached into his coat pocket and pulled out a folded-up piece of paper and handed it to me.

"Willie ain't here," he said simply, tapping the ash off the tip of the cigarette.

Robbie had been acting funny toward me ever since that first funeral I did. I guess he felt like I was a suck-up or something, because I was always on time and did everything Mr. Ray asked me to do. Plus Mr. Ray was looking out for me and I think Robbie was a little jealous, since that was his big brother. But I didn't pay Robbie no mind.

I unfolded the paper Robbie gave me. It was a note from Mr. Ray saying that he had a cancer support meeting he had to go to and he forgot to tell me, and that he would've called but young people don't answer cell phones, they only answer text messages, and could I teach him how to text and he'd see me tomorrow bright and early to go see my dad.

I folded the paper back into a small rectangle and slipped it in my pocket.

"Got it," I said to Robbie, who also could not ruin my mood no matter how he was acting. "Have a good Thanksgiving."

Without work my schedule was wide open, but I didn't really have anything to do. Chris was still at school. I thought about hitting Fulton Street and walking up to Cluck Bucket to see if Lovey was there, but then I remembered that she had to meet with some people about her grandma's paperwork, like insurance and all that kind of stuff I didn't really understand, stuff that no teenager should have to worry about. But I could tell from our text messages that she wasn't a normal teenager. She had that same thing I had when I first went back to school, that grown-ness about her—maturity—except she had it times two. No, times ten.

So for the first time in three months I was on my own in the middle of the day, which is totally different from being alone at night. At night it seems like all the bad things creep in, like the fact that I can't see my mother again, and that I didn't want my father to get out of the hospital because then he couldn't get into the bottle. But in the daytime when you're alone, all you think about is what to do before nighttime comes. Either that, or you try to think of things to do to take the place of the something you've been trying to avoid doing. Everybody got that thing they keep putting off, for whatever reason. And that's how it was for me. I knew what I had to do, but I kept using the funerals and work and hanging out with Chris all as excuses to not do it. But on that day I felt like a giant, like nothing could stop me or break me down. So I decided to do what I knew I needed to do—go see my mother.

The A train. Mom used to call it the world's best traveling circus. There's always a couple kids busting out their latest dance routine, flipping and pop-locking up and down the aisle while the train rocks back and forth. Or how about the two brothers who get on with bongo drums to provide some theme music for the ride. And of course, the salesmen, whether it be kids selling candy or dudes moving DVDs, one for five, three for ten. Everybody puts on a show in the A train circus, not to mention all the clowns who get on. From the girl who pretends like her cell phone is a boombox and we're still in the eighties, blasting her music loud enough for the whole train to hear, to the middle-school kids who try to crack as many jokes on as many people as possible, you just have to know what you're getting yourself into when you take the A. But it's the only train in my hood, so I don't really have a choice.

Luckily for me, it was the middle of the day, so the train was pretty empty. Just me, a woman dressed in workout clothes reading a book, and a homeless man all the way down at the end. He was alive, even though his dry skin made him look like he was dead. A zombie.

I rode for about ten minutes, shooting through the tunnels underground, the tracks screeching and knocking like a rocket about to take off. The conductor slammed on the brakes every time he came to the next station. The doors would open. No one would get on. Then, the doors would close again.

When we got to Hoyt Street, the woman with the book got off. Just me and the homeless man were left. And if it were any other day, I would've thought to myself that me and him were the same. Living and dead. But I didn't because it was my good day. On my way off the train I dropped a dollar in his cup, something I never do, hoping to make it his good day too. That's what girls do to you, I guess.

I transferred to the R train and zipped four or five more stops before getting off at Twenty-fifth Street, which was pretty much like getting off in another state. Quiet. Trees. It even seemed like the sidewalks were bigger, even though I knew they probably weren't. I used to come to this part of Brooklyn all the time before my mother died. Every summer when I was a kid she would bring me to Prospect Park, which wasn't too far from where the cemetery was. We'd just walk around and talk. Well, she did most of the talking, which was really just joke after joke about silly stuff. Like how black people named the butterfly, butterfly. Before that, she said, they were called "flutter-bys," which, when I think about it, made a lot of sense. But black folks put a twist on it, switched it around—or as my mother said, put some funk on it—and made it butterfly. She told me later that was a joke she heard from her father, who was told that story by someone else. Either way, it was funny, and I'll probably tell it to my kids. Maybe even in that same park.

Even though I had been in this area a bunch of times, I don't think I ever noticed how peaceful it really was. Maybe I was too young. Maybe I was too busy laughing, making all the noise. But now that I was alone, walking toward the cemetery in the middle of the day (couldn't have done it at night—would've gone from peaceful to scary), I realized it was probably the perfect place to be buried. I know that's a weird thing to say, but it's true. Not a whole bunch of noise or nothing. Just peace and space.

When we came here after the funeral to do the whole burial thing, one of the ladies who works at the cemetery gave my father and me a piece of paper with a map on it, leading to my mother's grave. That's how big this place is. You gotta have a map! I mean, all my life living in New York City, I never even thought about the fact that most of the people who live here die here, and I couldn't help but wonder if most of them get buried in this place.

I stood at the gate and looked out at all the tombstones, white and gray, sprouting from the ground like weird teeth. Most tombstones look exactly alike, and even though I think my memory is pretty good, trying to find my mom's grave without directions would've been like running around in one of those mirror mazes they have at Coney Island.

The map said to follow the road straight, make the first left, then follow the path over the hill. As I walked, the wind picked up, blowing my suit jacket open and making my eyes water. Like I said, if this was nighttime, this would've been a scary moment for me. I walked and looked at every headstone I was passing. Holmes, Forsythe, Briscoe, Wilson, Waymon, Flushing, Carson, Morton, and on and on. As I read the names of the tombstones in my head, it was almost like a weird roll call, like I was saying hello to all these people. Thinking of their families, their funerals. Dwyer, Piedmont, Lee, Miller (no relation), Radison, Former. The names kept coming as I walked into the wind, pushing myself up the hill, my suit jacket now a black cape flapping behind me.

And just like the map said, over the hill, there it was, with a bunch of sad-looking flowers dozing in front of it. IN LOVING MEMORY OF DAISY MILLER carved into a big—well, more like a medium gray stone.

"'In Loving Memory'?" I said out loud. "Is that what you would've wanted on there? 'In Loving Memory'?"

I chuckled because it was weird to talk to myself, even though I wasn't really; I was talking to her—my mother—which was weird too. I was also laughing, because if me and dad weren't so screwed up about the fact that my mom was going to die, we could've talked to her about what she really would've wanted on her stone. It probably would've been something like IN LAUGHING MEMORY, or even something like LOL, which she was totally obsessed with when she first learned how to text message.

I stood there staring at the marble block, trying to imagine what LOL would've looked like, when the feeling of being a giant that I had carried with me all day started to wear off. I wasn't expecting that to happen, even though when I think about it now, I should've known it would.

"I don't know why I'm here," I said to the tombstone. To no one. To her.

"I don't know what I'm doing here." I felt nervous, antsy. Stupid tears marched up my throat. A few more words and they'd be at my eyes. "I don't know what *you're* doing here," I managed to get out, but decided that those would be the last words I'd say. Not that I would be able to say anything else, anyway. If I opened my mouth, even a little bit, whatever was left in me would come pouring out.

I bit down on my bottom lip and looked out at all the other tombstones. After a few seconds everything blurred into hills of gray. So many burials, and here I was wishing that I could bury a few things of my own. Bury the fact that I'm standing at my mother's grave after she left me in the world to fend for myself. Bury the fact that my father is a drunk and now can't even walk, so he can't help me. Bury the fact that almost every kid in my school thinks I'm a damn crackpot. Bury the fact that I'm empty. Empty. Empty! I wish I could bury every damn thing!

I dropped my head, now dizzy with anger. My eyes, going in and out of focus, locked in on the bunch of flowers on the ground—most of which I recognized from the funeral.

I squatted down and stared at them.

"Look at this," I managed to squeeze out under my breath. "Look at your flowers, all dry and wrinkled up like trash. Like crap." I poked a petal. It crumbled. "They're all cracked up and brown and nasty. Overrated and overpriced, all for what? They're dead. *DEAD*. I just don't get why you were so head over heels for stupid flowers. Why everybody is. Look at them. They're wilted already. So damn stupid." I stared for about five more seconds before the anger came crashing over me like a wave. And before you knew it, I had grabbed a fistful of the flowers by their brittle stems and began beating them against the ground. I banged them on the dry grass over and over again, as if I were hitting a drum, the leaves crunching and exploding into chips and tiny shards. "Stupid, stupid, stupid!"

I went on and on until I had totally destroyed the flowers. It was like they had become ashes in my hand and I didn't even realize that there was nothing left of them until I was pounding just my fist on the ground. "Stupid," I whimpered one last time, now trying to catch my breath.

I stayed a while longer, not saying anything. Just trying to calm down. Just trying to be there. With her. I really felt like she was with me. I couldn't hear her, but I felt like she could hear me, and that helped me, sort of, get myself together. I thought I should maybe apologize for what I did to her lovelies. But I decided to skip that and just say what I really came to say.

"Mom," I started. I took a deep breath like I was actually standing in front of her about to break some big news. I continued, "I met a girl." It seemed like such a small statement after all the crying. But I continued anyway.

"Her name is Love. Her real name. And it's nothing yet, but I like her a lot."

Then I stood there staring at her name. DAISY MILLER. I was going to ask my mother to make me and Love work out, like maybe she had some kind of magic power, or could ask God and the angels to fool around with Love's mind to make sure this whole thing goes smooth. But then I imagined that LOL on her tombstone again and suddenly felt too silly to say anything else.

CHAPTER 10
HOMEMADE AND
HOMELESS

"Are they at least gonna give y'all turkey?"

"Hope so," my father said, reaching for the dinner menu. "Says right here, turkey, stuffing, mashed potatoes, cranberries, and a roll, with a choice of sweet potato pie or pumpkin pie for dessert."

"Sounds good."

"Yeah, it does, but let's see if it actually *tastes* good. If it tastes anything like this shit they been serving, I'm a beg Dr. Fisher to get Dr. Winston to come put that tube back down my throat." He laughed and reached for the remote control.

Thanksgiving morning at the rehab center, unfortunately, was the same as every other day, except for the construction paper turkeys pasted all along the walls of the waiting room. My father was propped up in his bed, his legs elevated and wrapped.

"It'll probably be pretty good," I said, smiling.

He paused for a second. "Not as good as your mother's."

I nodded in agreement and looked away.

He was right. There wasn't going to be any Thanksgiving dinner as good as hers, for us, ever again. It was like magic the way she made so much food, all by herself, and we never really saw her do it. I mean, one minute you'd see her snapping string beans and cutting corn off the cob. Then you'd see her stirring a pot of brown liquid with turkey neck bones floating at the top. Then you'd see her performing surgery on the turkey, which was always the grossest thing in the world, shoving her hand up its butt and pulling out all the slime. Then you'd hear the eggs cracking and the mixer running. And then, all of a sudden, dinner would be ready. Turkey, mashed potatoes, greens, stuffing, cranberries, corn, biscuits, pies and cakes, and a special tea she made to go with it all. No measuring cups. No boxes or cans. When she cooked Thanksgiving, Brooklyn Daisy went on break and Carolina Daisy ran the show. It's the only time she wouldn't let me help. This meal was hers, and hers alone.

"Yeah, you right about that," I said. I was trying not to make this a sad thing, but the whole vibe in the room changed. So I went with it and hoped for the best. "I went to see her yesterday. Her grave."

My father shimmied up the pillow behind him.

"How was she?" He caught himself. Pressed his lips tight. Tried again. "I mean, how was it?"

"It was good," I said. Then I thought about it. "She was good." I had told myself no crying on Thanksgiving, and I was determined to stick to it. But I could feel the rumble.

My father looked out the window, which he did every time *he* wanted to keep from crying. He took a deep breath and blew out like he was smoking an imaginary cigarette.

"I'm glad you went," he said. When he looked back at me, his eyes were glassy. "When I get outta here, and can walk again, maybe we can go together." His voice sounded strained.

I gave a shrug. Part of me wanted to ask him what he had been going through, trapped in the rehab wing of the hospital, not being able to really move on his own, forced to just lie there with his own thoughts all the time. I wondered if he ever cried when he was alone, or if he ever called out for her, or if he was having dreams about her like I was every night. Mainly, I wondered how he was dealing with it. I had the funerals. And now I had Lovey—someone new to talk to, and someone new to be excited about. But what did he have besides new metal bones in his legs?

We sat in silence that felt peaceful and heavy and weird and sad—pretty much everything but happy. So I changed the subject.

"So, I'm having Thanksgiving dinner today with a girl." Just came right out with it.

Dad squinted his eyes like he didn't believe me. "Who? I thought you were eating over at Willie Ray's."

"Nope. I'm eating with this girl I met named Love."

Of course my father looked at me sideways like I was losing my mind.

"Love, huh?" The mood of the room went instantly light again.

JASON REYNOLDS

"Yes, that's her real name, Dad. Love."

He snickered. "Okay, okay. Well, does her crazy parents—'cause they gotta be crazy to name her Love—know you coming to crash their table?"

"No parents, man. She lives alone. Folks passed away."

"Ah. Wow. Sorry to hear that, man," he said, now regretting the joke he had made. "Where'd you meet her?"

I was a little embarrassed to tell him.

"At her grandmother's funeral."

"You pick up women at these funerals? That's why you like this job so much!" He howled, but I didn't laugh at all, because that's not the reason I loved the funerals, and if he knew the real reason he wouldn't have found it so funny.

Noticing I wasn't sharing in his joke, he eased up.

"Okay, son, well, let me ask you this. She smart?"

"Yeah."

"She in school?"

"Yeah."

"She gotta job?"

"Yep."

"Nice?"

"Of course."

"Pretty?"

I just squished my face up, like it hurt me to think of how pretty she was.

My father busted out laughing again.

"Well then, enjoy your dinner. And if for some reason you feel like having *dessert*, think twice, son. One slice of her pie could equal a lifetime of your cake, if you know what I mean."

"What?!"

Mr. Ray and I left the hospital around noon. The second we got in the big black car he picked up the discussion we'd been having on the way to the hospital a few hours earlier.

"So, have you thought about what you're bringing?" he asked.

He had been explaining to me—really, it was more like preaching—how you never go over nobody's house empty-handed. Especially when you're going for dinner.

"Naw, I can't really think of nothing, and to be honest, I don't even think Love would trip if I didn't bring anything. I mean, we both said we were just gonna eat leftovers."

Mr. Ray looked at me like he couldn't believe what I was saying.

"You really green, huh?" he said, eyes back on the road. He began rolling the sleeves of his white shirt up to his forearm. Mr. Ray wore a suit, even on holidays. But he didn't wear a tie, so I guess to him he was dressed down.

"Matt," Mr. Ray said, putting on his blinker. "Trust me. You want her to like you, right?"

"Of course."

Mr. Ray jerked the car over the side of the road, pulling up in front of a bodega.

"Then don't show up empty-handed."

In the store I walked down the aisles looking for something that Love might like. Mr. Ray told me that this whole process would've been so much easier if we were older, because then I could just get a bottle of wine and be done with it. But because I can't buy wine, I'm stuck trying to figure out whether or not to go with soda, juice, cookies, or chips.

"Man, don't go with chips," Mr. Ray demanded.

"Why not?"

"Breath. Can't risk it. You might luck up and get a kiss."

Didn't even think about that. Chips were out.

"And soda isn't a good choice either, because girls her age are trying to make sure they don't get no unexpected bumps on their faces."

"Pimples."

"Right."

We walked up and down the cluttered aisles as he continued to shoot down my options.

"And juice, well, juice ain't bad. But we don't know what kind of juice she likes, and you don't want to bring grape when she loves apple. And Lord knows, she might even like one of these fancy ones with the kiwi and passion fruit and all that mixed up in there. So cookies it is."

Dude was nuts.

"Yeah, but I don't know what kind of cookies she likes either," I explained.

"Chocolate chip," he said right away. "I ain't never met a person that didn't like chocolate chip cookies."

Me neither, I realized. I started looking around the bodega for the cookies. Oreos, those nasty wafer things that taste like dirty air, and those cheap strawberry cookies. No chocolate chip? I looked and looked. No chocolate chip! Then, out of pure instinct, I went for the eggs. And the flour. Some sugar. There were chocolate chips in the house from when my mother and I baked cookies for my dad's birthday.

"But what if *she* don't like them?" I said, as I tried to nonchalantly put the ingredients up on the counter.

"What's all this?" Mr. Ray asked, confused.

"Well, they didn't have any chocolate chip cookies, so I'm just going to make some," I said, matter-of-factly.

He studied me hard. "You serious?" he asked. "You know we could just try another store down the block."

"Naw. I think I'd rather just make them myself," I said, a little embarrassed. "They'll be better, and it's easy. No big deal." No big deal? Who was I kidding? *Huge* deal!

Mr. Ray just looked at me strange. Who knows what he was thinking. Probably that I was weirder than he thought.

"But answer my question." I put a ten-dollar bill on the counter. "What if she doesn't like chocolate chip cookies?"

Mr. Ray snatched the money off the counter and gave it back to me, replacing it with his own. He collected his change, grabbed the bag of cookie ingredients, and turned back toward me.

"Then run."

✖   ✖   ✖

JASON REYNOLDS

Love had texted me her address and what time to be there the day before.

815 Greene Ave

Be here around 2:30 :)

I'd been surprised—I had no idea she lived so close. Greene Avenue was only, like, ten blocks from me. Definitely walkable.

That gave me about two hours now to make the cookies. I broke out the sifter, the mixing bowl, the mixer, some measuring cups, and the old wooden spoon my mother loved to use. Then, finally, I opened up the notebook—THE SECRET TO GETTING GIRLS, FOR MATTY—and flipped through until I found the recipe.

Daisy's Damn Good Choco Chip Cookies (for Matty)
What you need:
1 cup of white sugar
1 cup of brown sugar
1 cup of veggie oil
an egg (no shells, son)
1 tblspn of milk
4 cups of flour
a pinch of salt
a pinch of baking soda
a few drops of vanilla extract
2 cups of choco chips (nonsweet)

What to do: Mix up everything but the choco chips. Those go into the batter last. Then scoop out two

pinches of batter at a time (or you'll have cookie pan-
cakes) and put them on a nonstick pan. Put them
bad boys in the oven at 350 and let them bake for
ten minutes. Boom. You got yourself some damn good
choco chips. Love ya, Matty, but I'll tease you if you
burn these.
Mom

I could actually hear my mom's voice while reading the recipe. I checked to make sure we had everything—the vegetable oil, the brown sugar. Check and check. The vanilla extract. Check. Everything was there. For a minute it felt like fate, but then I realized it wasn't that deep. I was just baking cookies, and my mom cooked a lot, so of course we had everything. It's like walking into a funeral home and being surprised there are caskets.

I measured and poured and pinched and mixed until the batter was done. (My mother was a master pincher.) Then I poured the chocolate chips in, and some honey, which I just added because I figured it would be a nice touch. I stuck my finger in the batter, which my mother would've tripped about, but I just had to. She used to let me lick the spoon, but my finger? No-no. I gave it a taste. Oh . . . man. Slammin'. Then I scooped out little nugget-size chunks and lined them up on the pan, eight rows of four, and into the oven they went.

I checked my phone. One o'clock. I was tempted to run upstairs and wash up and get dressed, but my mom always said never to leave the stove. I had already set the timer for ten minutes, so might as well wait. Plus, the recipe clearly stated that she'd laugh at me if I burned these cookies, and I kinda felt like she would figure out a way to let me know she was laughing. Even if it was by showing up in a dream or something. So I sat at the kitchen table and waited, flipping through the notebook—through the recipes.

Daisy's Friggin' Fried Chicken, for Matty
Daisy's Sweet-ass Sautéed Spinach, for Matty
Because He Needs His Vegetables
Daisy's Dirty Shrimp and Grits, for Matty
Daisy's Carolina BBQ, for Matty
Daisy's Pineapple Upside-down, Right-side Up Cake,
for Matty (Relax, It's Just a Pound Cake, Son)

And on and on. I flipped page after page, reading her little notes to me, smiling to myself, a part of me aware that this was the first time seeing her handwriting didn't crush me. The first time I'd even wanted to cook anything. Did I feel sad? A little. But I also felt, I don't know, different. Like something about it all was kinda calming.

Ten minutes had passed and the smell of baking cookies had started to sneak from the oven door and float around the kitchen. It's a smell I've smelled a million times, but it never gets old. The oven dinged. I opened the door, and there they were, thirty-two perfect little pieces of chocolatey heaven. At that point, I knew for sure this was a better idea than just buying a bag of cookies from the store. Like my mom used to say, food is better when it's cooked with love. Well, these were cooked with like, but *for* Love, so . . . pretty close. I slid the tray out, took a bite, and at that moment, *yeow*! Burned my tongue. But hadn't burned the cookies. I felt like Mom and I had done all this together.

I also hoped she was right about, y'know, cooking being a way to get girls.

I glanced at the clock—shoot! I needed to get dressed. *What to wear, what to wear.* I knew I couldn't wear my suit. That just would've been ridiculous, showing up in an all-black suit—the same black suit she met me in. The one, in fact, I wore to her grandmother's funeral. Not good. But when you wear a suit every single day, it's hard to *not* wear one. Like Mr. Ray. He was dressed up on a day off, not because he wanted to be, but because he probably doesn't know how to not be. As a matter of fact, I've never seen him in jeans. I bet he doesn't even own none.

I jumped in the shower, because even though I love the smell of baking cookies, I didn't want to smell like them. Reeking of sugar might've been a turn-off. After I washed up I looked through my closet at clothes I hadn't thought about in three months. I pulled out a few different things, colorful Polo shirts, blue jeans, khakis, sweaters, but I didn't feel comfortable in none of it. So I went with black jeans, a black T-shirt, a black jean jacket, and black sneakers. I looked in the mirror. Simple and comfortable, and close enough to my everyday uniform.

Then I noticed sharp lines running through my shirt, making it look more like paper than cotton. My jeans were stiff, and creased in weird places. And for the second time that day, I could hear my mom loud and clear: *Take pride in the way you present yourself,* followed up by, *And ain't no pride in looking like a tumbleweed. Go run some heat over them clothes and knock them wrinkles out before people think I ain't trained you.*

Yeah. Mom was right, as usual. I was a mess. So I started over, this time ironing till everything was smooth and flat. I looked in the mirror again. No wrinkles. I looked ten times better. Presentable and trained.

I packed up the cookies, grabbed my coat, and headed out.

2:05. I texted Lovey.

On my way

Then I texted Chris.

On my way

Just as soon as I locked my front door, my phone buzzed.

1 TEXT MESSAGE

It was from Chris.

Good luck champ lol

Then another message came through.

1 TEXT MESSAGE

This time from Lovey.

Good ;) *I live on the first floor.*

The ten blocks seemed like they lasted forever. I was walking fast enough to not be late, but slow enough so that I wouldn't start sweating. I didn't want to get there and not be fresh, especially after all that ironing. I also thought about how showing up with a plastic bodega bag didn't exactly match my whole look, so I trashed it and just carried the cookies in a Ziploc.

815 Greene. A three-floor brownstone, pretty much like every other house in the neighborhood. A seven-step stoop, an old-school buzzer box, and Christmas lights in one of the neighbor's windows that I could tell had been there all year long.

Lovey said she lived on the first floor, which is always buzzer number two, because buzzer number one would be the ground floor, basement apartment. At least that's what I hoped.

I pushed the button. It made that weird noise that sounded like someone being electrocuted.

"Hello?" Love's voice came crackling through the speaker, loud but sweet.

"Hey, it's Matt."

"Okay. Be right down."

Then, I got nervous. I was good all the way up to that moment, but once I knew the date was actually going down, robot face started to appear. My stomach got tight, and my palms started feeling slimy as I held the bag of cookies with both hands as if I were presenting a cake.

I heard her apartment door open inside. Then the footsteps to the front door. Then the turning and clicking of the locks and the wiggling of the doorknob.

"Hey," she said with a big smile, swinging the door open. She was dressed in jeans, a sweater, and a light jacket. Her hair was pulled back in a ponytail, and her face was perfect, and I don't even think she was wearing makeup. She leaned toward me for a hug, wrapping one arm around me lightly. I did the same. The cookies pressed up against her stomach.

"What's this?"

"Well," I started, nervous. "I didn't want to come empty-handed."

Her eyes grew bright. "That's sweet."

Instantly, I thanked God for Mr. Ray.

I didn't even get a chance to tell her they were homemade before she added, "The kids are gonna love these."

Robot-mutant-infant-animal-face.

"Kids? You . . . you got kids?" My voice shot up to soprano.

"Ha! Boy, please. Picture that. I'm talking about the kids down at the shelter. That's where we going."

I was confused. "Oh, I thought . . ." I started to say but got too embarrassed to finish.

"You thought what?" she asked. Then it came to her. "Oh, you thought we were eating here?" She started laughing, but not in a mean way. "I told you, you might be a killer. I mean, now you know where I live, but I ain't about to let you in!" she joked. "I'm kidding, I'm kidding. It's just that my grandma cared a lot about those folks in that shelter, especially the kids. I just feel like I need to do this. Y'know, keep her tradition alive. Plus, they're expecting me to handle the newspeople this year."

"Newspeople?"

"Yeah. Every year, the news comes down and does a spot about what Thanksgiving is all about. They film a little bit, ask a few questions, and air it later tonight. It's no big deal, but it's cool."

"Sounds like it," I heard myself say, but my brain was thinking, *Shelter? Newspeople?*

"Grams used to always talk to them, but now that she's gone, I guess it's on me," she explained. I'm not sure if I looked disappointed—I can never tell—because Lovey added quickly, "But I totally get it, if you don't wanna come."

"No, I'm down," I said, recovering. I wasn't going to blow this. "I never been to a shelter, anyway. Something new."

I wasn't mad about not having a private dinner with Lovey in her house. Just disappointed because I had worked myself up so much to be ready for it. But at the end of the day I was actually kind of happy we weren't eating there. Being around other people—even though they were homeless people—made it less like a date, less serious, which for me was a good thing, because I really didn't know what I was going to do or say once we got alone, other than offer her homemade chocolate chip cookies and hope she didn't say she didn't like them.

"Cool." She took the cookies and tried to place them in a plastic bag on the floor in the hallway. Actually, there were a bunch of plastic bags. "Help me with these."

She handed me a couple, filled with what I guessed was food wrapped in aluminum foil like big silver boulders. Whoa! They weighed a ton. We shuffled down the sidewalk to the bus stop. I did my best to pretend like the bags weren't heavy. But they were heavy as hell. Like, heavy enough to pull my shoulders right out the sockets.

On the way Love talked about how her grandma had turned the shelter around.

"You know how it is. People judge people. We all do it. But

homeless people get it the worst, 'cause they smell bad sometimes, and some of them have issues, but Grams treated them all like people," she explained. "That's the difference with this place. You go to some shelters and they serve food but won't actually say a word to the people living there. Or they'll let them sleep there for a night but talk to them any kind of way." She stopped for a second to rest, swapping bags from one hand to the other. I was so glad we took a break, because it felt like my arms were literally going to fall off. She flexed her fingers, trying to get the feeling back, I guessed, because I was doing the same thing. "But Grams got to know them. I mean, these people are like family to me. I've been around them basically my whole life. Honestly, if the shelter could pay me, I would've kicked the Bucket a long time ago," she said, talking about Cluck Bucket.

"What? You would leave your big-time job in the hood?" I teased, and hoped she got it. The worst thing that could happen was to flop a joke right now. Luckily, she started laughing.

"Yep. I'd let go of all the glitz and glamour of chicken grease to help people," she said, dramatic. Awesome.

Before I knew it, we were there. A HELPING HAND SHELTER was painted on a wooden sign that was nailed to the door. The sign was old, and a lot of the paint had chipped and cracked. There were a few guys outside all huddled up. One was holding a handful of cigarette butts while the others sifted through, picking out the ones that still had a little tobacco left in them.

"Hey, boys," Lovey said.

They all seemed excited to see her.

"Miss Lady." A tip of the hat.

"Lovey, how you, sugar?" A nod.

And so on.

I pulled the door open and waited for Lovey to walk in. Mom said being a gentleman works.

"Just make sure those things don't spoil your appetite. It's Thanksgiving!" Lovey was saying to the men, like somebody's mama. Those guys were old enough to be her grandfathers, but they showed her respect. Then she went inside the building, thanking me for holding the door.

I expected the inside of a homeless shelter to look like the inside of a prison, even though I had never been inside either. But you know how prisons are on TV, all metal and gray and filled with angry people eating slop and sleeping on concrete slabs. It's embarrassing to say that, but it's true. I thought I was going to be walking into death's waiting room. But it wasn't like that all. The walls weren't gray. They were a light purple, with pictures of smiling people painted on them. Two girls with jump ropes, a boy doing a handstand, a man with long arms and legs spinning a basketball on his finger, a woman standing next to a younger girl stirring a pot.

"That's me and Grams," Lovey said, catching me staring at the mural. "We had the kids paint pictures of people who inspired them. Pretty sweet, right?"

"Absolutely," I said. She was gazing at the mural like it was her first time seeing it.

"Let me give you the tour."

We walked down a soft pink hallway and popped into different bright-colored rooms. In most of them there wasn't much to see. A desk here, a file cabinet there. Then we got to the brightest room, the children's room.

"Here's all my kids," Lovey joked.

I laughed at how shocked I was when I thought she was saying she had kids, back at her house.

"It's crazy how good you look after having"—I did a quick count—"eleven munchkins."

Now Lovey busted out laughing and knocked her elbow against my arm.

We watched as the children acted like children, jumping around, laughing at everything, screaming at nothing. Being kids. I was amazed. It was almost like they didn't know they were in a shelter.

"Miss Lovey!" A little cinnamon girl with a million braids in her hair came up and wrapped her arms around Lovey's legs.

"Hi, Danielle." She rubbed the little girl's back. "You being good?"

Danielle pulled away to look in Lovey's face. "Yes." Then she looked over at me. "This your boyfriend?"

Lovey bugged her eyes and squatted down to look Danielle in the face. "What you know about boyfriends?" she teased, tickling the little girl under her arms. Danielle fell to her knees giggling. I just watched and smiled, happy to hear laughter, and happy Lovey didn't say no.

From there we hit the last spot on the tour, the dining room, which was the biggest room of them all. It pretty much looked like my high-school cafeteria, with the floor that looked like a checkerboard and the wobbly brown tables. There were a bunch of men and women in there, mopping and setting up chairs.

"This is where we're gonna eat," Lovey said, walking through the room with her arms spread wide. "And over here's the kitchen."

There were a few more volunteers washing out pots and pans and getting trays ready. We set all the bags down and Lovey introduced me to everyone. A tall, lanky, white guy named Carl. A short, Spanish woman (with the softest hands ever!) named Rita. An old lady named Maggie who reminded me of my sixth-grade teacher, Ms. Clayton.

"This is his first time, y'all," she said, calling me out.

We unpacked all the stuff she brought, which really was leftover fried chicken and mashed potatoes from her grandmother's funeral. I noticed that there was tons of other food lined up on the counters, including a couple of already cooked turkeys, a few hams, and a whole bunch of pies and cakes. Lovey put the cookies on the counter.

"For the kids," she announced.

Then, another lady came in carrying a bag of those can-candle things that we always use at the funerals to keep the food warm.

"Hey, everybody," the lady said. "I got the heaters, but I don't know how to get 'em going."

This was my shot. I wasn't sure what I would be able to do, but I knew exactly how to do this one thing.

"I do," I spoke up.

Lovey looked up at me, surprised. I could tell she wasn't expecting me to jump right in like that, but hey, I was trying to make a good impression. She grabbed the turkey knife and started wiping it off. Her eyes followed me as I grabbed the cans from the lady and used my house key to pop the lids off like my dad did with beer bottles. And as cool as possible, I struck a match and got the fire started.

CHAPTER 11
CANDY MAN

"Dinner is ready. Everybody come down to the dining room." Lovey's voice came blaring over the intercom speakers throughout the building. "I repeat, dinner is ready. Everybody to the dining room . . . before I eat it all!"

You never really know how many people are in a place until they all come to one space. Also, you never really know how many people are out there struggling, hungry, until there's free food available. Folks came from everywhere. Men, some old, some young. Some with canes and walkers, wearing busted shoes. Some with shirt and tie on, and old seventies thrift-store jackets. Ladies, some toothless, in oversize men's clothes, and some looked perfectly fine. Teenagers, acting all cool as usual, doing their best to not fit in with the homeless crowd, even though they were homeless themselves. And of course, the kids—some adorable, and some badasses.

As they all formed a line at the food table, me, Lovey, Carl, Rita, Maggie, and a few other volunteers all stood behind the dishes we were serving. Lovey had the turkey. I got the chicken.

"A'ight, now this is simple," Lovey said to me, "Everybody who wants chicken can get a piece. Just make sure you save the drumsticks for the babies."

"Got it."

Honestly, I didn't think it was going to go as smooth as it did. Everyone took some of everything, piling their plates up with mountains of food, but nobody was piggish about it. The only problem I ran into—which I thought was going to ruin everything—was that every single person wanted a chicken breast.

"Leg, wing, or breast?" I asked the most interesting-looking old man I had ever seen. His skin was dark and shiny but his eyes were a cold blue. His hair was long and cornrowed straight back.

"Well, I'm known to be a breast man," he said, flashing a devilish grin. The woman behind him, a tiny old lady who, to me, fit the description of the perfect grandmother—small, wrinkly, glasses, and feisty as hell—slapped him on the back of the head.

"What?" he yelped, turning to her. He opened his arms and pulled her in for a hug. "I'm talking about chicken, darlin'. Chicken." He glanced at me. "Right, young man?" Again, with the grin.

"Of course, of course." I played along, while he stroked the shoulder of who I figured was his girlfriend. The flyest of homeless senior citizen couples I've ever seen, that's for sure. I continued. "But I got bad news, we're all out of breasts."

"Out of breasts!" the man barked.

"Out of breasts!" his girlfriend repeated.

You see where this is going?

The phrase "out of breasts" shot down the line faster than the old couple could move to the next tray, which was Lovey serving the turkey.

Lovey looked over at me with the "yikes" face. Then she looked at the couple and said, "Hey, hey, don't be like that, Mr. Watts and Ms. Bingham. We got plenty of turkey." She piled on the white meat. A little extra for them.

"They got plenty turkey!" Mr. Watts yelled, Ms. Bingham's voice coming shortly after. And on down the line it went again, now calming the rumble the lack of chicken breasts caused.

"You almost started a riot," Lovey said, balling up a napkin and throwing it at me.

"Close one."

Other than that, everything was cool, and it was awesome to see the smiles on everybody's faces, their eyes lighting up with every plop of macaroni and every slice of turkey.

Once everyone else was served, Lovey and I took a seat next to a few of the kids and dug in.

After about five minutes of nothing but the weird sound of about a hundred people chewing, Lovey said, "Turkey good, huh?" She stuffed more in her mouth.

"What you think?" I joked, showing her my plate, which had nothing left on it but knife marks. Chris would've been proud. Mom would've been pissed. "No cavemen live in my house," she would've said.

Lovey bugged her eyes out. Then she picked up her cup of punch and took a sip. "Crazy that a lot of it was cooked in a homeless shelter."

"I know. Kinda unbelievable," I said. "Thank you for inviting me."

"Did I invite you? Or was it more like I bamboozled you?" She put her hands together like a fairytale witch casting a spell.

"Ah. Definitely bamboozled."

When everyone was done eating, me and the rest of the volunteers grabbed trash bags and walked around to collect all the empty plates and cups. Lovey walked with me, talking to everyone while they threw their scraps and bones in the black bags. Whenever we got to a kid, she called out, "Dunk it!" One little boy picked his plate up, folded it in half, and slammed it as hard as he could into the bag.

"Two points!" Lovey howled. "You see that, Candy Man?" She looked over at an older guy, long and skinny, sitting there smiling away at the kids. "Better watch out before little man is better than you."

I looked over at the guy called Candy Man and instantly recognized him. He was the same guy I shared the train car with the day before, when I went to see my mom's grave. He looked much better than he had yesterday. He had on slacks and a white V-neck T-shirt, tucked in, old-man style. He was shaved, and even though his skin was still dry, he seemed to be way more alive than he had been on the train.

"He better be better than me," Candy Man said. "All of y'all better be better than me, hear me?" he commanded, dropping his own plate in the trash.

"I'm gonna be famous, watch," the boy who dunked his plate said. He ran up to Candy Man and flung himself at him, wrapping his arms around Candy Man's legs.

"Oh, yeah?" Candy Man patted the boy's head. "Then I better get your autograph now!"

Another little girl came over and joined in on the hug. "Me too!" she squealed. "I'm gonna be famous too!"

And another. And another. Even Danielle, the little girl who asked if I was Lovey's boyfriend when we first got there, ran over to pile on. It was as if Candy Man was the king of the shelter.

After we finished with the trash, it was chill-out time, where everyone just did whatever they wanted. The smokers went back outside to puff burned-out cigs, some of the other grown-ups played card games and board games, shouting at each other while slamming cards down on the table. Some played chess, of course. Most of the teenagers took off, and all the little kids lined up to have their pictures taken by Lovey, a thing they apparently did every holiday.

"What's the deal with Candy Man?" I asked Lovey while she unpacked her fancy camera and started attaching the lens to the body.

"Candy Man is a trip, but the kids love him because he used to be a star." She turned the lens until it clicked. "His real name is Martin. Used to play ball for the Knicks."

The Knicks? Sweet! I mean, well, kinda sweet. Not so sweet that he's homeless now. But still.

"So—what happened to him?" I asked Lovey.

She lifted the camera to her face and pointed it toward me faster than I could tell her not to. *Snap!* The flash was blinding. She looked at the photo and smirked at what I knew was robot face.

"Drugs," she said, plainly. I was still stunned as she turned toward all the kids. "I gotta try to get as many of these done as I can before the news folks get here," she said, still talking to me. But then she switched to her mom-babysitter-teacher voice. "Everybody ready to cheese!" All the children screamed as if she had just told them they were going to Disney World. They stood in line, practicing their snaggle-toothed, buck-toothed, and no-tooth smiles.

"And what about you, Mr. Miller?" She had turned back toward me, a flirty grin on her face. "You ready to cheese?"

I put my hand up. "You just took one of me."

"Ah, but that was just a test shot. Now, for the real one."

I waved my hands. "Naw, naw, I can't. I suck at it."

"At what?" she said with some bite in her voice.

"At smiling," I admitted.

She squinted at me as if she didn't believe me.

"Well, we'll have to work on that." She reached over and pinched my cheek like I was one of the kids.

And just like that, a smile came out.

I noticed Candy Man sitting alone with his chessboard, begging some of the other guys to sit and play.

"Why don't one of y'all take on Candy Man?" I asked a man with a toothpick sticking out from the side of his mouth. He was one of about five guys all standing around playing chess and talking trash. I knew it really wasn't my place to bust in and say something like that. I mean, I didn't know any of these guys, but I figured me being with Lovey, and serving them all food, was enough of a pass for me to say something. Stupid.

Suddenly, all eyes were on me. It was like I had just said, "Yo, your mama got next," or something crazy like that.

"What?"

Then the man with the toothpick moved his hands like he was telling everyone else to calm down.

"Candy Man ain't no fun to play," he said, sizing me up. He pulled the wooden stick from the side of his mouth. "He too damn good, and when you get beat by somebody over and over again, it just ain't no fun no more."

"Hey, Cedric, don't even bother explaining it," one of the other guys, a red-headed freckly faced one, said. Then he looked over at me. "Why don't *you* just go play him and see for yourself."

"I'm not that good."

"Scared?"

Come on, what are we, in middle school? That's what I was thinking. But what I said was, "Scared? It's just chess. I'll play him."

I walked over to Candy Man. At first I thought all the other guys would follow me over, y'know, to build up the drama like an after-school fight. But no one even bothered. I guess they figured I'd get blown out anyway, so what was the point? I slid the chair out and took a seat in front of Candy Man. And without saying anything, I moved a pawn.

Candy Man rubbed his hands together as if he was trying to warm them up. "All right, some competition."

"Won't be much, man. I ain't really that good."

"No shit," he said, cocky. "I could tell by your first move."

This is how the game went down. I moved, then he moved. I moved again, and then he shook his head, and moved. I moved again, then he looked up at me like I was crazy. Then he moved. Then I moved, and he knocked over my king. Eight moves. Checkmate. The fastest war in history.

"Good game," he said, obviously embarrassed for me.

Toothpick and Freckles were right. He really was that good. I shook his hand, then slid my chair back from the table.

"Wait, you leaving? One more game, c'mon," he begged, setting the pieces back on their original squares.

"I think I've had enough abuse for one day," I said, confused as to why he would want to play me again. Three more minutes of total wackness? For what?

"Come on, come on, sit down," he said. "We don't have to play if you don't want to." Candy Man suddenly transformed from a champion to a child, and I suddenly got it—he was just desperate for some company.

I turned around to see what Lovey was doing. The news crew had just shown up, and they were filming her as she handed one of the kids a cookie. I had time to kill.

I eased back down in the chair and pulled up to the table again.

"So," Candy Man started. "What's your deal?"

Not really a good ice breaker.

"What you mean?" I responded.

"I mean, you ain't never been here. At least, I ain't never seen you. And today you show up to help. So what's your story, *Good Samaritan*?"

I looked over my shoulder again, to see what Lovey was doing now, sort of hoping she'd come and save me.

"I came with Love. You know Love?" I said, pointing over at her.

Candy Man leaned forward. "Yeah, I know her. Of course I know her. Been knowing her her whole life," he said, snappy. "The question is, how *you* know her? You her boy or something?"

Hell yeah, I'm her boy.

"No sir. Just a friend," I replied, nervous that he'd try to check-mate me in real life.

Candy Man eased up a little. "All right then," he said, looking down at the chess pieces all lined up perfectly. "'Cause she special. Her grandma was special, her mama was special, and she special."

"Yes sir," I said, nervous, and way confused about this whole conversation we were having. I mean, I tried to leave the table, then he begged me to stay just so he could grill me about Lovey? Yeah, fun times.

"Where you from?" he asked, straightforward.

"Right here. Brooklyn. Bed-Stuy. You?"

"Harlem. But not Harlem today. Harlem a long time ago. How it used to be. You probably don't know nothing about that?"

JASON REYNOLDS

"My parents used to live there." The conversation finally started to settle in and flow. "They used to work at a soul food restaurant up there, so I know a little something about it."

"Oh yeah?" His eyes lit up. "Which restaurant?"

"I never remember the name of it, but I think it was somewhere around One-thirty-fifth and Amsterdam."

He thought for a moment. "Can't place it, but I didn't live too far from there," he said, still trying to figure out what restaurant it was. "What's your folks' names? If they was uptown, I might know 'em, and if I don't, they probably know me." He smiled. All gums.

"My father's name is Jackson," I said. "Jackson Miller. And my mother's name was Daisy."

"It *was* Daisy? What's her name now?"

"She passed away," I said, fast. As I said it, it dawned on me that this was the first time I had really thought about my mom since I had been at the shelter. I looked down at the chessboard to avoid any look Candy Man might have been giving. If it was a pity face, I didn't want to see it. And if it was a stupid, no-big-deal face, I didn't want to see that one either.

"Oh," he said, stuck. "I'm sorry to hear that."

"Yeah, it's cool. So what about you?" I flipped the conversation on him quickly. Didn't want to give it time to simmer and bubble. Just wanted to move on.

"What about me?"

"What's your story? Love told me you used to play ball."

"Yeah, I used to. Played a few years for the Knicks."

"I heard!" I tried to contain my excitement. Like I said, I'm not even a big sports dude, but actually meeting somebody who played in the pros was big. Couldn't help it.

"What was that like?"

Candy Man ran his hand along the back of his head. "Y'know, it was the best thing that ever happened to me. And also the worst."

"Oh yeah?" I pretended to sound surprised. "Why you say that?"

Now it was his turn to look down at the board. I wasn't trying to put him on the spot, but it just kind of happened.

He turned a pawn on its side and spun it like he was spinning a quarter.

"Partied a little too hard." He gave the pawn another spin. "Started putting that shit in my veins." Now he flicked the pawn away. It skittered into one of mine, knocking it over. "It was like one day I was standing at the foul line shooting free throws, and the next day I was fifty, sleeping every night on the street. And the crazy part is, I don't remember nothing in between."

"You ever been married?" I asked.

Candy Man snapped his neck back and then he started laughing. "Naw, son. Only thing I ever been committed to is rehab. And even that ain't work out so well."

"No kids?"

"The little youngins running round here are my kids." He looked me straight in the eyes. "And Lovey."

I know he said that we didn't have to play another game, but I picked up the two pawns, reset them, then made a first move. Might as well.

He moved after me.

"And this is one of our new volunteers." Lovey came out of nowhere. The smell of fruity perfume and food came down on me as she approached the table. She interrupted my next move (not that it would've been a good one) and she brought the whole news crew with her. The guy with the big camera, the dude holding the light, the lady in the stiff suit—everybody.

"Hi, I'm Connie Whitlock of New York One. Would you mind if we just ask you a few questions about your experience as a first-time volunteer here at Helping Hand?"

I looked at Lovey. And even though I always suck at this kind of thing, her face made me say yes.

Damn girls.

"So what's it been like, spending your turkey day here at the shelter?" Ms. Whitlock, who my mom used to watch all the time, asked in that weird, phony voice newspeople always talk in.

"Well," I started as I stood up and tried to get my thoughts together. Ms. Whitlock held the mic just under my chin like a mother holding an ice cream cone for a kid to lick. "It's been cool. I mean, I've never done anything like this before, and when Love, here, invited me, I thought maybe I'd come and everyone would just be bummed out—" Argh! *Bummed out?* Stupid, stupid, stupid. "I mean, like, I thought folks would be sad to be in such a tough situation for Thanksgiving," I went on hurriedly, trying to recover. "But when I got here, and started helping, I realized that most of these people are kind, and just grateful for a hot meal and someone to talk to. We all can relate to that."

"Fantastic!" Ms. Whitlock exclaimed like she was reading it off a cue card. "And there you have it, folks. Love Brown, the granddaughter of Gwendolyn Brown, has taken the baton and keeps the giving tradition alive here at Helping Hand Shelter. I'm Connie Whitlock, and from all of us here at New York One, have a happy Thanksgiving, everyone. Now, back to you, Carla."

The guy holding the big camera said, "Clear," and then Ms. Whitlock and Lovey shook hands and talked a little longer as I dropped back into my seat to continue with the whooping that was waiting for me by Candy Man.

I moved my own knight.

Candy Man moved it back, and moved another one of my pawns. Then he looked at me and said, "I just want it to last a little longer."

Ouch.

Then he moved his knight.

"Take it easy on him, Candy Man, I don't want you to beat him so bad he too scared to come back down here." Lovey was interrupting again, this time by herself—the newspeople had left. She propped her camera up to her face for a shot of the chessboard. "I like him, so don't scare him off." She flashed a smile as she turned the lens, zooming in and out.

Candy Man gave his best cheese back. "I'm taking it easy," he assured her with a wink.

"Good, because you don't want *me* to sit down at this table."

Candy Man leaned toward me. "She's the only person here who ever beat me."

Then Lovey leaned toward me. "That's because I'm the only person he lets win."

For another hour Candy Man went on and on, telling stories about Lovey, and how she was when she first started coming to the shelter with her grandmother. He talked about her big brown penny eyes, and how even though she was adorable, she was tougher than most of the boys.

"Man, she'd have holes all in her little jeans, and her knees would be bleeding, because she was outside wrestling with the boys," Candy Man remembered. "But she wasn't no baby. She was tough and she never cried. Never. The boys, though, forget about it. They'd be boo-hooing all over the damn shelter until Gwen came and gave them hugs and whatnot."

This was, I think, the third story. The first one was about how Lovey would growl at boys, like a wolf or something. That one was funny. And the second one, Candy Man was laughing so hard I couldn't understand what he was talking about, but I know it had something to do with boogers.

Lovey gave Candy Man a terrible look.

"Why you always gotta tell these stories?"

"That's why I let her win, son"—he totally ignored her—"because, truth is, I'm scared of her."

"Candy Man!" she yelped, and punched him lightly in the arm. He hooted and held his arm, hollering about how he was thinking about trying to go back to the NBA, but now she'd permanently injured his arm, so he couldn't.

Then he reached for her and pulled her in tight for a hug, like the kind that fathers give daughters, or mothers give sons. Then I shook his hand and told him it was nice to meet him.

"Good to meet you too, son."

"Matthew," Lovey reminded him.

"Yeah, Matthew," he said, pointing at me.

The night was perfect for a walk. The sun had gone down just behind the brownstones, making it seem like all of Bed-Stuy was glowing. And it was crazy warm for the end of November. A breeze swept down the block and around me and Lovey as we started on our journey home. Neither one of us questioned whether we should catch a cab, or a bus, or jump on the train. It was obvious, walking was the only option.

"Bummed out?" Lovey started teasing. I knew she was too quick to miss that slipup, and something told me I was going to pay for it. "Bummed out, Matt?" She exploded into laughter. "I can't believe you really said that!"

"You threw me into the fire! I didn't know I was gonna be interviewed. You set me up!" I threw a fake glare at her, but that only made her laugh harder. But I got her to ease up as soon as I asked her if that's what she sounded like when she used to howl like a wolf when she was a kid.

"Hey, watch it," she said, wiping laugh-tears from her eyes.

"Okay, okay. But, seriously, is Candy Man always that funny?"

"Martin 'Candy Man' Gandrey is a trip," Lovey said. She made air quotes when she said *Candy Man*. "You caught him on a good day. A sober day. Sometimes he's all there. And sometimes"—she sort of shrugged—"he's not."

"Martin Gandrey?" Where had I heard that name before?

"What?" Lovey asked.

"Nothing. Just feel like I know him," I said.

"Please. Everybody thinks they know that dude," Lovey replied with some snark.

"Yeah, I bet," I said. I mean, he used to be famous. Might've heard his name anywhere. I continued. "Anyway, back to the point. Today he wasn't high, right? So was everything he was saying true about you? You really that tough?"

She sighed and shot me a smile. "When I need to be. Does that scare you?"

Then she started cracking up again, totally ruining the whole cool thing she had going for her. Once she got through her silly spell, she said, "Look, I lost my mom when I was seven. Never knew my dad. I had to be tough. It was the only way I could deal with everything."

"Yeah, I get it." My eyes were drawn to the windows of the connected houses. Families, laughing and leaning back in their chairs at the table. Kids running around. Football on the big screen. "I can understand that."

"But I'm much better now. Much sweeter." She blinked her eyes at me all fast.

"Oh yeah?"

"Yep, and I can prove it."

Those penny eyes, as Candy Man called them, were twinkling

or sparkling or whatever it is girls do with their eyes, and driving me crazy. I wasn't sure how she was going to prove it, but I had a feeling I was going to like it.

"Okay, so prove it," I said, stopping in the middle of the block. I don't know why I stopped walking. I guess I was trying to let her know that I was ready for what was coming, and pretty much hoped it was a kiss.

Lovey stopped and turned toward me. Then she reached into her jacket pocket and pulled out a wad of paper towels. She unwrapped what seemed like a hundred pieces of paper towel to reveal . . . a cookie.

"You know what I had to do to save this for you? Those kids are maniacs when it comes to anything chocolate chip related. This was the only one left, and I thought it would be rude for you not to have at least a little of what you brought to the table, especially since you *made* them."

I couldn't believe it. She saved me a cookie. And if she saved me a cookie, that meant, yeah, it did, it meant she was thinking about me. Supercool.

"How you know I made them?" I asked. I'd never gotten around to telling her that.

"I could just tell by the way the kids were eating them. Plus, some of the cookies looked a little funny," she teased.

"Yeah, but they don't taste funny," I bragged, breaking the cookie down the middle. "Want half?" I asked, remembering what Mr. Ray told me to do if she doesn't like chocolate chip cookies.

"Are you kidding? I was gonna be so pissed if you didn't offer!"

She held up her fist, then grinned. "Chocolate chip are my faves."

Thank God.

I don't know how many blocks we walked. Twenty, maybe thirty before finally making it back to her house. But then, at her stoop, she made it clear that I couldn't come inside. I mean, she didn't say it, but she didn't open the door, either. She just kind of stood there, and we had another movie moment where both people get super weird about what to say and do next and so they both just act crazy. Yeah, we did that. Again. Just like at her grandma's funeral.

"So," I said.

"So," she repeated.

"Thank you so much for inviting me to dinner," I said, trying to be cool without seeming like it. "I never experienced anything like that before. It was a different kind of Thanksgiving, but just as good."

"I'm glad," she replied, her hands behind her back. "And you're welcome."

"Um, how often do you do that? Every holiday, right?"

"Yeah, we do the big dinners for all the holidays. You thought this one was crazy, wait till you see the Christmas one." She caught herself. "I mean, if you're around."

"I'll be around," I said, quickly. "So, y'all do it for Christmas?"

"Yep."

"New Year's Eve?"

"Oh man, homeless people dancing all over the place," she joked.

"Sounds amazing. And what about Valentine's Day?"

Lovey's face dropped. It was almost as if all the blood were draining out of her. Like . . . the pennies became stones.

"What?" *Damn. What did I say?*

"I don't do Valentine's Day," she said, plain.

"You mean, you don't do it at the shelter?"

"I mean, I don't do it at all," she snapped. She whipped around and started fumbling with her keys trying to get the front door unlocked.

"Wait, did I say something wrong? I wasn't trying to say nothing like we was going to spend Valentine's Day together or anything like that, I just thought . . ."

"No, it's fine," she said, finally getting the door unlocked. "I just don't do it, and I think you should leave now."

She kept her back to me as she flung the big wooden door open. I thought that if I waited, she would at least turn around and look me in the face. But she didn't. She just slammed the door behind her. I stood there at the top of her stoop, which thirty seconds ago felt like standing at the top of a mountain, and I crumbled, shocked, as the glow of the day faded to nothing.

Okay. Okay. Okay, I told myself, *that's the way it goes.* Just like Mr. Ray said, sometimes you win, and then you turn a card and lose. And clearly, I had turned something like a two or three and I didn't even see it coming. All I knew was that a day that had gone so well, a day that was so different from any day I had ever had, the first day I wasn't totally dazed and numb, all zoned out because of my mom being gone and my dad being all jacked up, suddenly became just like every other day before it. A mess. And just like with those days, I had no idea why it was happening.

I got home, looked at the notebook on the table, slammed it shut, and stormed up the steps to my room. I threw myself onto the bed with all my clothes on. It wasn't really that late, but there was nothing else for me to do but try to go to sleep. I just wanted the day to be over, and for tomorrow to go back to normal, where I would get up, put on my black suit, go see my father, then go to a funeral and watch other people hurt. Forget about being happy and feeling alive. Most importantly, forget about Love.

CHAPTER 12
LIKE SEEING A GHOST

Doorbell. Who could be coming here so late? I checked my phone. 10:40 p.m. I wasn't 'sleep, just doing everything I could to ignore Chris's text message begging me for details, and trying not to text Lovey to see what the hell I did to blow the night.

Doorbell, again.

The last time this happened I got only bad news. Well, *more* bad news. I bopped downstairs and thought, *At least this time I'm dressed.*

"Who is it?" I called when I reached the door.

"Mr. Ray."

I felt like I was having déjà vu.

I opened the door and there he was, holding what looked like two metal Frisbees.

"I brought you some food. In case you hadn't eaten," he said, coming in.

"Thanks, but I have," I told him. He didn't seem to hear me. At first I thought it was a little strange that he had shown up so late, but he was always checking up ever since he declared he'd look out for me after the Cork/Dad fiasco, so maybe this was just one of those times. He set the food on the table and unwrapped one of the plates. Colors and sauces all mixed up. Looked good. But I wasn't hungry. Even if I hadn't already eaten, I wouldn't have been hungry.

Mr. Ray moved toward the living room, and I stood behind him watching as he held the food and limped. That's when it hit me. The newspaper clip in Mr. Ray's basement—the one separate from the rest. A crushed knee. A crushed dream. Martin Gandrey. It was like Mr. Ray's offbeat stride turned the light on in my brain, and I could suddenly remember exactly who Candy Man was and where I had heard that name. He was the guy who fell on Mr. Ray and ended his career all those years ago. *Shoot, shoot, shoot!*

We both took a seat on the spaceship.

"So, how was your date?" he asked.

"Actually, pretty good until the end." I turned the TV on, now nervous. I wasn't sure if I should tell Mr. Ray about Candy Man or not. I mean, I could, but what for? What good would it do?

Mr. Ray lifted his eyebrows almost to his hairline. "Oh yeah?"

"Yeah. Everything was cool, the cookies worked—"

"What'd I tell you? Told you, man. Chocolate chip always wins," he interrupted.

"Yeah, yeah, I think it had more to do with my baking skills," I boasted. "Most of them went to the kids, anyway."

Mr. Ray looked as confused as I had when I heard about *the kids*.

"We went to the shelter," I explained, letting Mr. Ray off the hook. "That's where we spent the day. And to be honest, it was pretty cool."

"Oh, okay. Y'know, I've been meaning to volunteer there for years, but I never have time." Mr. Ray stabbed at his mac and cheese. I swallowed hard. If he volunteered there, he'd probably bump into Candy Man, and who knows what would happen.

Mr. Ray continued. "So what happened at the end of—was it still a date? I mean, shelters aren't exactly first-choice date spots."

"It was still a date," I said, short.

"Okay, okay. Well, what happened at the end that threw it off?"

"I asked her about Valentine's Day, that's all." I punched at the buttons on the remote. "And she flipped on me!"

"Ohhhhh," Mr. Ray moaned.

"What? You know what it is? Why Valentine's Day pisses her off?"

Mr. Ray took a fork-full of everything and stuffed it in his mouth.

"You know, don't you?" I asked, urgently. Mr. Ray just chewed his food. "Mr. Ray? Are you going to tell me or what?"

He swallowed and said calmly, "Matthew, I can't. It's not my place. And I need you to understand that." He took the remote and found the football game. I leaned back on the couch, frustrated. Yeah, I understood why Mr. Ray couldn't say what he knew. Loose lips sink ships, my mom used to say, and I went to school every day on the *Titanic*, so I got it. But still, I wanted to know.

But I got myself together. "What about you? How was your Thanksgiving?"

The score on the game was zero to zero, fourth quarter, making this the most boring game ever. At least that's what it seemed like to me, and Mr. Ray apparently felt the same way because he turned the channel again. News. He looked at the TV screen as if it were the reporter who just asked him a question. He never looked at me. "I had dinner in the basement," he finally said, his voice empty. And I suddenly knew why he really came over. It wasn't to check on me—at least not *just* to check on me. He just wanted to be around someone. He was just like Candy Man waiting on one more game of chess. I got it, and I knew I didn't need to comment on it, so we just sat there, swallowed by the giant burgundy couch, watching the news, when suddenly I sat forward—Connie Whitlock came on the screen. Her head seemed larger than it did in real life.

"Good evening, folks. I'm Connie Whitlock, and today was a special day, not only for people fortunate enough to break bread with family, but also for the less fortunate, who today also got to share in a family meal, thanks to the good people down at Helping Hand Shelter."

I slapped Mr. Ray on the arm. "Hey, this is about the shelter. She interviewed me today. I'm about to be on this thing!" Strange— even though I'm not the smoothest person when it comes to things like interviews, I was superhyped to see myself on TV. Who wouldn't be?

First, Lovey (who looked even better on-screen) talked about the history of Helping Hand, and about her grandmother, Gwendolyn Brown. She and Connie were walking around the shelter—they got some really cool footage of all the kids waiting in line to get their pictures taken, the massive pots and pans and trays for the food, and some of the other volunteers. And then, I was up.

"*. . . I thought maybe I'd come and everyone would just be bummed out . . .*"

I was hoping they'd edit that out. But, they didn't.

"Bummed out!" Mr. Ray shouted, heaving with laughter. He pounded his leg and threw his head back like old men do, cracking up. "Man oh man," he panted. "If I was that dude sitting next to you, I would've been pissed!"

"Who, him?" I pointed to the screen. "Crazy thing is, he didn't seem to even catch it," I said. Then I took a deep breath and looked away from the television, away from Mr. Ray, and said, "The other crazy thing is that his name is Candy Man." I tried to laugh it off, and hoped this didn't go bad. I'm not even sure why I said it, but it just seemed like the right thing to do. If Mr. Ray hadn't mentioned him, I would've let it slide, but he gave me an opening, so I took it as a sign. Maybe Mr. Ray could find closure or something. I didn't know.

Mr. Ray's cackling tapered off. "Wait, what did you say?" He caught his breath. "What's the guy's name?"

"Him?" I pointed to the guy who was sitting behind me on the screen again. "They call that guy Candy Man."

Mr. Ray leaned into the TV to get a better look. He leaned so far that his butt was up off the couch. He studied the man for at least ten seconds, while Connie Whitlock wrapped up the report.

". . . have a happy Thanksgiving, everyone. Now, back to you, Carla."

Mr. Ray flopped back down on the couch, his face stricken, like he had seen a ghost.

"I'll be damned," he muttered. Then, "Sonuvabitch."

Mr. Ray had a sick look on his face. As if the mac and cheese was spoiled and was suddenly tying his stomach in knots. He wiped his forehead, his eyes, and his mouth all in one motion, then said, "Martin Gandrey."

I bit down hard on my bottom lip. "I didn't want to tell you."

"Martin 'Candy Man' Gandrey," he repeated again, ignoring me. Mr. Ray stared at the TV. The news had gone on to the next story. Fire in Bushwick.

Fire in Mr. Ray.

Fire in my mind.

"That's him, Mr. Ray."

Mr. Ray turned back toward me, his eyes lost, his mouth frowning. "That's him."

CHAPTER 13
516

"HELLO?" MY DAD SAID, GROGGY, OVER THE PHONE.

I wiped the sleep off my face and cleared the night before from my throat. I wasn't sure what time Mr. Ray left, but I know he stayed past midnight going on and on about Martin Gandrey.

"Dad, I'm sorry I didn't make it in. I overslept. Long night." I looked in the mirror. The couch cushion left lines in my cheek.

"Oh, really? Long like you ain't your mama's little boy no more, long?"

"No, man." I rubbed my eyes. "Not like that at all. Mr. Ray came over and we just sat up talking for a while. I think he was having a tough day."

"Ah, I've had quite a few of those myself," my dad said. He pulled the conversation back. "How was Thanksgiving?"

"It was cool. Different, but cool. Yours?"

"Terrible. Hospital food is running straight through me. I been up all night too, but I been calling on God and releasing the devil!" he howled out, his staticky voice popping in my ear. "So I'm glad you ain't come in here this morning. Damn room smells like a war zone."

We talked a little bit more as I slipped on my suit. Then I told Dad I'd see him Monday, and ran out the front door to see if Mr. Ray was sitting on his stoop.

"I'm so sorry, Mr. Ray," I said, running across the street, shoes untied and shirt untucked. "I overslept."

Mr. Ray sat there smoking a cigarette, flipping through the last few pages of the newspaper. I noticed he wasn't wearing his tie.

"No biggie, son," he said, lowering the paper. There was tired in his eyes. "No work today, anyway. People typically don't bury folks the day after a holiday." He took a pull of his cigarette and blew the smoke into the air. "Can't blame 'em for that."

"Oh, okay," I said, sort of disappointed and sort of relieved. "What time did you leave last night?"

Mr. Ray tapped the ash on the step. "I don't know, one or two. You were passed out. Snoring and everything. Then I came on back over here, and just sat up and thought for a while. Candy Man." He took a quick pull on the smoke. "You know I wasn't really mad when you said that was his mug on the TV screen."

"You weren't?" That was a relief.

"Naw . . . it was more like . . . it hurt. It was sad to see him that way, y'know?" Mr. Ray flicked the cigarette butt out onto the sidewalk. I watched it hit the ground and roll a little, still smoking. "Like I told you, life ain't shit like chess."

Mr. Ray snapped his newspaper and lifted it back to his face. I couldn't read his mood. Couldn't tell if he was in a bad one or a good one. Maybe neither. Maybe both.

"Two days off in a row?" I changed the subject, which I realize now was one of my better talents. "What you gonna do?"

Mr. Ray folded the paper and slapped it flat on his knees. "Well, after yesterday and last night, I think I'm just gonna sit right here and enjoy the sunshine."

I took a seat next to him and looked across the street at my house. It was weird how even from the outside you could tell something had changed. It was like even the house didn't look as alive. Like some of it had died too. I'm not sure if it was just because for the past few months fewer people had lived there, or what, but it definitely looked different. Darker.

My phone buzzed.

1 TEXT MESSAGE

Sleep?

It was Lovey. My stomach turned over. Part of me wanted to smile, and part of me wanted to be upset.

I tried to cover the phone. I didn't want Mr. Ray to see and start teasing.

Nope wassup? I texted back, trying not to sound desperate.

Buzz.

Nothing just chillin at home

U work today? she asked, as if everything was cool between us.

I didn't know Lovey well enough to know how she really was, but I hoped she wasn't one of those girls who cussed you out and then acted like it never happened the next day, making you feel all crazy. That's not cool.

Nope wassup? I repeated.

I tried to play off the texting as smooth as possible. I wouldn't look at Mr. Ray, who was now reading the last page of his paper and pretending not to hear the constant buzzing.

Buzz.

I'm off too, she texted.

I didn't really know what to text next. I mean, first she got all mad at me and now she's texting. What was up with that? And still, I wanted to see her. But after the whole Valentine's Day drama, I didn't know how to ask.

"Tell Lovey I said hello," Mr. Ray said through the newspaper.

"What you talking about?" I faked a laugh. Awkwardness was such a natural thing for me.

Mr. Ray lowered the paper and just glared at me. "Uh-huh. I'm old, Matt. And when you old, certain things you just know. This is one of those things." He raised the paper back up. "What's that look?" He dropped the paper again to catch my eyes. I turned away.

"You know what this look is, Mr. Ray. Tell me why she got so mad at me yesterday?"

Mr. Ray sighed. "I can't tell you, son. You know I would if I could, but what kind of man would I be?"

"I know, and I feel you. But what am I supposed to do?"

Mr. Ray flashed a grin. "You need to get to clicking and clacking on your little fancy phone there to figure out a time for y'all to talk. Really talk. Not this mess y'all doing right now."

"Texting."

"Whatever."

Dang. Mr. Ray was right. We needed to talk, plain and simple. And seeing as though *she* was texting *me*, she clearly was opening the door. I just had to be man enough to walk through it.

Buzz.

Come over? she texted.

Come over?

My stomach started twisting up with nervousness and excitement and fear and weirdness. But my reply came across cool as ever. I understood where Mr. Ray was coming from about talking, but at the same time, thank God for text messaging.

Be there in 20

I glanced up at Mr. Ray, who was just looking at me smiling. Before I could even tell him that I was about to leave, he bounced his eyebrows like a weirdo.

"See ya later, Matt," he said all singsongy as I hurried off the stoop.

I was hoping that on the way to Lovey's house I'd have a chance to get myself together and work out all the nerves, so that when I got there, I wouldn't have to worry about becoming a robot or an alien or anything like that. But since this is Brooklyn, and I'm Matty

Miller, of course my quiet walk was interrupted before I even got to the end of the block.

"Yo, Matt!" someone called behind me.

I turned around and Chris was skipping toward me, his shoes only halfway on, the heels flopping.

"Yo man, you couldn't hit me back?" he said, talking about texting me *What happened?* right before Mr. Ray showed up last night. I never responded, because what happened was, well, I didn't even really know.

"Man, my bad, but I wasn't feeling that well. Went to bed early. Long day," I said, walking backward.

"How was the date?" he asked. Then, realizing that I was on the move, "Where you going?"

"I'm going to Lovey's house to hang out." I held in a smile. "Down on Greene."

Chris's eyes bugged out. "Word?" He looked at me funny. "Well, I'm going that way too, to the barbershop."

What could I say? He was my best friend. Even though I wanted to walk by myself . . . he was my best friend.

"So forreal, tell me about yesterday," he demanded, pausing to tie his shoes. He told me that he saw me pass the building and ran outside to catch me, which is why he was all over the place.

"Ain't really nothing to tell."

"What? Yes there is," he said, this time assuming that I *had* had some crazy time with Lovey.

"Man, not like you think. She took me to a homeless shelter and we spent the day there."

"Oh," he said, awkward. "That's . . . um . . . different." He thumbed a smudge on his left shoe.

"Shut up, man."

"What?" Chris stood up and stretched his arms out. "I'm just saying I never heard that before. A date at the *shelter*."

"Dude, you're not funny."

"I'm not trying to be, Matt." He was lying. He was totally trying to be funny. "I'm just trying to understand."

A woman pushed a stroller up the street. Me and Chris stepped to the side so she could get by.

"Let me get this straight," Chris said as we continued to walk. "You ate turkey with a bunch of bums?"

"Don't call them bums! But yeah, I did. And it was pretty dope," I said, serious.

"Ah . . . all righhhhhhht. Huh. So after that you better had at least been rewarded with a smooch," Chris finally said.

"Not even."

Chris stopped short. "What?!"

I kept moving. "It didn't happen."

"What do you mean, it didn't happen?" His footsteps quickened as he tried to catch up. "Why not?"

I kicked at an empty potato chip bag that the wind was blowing around like a leaf. A salt-and-vinegar leaf. "The thing is, it was all going smooth. A great time at the shelter, a sweet walk home, vibin'. But then I asked her something about Valentine's Day and she lost it. Like, she totally flipped and just shut me down."

"Wait. Let me get this straight. You mention Valentine's Day, and she spazzes on you? What the hell kinda girl does that?" Chris yelped.

"That's what I'm saying! And now I'm going over her house so we can talk about it." It was my turn to stop short. "Oh. We're here."

Chris looked up at Lovey's house, then looked at me, still stuck somewhere in his head.

"Wait right here. I want you to meet her."

I ran up the stoop, skipping every other step, and jammed my finger into the buzzer.

"Who is it?" Lovey's voice came through.

I cleared my throat. "Matt."

A few moments later there she was, standing at the front door in jeans and a sweatshirt, her hair down but pulled back behind her ears. The gold chain with her mother's name hung around her neck.

"Hey," I said, my heart beating crazy fast. "I want you to meet my boy, Chris." I stepped out of the way, so she could see him. "Chris, Love. Love, Chris."

"Hey, Chris." She stood in the doorway and waved.

"Hey," he said, running up the steps to shake her hand. He wore a stupid smile on his face, and I knew he was sizing her up so he could run down all of his crap about how he could tell she was crazy just from the handshake.

"Matt, I'll holla at you later," he said. "Nice meeting you, Love."

As he walked down the steps, he looked back as I closed the door. Big stupid smile still there.

Lovey's apartment looked exactly like a grandma's place is

supposed to look. Old. Comfortable. Warm. Brown and green and orange. Big sofas, small TVs. Old-school.

"Shoes off," Lovey commanded, as we came into the front room.

I slipped my hard black dress shoes off, glad I didn't have any holes in my socks.

There were photos everywhere, some framed and propped up on tables, some just pinned to the wall. There were tons of pictures of flowers, but most were of her and her grandmother, who I recognized from the funeral. As a matter of fact, a lot of the photos were the ones that ended up in the funeral program.

"You want something to drink?" Lovey asked while I took a seat on the brown couch in the living room. The couch was soft, and I could tell that a lot of butts had been on it by the way I sunk down in it, just like I do when I sit on the big burgundy spaceship in my house.

"Sure. Anything is good."

Lovey bumped around in the kitchen while I kept looking around at all the old trinkets and pictures. There was a framed piece of cloth with BLESS THIS HOUSE sewn into it on the wall next to a picture of Jesus, next to a picture of Martin Luther King Jr., next to a picture of Lovey, young and weird looking. It was a school photo, one of the ones with the bookcase background. Lovey had pigtails, and that same chain around her neck. In the picture the chain was a lot longer.

"I know you happy you didn't have to work today," Lovey called out from the kitchen. "I know I am."

"I don't know, I was actually kinda disappointed. I mean, I don't hate my job. Matter fact, I kinda like it," I explained as Lovey came into the living room holding two glasses of orange juice.

She handed me a glass and plopped down on the couch next to me, looking surprised.

"Really? You like working around dead people? Funerals? Sad families?"

I took a sip.

"I know it sounds kinda weird, but something about it does something for me. Like, I like working with Mr. Ray. He's just mad cool." I could've stopped there. That sounded normal. But suddenly I had to tell her. I *wanted* to tell her. So . . ."But I also sit in on the funerals, and sort of, I don't know, be a part of them."

"Wait. So you're saying you like sitting in on funerals of people you never knew?"

I took another sip. A bigger one. A gulp. It was honesty time.

"I guess so. Yeah."

"*Yeah*, that's pretty weird," Lovey said, standing back up. "Why would you want to be around sadness all the time?" she asked.

Dang, I was freaking her out, but now I was all in. I could feel my stomach knotting up.

"I guess because seeing other people deal with what I've had to deal with, y'know, with losing my mom and everything, makes me feel less . . . lonely. Like I ain't the only person going through tough times."

I switched the glass from my right hand to my left hand, wiped my right hand on my jeans, and switched the glass back.

"I guess I can understand that." To my surprise her face suddenly relaxed. She leaned against the arm of the couch. "So what about Grams's funeral? I mean, I know you were there to work, but, were you *there*?" she asked.

"Yeah." My eyes went back to my juice. I couldn't look at her, suddenly ashamed. "I was . . . uh, sitting in the back row. It's hard to explain. It's like . . ." I tried to figure out the best way to say it. "It's like, I always look for the closest person to whoever passed away, y'know, like maybe a daughter or a son, or a wife or husband. That's who I focus on. And this time . . ." I glanced up at Lovey just for a second, then I dove back into my glass. "This time . . ."

"This time I was the closest person," she finished my sentence.

I nodded, embarrassed. "Yeah. You were the closest person."

I raised my eyes again. Lovey's mouth looked like it was going back and forth between a smile and a frown. "Wow," she said in disbelief. "And what did you see?"

I gulped down the last few swallows of juice and ran my finger over the rim of the glass.

"Someone with a lot more strength than me, that's for sure. I mean, I could tell you were sad, but not falling apart like I was—" I caught myself. "I mean, am. When my mother died, it felt like my entire body was flipping and turning inside out. Like everything in me was falling apart, and usually that's what I see in other people. But with you, I don't know. I guess I saw some kind of peace, or something. Like you were somehow more together about it all."

Lovey didn't say anything. She just made a sound with her mouth, like a grunt, that I couldn't read. I couldn't tell if the grunt

JASON REYNOLDS

was a good thing or if it was the sound that came right before she kicked me out of her house.

"And what did you see yesterday?" she asked.

"What you mean?"

"I mean, *yesterday*." She fiddled with the chain around her neck, twisting it so that the clasp was in the back. "When you asked me about Valentine's Day. What did you see then?" Her voice got softer as she sort of seemed to be shrinking.

"Honestly, I don't know what I saw. You just shut down."

And for the first time I saw hurt in her eyes. The pain, a chink in her armor. I finally saw a little bit of me. Whatever she wanted to say next, she swallowed, and instead reached down, grabbed my empty cup, and went back into the kitchen. I could hear the water running. The glasses clanged together, ringing out like a bell. Then the water stopped, and a few moments later Lovey walked through the living room into what I guessed was her bedroom. Fifteen seconds in there, then she was back.

"I wanna show you something," she said, gazing at whatever was in her hands. "And I don't know why I'm showing you this, because I just met you a few days ago, but I'm gonna show you anyway, because"—now she looked up, right at me, her eyes turning me into dust—"because, I don't know." The weird thing was that I understood exactly what she was trying to say, and I was right there with her.

She held out her hand, and in it was a picture. It was obviously an old photo because just like the one of me and my parents, it had started to fade and turn colors. It was also curling at the corners.

"Is that . . ." I looked at the young woman standing in front of a building holding a little girl in her arms.

"Yeah. My mom." Lovey pointed to the little girl. "And that's me."

From Lovey, to the photo, to Lovey again.

"It's me, trust me." She flashed the same kiddie smile the little girl in the picture had. "See?"

I smirked.

"This is the only picture I have of her," she explained. "She hated taking them. Hated it. Didn't like the way she looked in them."

I could relate.

"Well, at least you have this one," I said.

"Yeah, I guess," Lovey said, plain. "Recognize that building behind us?"

I studied the picture carefully. It was so faded, I could barely tell what was what, other than the obvious two people.

Then I saw it. The building number. 516.

"Hey, this is on my block! Chris lives in that building. Grew up there! What were y'all doing around there?"

"We used to live around there. In that building. Building 516. But I haven't been around there in a long time. I refuse to go. Even when the cab dropped you off the day of the funeral, I got a little nervous. Just being on that block."

"Pretty rough around there," I agreed.

"Don't I know it. See, this photo was taken about two weeks before Valentine's Day," Lovey started to explain, then she got all choked up. She held the photo, ran her finger over her mother's face as if trying to remember what her skin felt like. "It . . . um . . . ," she stuttered, "it . . . it was taken by the man who killed her."

I didn't know what to say. It was as if all the air in my body had been instantly sucked away. "I'm so sorry, Love. That must've been . . . terrible."

"You have no idea," she said, now sniffling. Tears slid down her cheeks and she backhanded them away. Then, she told me the story.

"We lived on the third floor. Ten years ago, for Valentine's Day, Mom decided to stay home with me and have a mother-daughter date. It was something we did all the time—our thing—and because she was dealing with this crazy dude that she really wasn't trying to be bothered with, it was the perfect excuse to not go out with him.

"All I remember is we were putting frosting on cupcakes when he started banging on the door." She paused, and her face looked as though she still couldn't believe it after all these years. "Banging and banging and banging. He started yelling all kinds of crap about how he knew my mom was in there"—Love's eyes, now puffy, lowered into slits—"and that the only reason she ditched him for Valentine's Day was because she had another man in the house, which, of course, wasn't true. So, Mom . . . she, uh . . . she told me that she'd be right back." Love shook her head. "But she never came back. I heard her outside the door, yelling at him to get out of the building. Then, I heard them walking down the hall, now both shouting at each other, him accusing her of cheating. He called her all types of names." She took a deep breath. "Then they hit the stairwell, which is where most people in that building went to argue, or fight, or just be loud. About five minutes later"—she toothed her top lip, and tears rolled from her eyes—"gunshot." She looked at me, ghostly. "That was it."

The knot in my tie seemed to have gotten tighter, like it had come to life and was choking me. I couldn't say a word. Nothing. All I could do was try to contain the burning sensation in my chest and all the thoughts crashing around my head. I tried to imagine the pain Lovey must've felt seeing her mother like that in the hall-way. The blood. How many nights the sound of that gun must've rang out in her mind, over and over again. I wondered if she blamed herself. And with all the hurt I felt for her, I also struggled with the idea that maybe . . . couldn't be . . . but maybe me and Lovey somehow shared that day, in different ways. My thoughts flashed to Chris. The sleepover. The gunshot. His mother yelling at us to get back. But . . . that couldn't be the case. Could it?

"You mind if I have some water?" I asked her, shaky.

Lovey was staring at the photo, one hand covering her mouth. She nodded, set the picture down, and, without saying another word, headed to the kitchen. I glared at the photo as if it were toxic, because it was dragging me back, dragging me back to ten years ago. Building 516. I shook my head. *Can't be true. It just can't be.* Valentine's Day. The funk of Chris's feet stinging my nose all over again. The tiptoeing through the dark. *Can't be.* The argu-ing from outside. Loud. Angry. The clicking of the lock. *Can't be.* The sound, the horrible, horrible sound. Gunshot. Screams. Dog barking. Screams. A child crying. Lovey? A child crying? Oh, man. *Can't be. It just can't be true.*

"You . . . uh . . . you okay?" Lovey was back with the water. But when I tried to take a sip, I couldn't swallow it, as if the water had somehow become too thick. My throat was so dry, but I just couldn't drink it. Couldn't get it down. My hands trembled so violently that I had no choice but to set the glass of water on the table before I dropped it.

"Yeah," I wheezed, squeezing my hands together. "But now I need to tell you a story."

CHAPTER 14
MY SIDE OF THE STORY

THE ONLY WAY I WAS GOING TO BE ABLE TO TELL LOVEY WHAT I needed to tell her was if I could get some fresh air, so we walked about ten minutes to Fulton Park as I tried to calm down. I could tell Lovey was nervous about what I had to say, but she was doing her best not to press me about it.

We sat on a bench directly across from the grossest couple ever. The girl was sitting on the guy's lap, and they were just . . . going for it. I mean, it looked like she was trying to eat his face. But all the other benches were taken by a man and his dog, an old lady sitting with a bunch of groceries waiting on someone to come pick her up, and the bird guy who feeds the pigeons whatever he has left over from his dinner the night before. I had no idea pigeons ate pizza.

Now that we were sitting, Lovey couldn't hold back any longer.

"Matt, can you just tell me?" She asked desperately. "You're making me nervous."

The girl across from us moved her mouth to her boyfriend's neck. Yuck.

"I know, I know." I turned to Lovey. "And I'm sorry. I wasn't expecting . . . to react like that. I guess I was just so surprised by what you told me."

"Oh . . . well . . . I'm sorry it did that to you," she said, uncomfortable.

"No, no! It's not that! It's just, I . . ." I was stuck. I took a deep breath. "Lovey, everything that happened to you—to your mother that night—I was there."

Lovey straightened up, as if someone had sent an electrical shock through her. "What you mean?"

"I mean"—I swallowed hard—"I was *there*. In 516."

A crease formed in Lovey's forehead. "I . . . don't . . . understand."

"I know." A guy on a bike road through the flock of pigeons, causing them to flap and flitter around, pepperoni hanging from their beaks. "I didn't know either. I had no idea it was you—your mom."

I couldn't read the look on her face, so I just plunged on. "Listen, I was sleeping over Chris's that night. And, y'know, after dinner, his mom sent us to bed, and all of a sudden we hear all this noise coming from the hallway." I had an urge to reach over and grab Lovey's hand. But I didn't. I paused a second to see if she would connect the dots. But she was just staring at me.

"People screaming. A man and a woman."

Lovey's eyes began to fill up again.

"I can stop," I said.

"No," she said, blinking away the tears. "No. Finish."

I guess that's what made her so strong—being able to just face reality straight up. I don't know if I would've wanted to hear anymore.

"You sure?" Now I reached over and put my hand on top of hers. It was just a natural reaction. Then after a few seconds I pulled it back. Also a natural reaction.

She nodded. "Yeah."

"Okay. I convinced Chris that we should go and see what was happening in the hallway. So we went to the front door, and when we opened it . . ." I stopped.

"What?" she asked. Then she demanded, "Say it." She grabbed my arm and squeezed. "Matt, say it!"

I swallowed. "The gunshot."

CHAPTER 15
SIMPLE WHAT?

THERE'S ONLY ONE OF TWO THINGS THAT COULD'VE HAPPENED after a conversation like that. Either we could've decided to never speak again, both totally freaked out by what I guess was fate, or a hell of a coincidence, or whatever, or we could've decided to see it as a sign to at least go on a real date. I mean, we definitely had a moment, even if it was caused by the worst possible situation ever. Lucky for me, Lovey felt the same way and chose real date. It took another few days of texting to get us back to normal, after all that damn *real* talking Mr. Ray was kicking. But he was right. And when I saw him, I thanked him.

"You understand now, why I couldn't tell you?" he said as we headed to the next funeral—Brendan Wilson, a firefighter who died while saving a family.

"Yeah, I do."

"Everything's cool between y'all?"

I looked at my phone and scrolled through the text messages from Lovey. "Yeah, I think so."

The only catch about going on a real date with Lovey was that she said she would only go if she got to pick the place, which for me wasn't really a catch at all. Naw, I didn't have to deal with the stress of trying to figure out where to take her, which would've been like rummaging through the bodega trying to figure out if I should bring juice or cookies to dinner all over again. Mr. Ray would've said to take her out for a meal, of course. Chris would've said movies. My dad would've said both. Too much pressure! So it was her call, and that was fine with me.

Next thing I knew it was date day and I was sitting in the back of a cab with her, the Jamaican driver slamming on his brakes every few seconds, and I had no idea where we were headed. I knew the guy was Jamaican because he had the flag hanging from the mirror. His car was old and still had a tape deck, and he spent the first few minutes of the ride rewinding and fast-forwarding, trying to find a song. He kept looking through the rearview at us, and then back to the radio, and occasionally, thankfully, he would look at the road.

"Where are we going?" I asked. All I knew was that Lovey had told the cabbie to drop us at the corner of Washington Avenue and Eastern Parkway. But that's it. She looked out the window, pretending to ignore me. But I saw her reflection in the glass. "You smiling!" I said. "Why don't you just tell me?"

Lovey turned and tried to shrink her smile. But she couldn't. "Why don't you just wait and see?"

I sucked my teeth. "Fine."

I never really been one for surprises, because every big surprise in my life has somehow been bad. I like things normal and consistent. Safe. Which wasn't really an option at this point, because we had already gotten into a cab with a man who was more concerned about his music than the car in front of us, or the ones coming toward us, for that matter.

The cabbie slammed on brakes for what seemed like the tenth time. He glanced at me through the rearview mirror and must've noticed the look on my face. Fear. He was scaring the hell out of me fooling around with that stupid, old-ass radio.

"You okay up there?" I asked, trying not to lose it or come across like a punk. Not on the first *real* date.

"Yeah," he said, looking back down at the radio, then back up at me. "Weh you ah-fret fuh?"

I looked at Lovey, who was looking out the window again, but I could tell she was sniggering.

"I'm not. I'm cool." Cool and about to puke! I looked around the cab for the guy's license and all that stuff, just to make sure I knew a.) whose name to say if something crazy happened, and b.) whose cab to never get back in. On the back of the driver seat I found his info. Ivan Renson, Island Cab Company, Brooklyn, New York.

With one hand on the wheel, one hand on the radio, and a heavy foot on the gas, Ivan Renson said, "Yuh need fi relax, mon. Mi 'ave it," and finally pushed play.

Bob Marley. I didn't know the actual name of the song, but it was one of the popular ones that everybody knows.

Rise up this mornin', smiled with the risin' sun, three little birds, pitch by my doorstep, singin' sweet songs, a melody pure and true, sayin' this is my message to you-oo-oo. Singin' don't worry about a thing, 'cause every little thing, is gonna be all right . . .

The cab driver sang loud and free, clapping his hands and rocking his head back and forth. He looked at me again through the mirror.

"Jus lissen ahn vibe out," he said, turning the reggae up louder. "Now, we go to Washington ahn Eastern Parkway, seen?"

I wondered if this was just his favorite song, or if he picks new music for every person who gets in his cab. Like, he figures out what would be good for the person to hear. I mean, the Bob Marley song *was* great riding music for us, even though he almost killed us just to find it. Lovey started singing it, and before I knew it I was humming along. *Every little thing is gonna be all right.* As the cabbie pulled up to the corner of Eastern Parkway and Washington Avenue, Lovey told him to go a little farther down Washington.

"Just to the middle of the block, then we're good," she said, reaching into her pocket. Of course, as soon as she started digging for her money, I started searching for mine, y'know, to be a gentleman.

She reached over and put her hand on mine, still in my pocket.

"I got it," she said, beaming. "I invited you, I pay. You get the next one."

The next one. Nice.

My mom would've loved her.

Mr. Renson turned around and gave me a pound, then opened

his hand and gave Lovey a gentle handshake and a wink. It was the first time I actually saw his face. It was slim and sharp, but his wild beard covered most of it. All I could see were his eyes and his bottom lip. If he hit someone, all he'd have to do is shave and he'd look like a totally different person. No one would ever find him.

When we opened the door there was already another couple waiting to take the cab. They looked cold, and were clearly in the middle of a fight. Mr. Renson hit stop on the tape player. As me and Lovey climbed out and the new people climbed in, the fast-forwarding and rewinding started all over again. I guess it was time for a new song. A song for them.

I popped the collar up on my coat to keep the chill off my neck. I looked around. Where the hell were we? So I asked her, just as "I Shot the Sheriff," a Bob Marley song I did know the name of, came blaring from the cab, pulling off.

Lovey wrapped a scarf around her neck. Then she smiled and reached for my hand.

"You promise to be open?"

"Of course."

"Well, this is what I wanted to show you," she said, turning around with a hand flourish. "The Botanic Garden."

The Botanic Garden? What? I was stuck. I mean, flowers? *Flowers?* But I liked Lovey, so I had to go along with it. And she knew that, which is why she stood there giving me her cutest face, and held my hand—which, by the way, felt like . . . more than holding my hand.

I didn't know what to say.

"Just come on," Lovey demanded, dragging me toward the gate.

Inside was like being somewhere far away from Brooklyn. And I have to admit, that part of it I liked. I mean, you couldn't even hear cars, like as soon as we walked through the gates, we entered some new dimension—some secret land where drama didn't exist. Only flowers.

"My grandmother used to bring me here," Lovey said as we walked around looking at what had to be millions of flowers. I looked at all the crazy names: Clematis, Chrysanthemum, Callicarpa. White, yellow, and purple.

"We'd come every week after my mom died," she went on.

"Why?"

Lovey brushed her hand against a plant. "Because it was Grams's favorite place in the whole city, other than the shelter. She just felt like it was good to keep living things around you, y'know, to remind you of the beauty of life. That was her whole thing. The beauty of life." A sweet smile lit up Lovey's face.

I looked at the name of the plant and tried to pronounce it in my head. Then I gave up. "I guess."

"You guess?" There was an edge to Lovey's voice. "Oh, I see. Too tough for flowers, right?"

"Naw, not even. I just don't get the hype. I mean, let's say I buy you some flowers tomorrow. You'll be all happy about it, and then two days later you'll be throwing them away. It's like they're these things that everybody waits to grow into something beautiful, and as soon as they do, they die. No disrespect to your grandma, but I don't think there's all that much beauty in that."

Lovey didn't respond. She just pulled out an old Polaroid camera, which I wasn't expecting. I figured she'd have her fancy one. At first I was going to ask her where she found that retro camera, y'know, for small talk, but I figured it must've been her grandma's and would pretty much come across as a stupid question. We looked at a few more plants before the silence just began to eat at me.

"So," I started.

"So," she replied.

"What do you think about my theory on flowers?"

"Oh. Actually, I agree." She held her camera up to her face and clicked at a sunflower (one I could at least pronounce). The camera spit out a picture. Lovey pulled it free and started waving it around until the image started to appear.

"So then why do you like it here?" I asked, surprised that she agreed.

She snapped a few more and waved them all. I have to admit it made me curious.

"Look at these," she said, holding the Polaroids up so I could see the images she had just taken slowly come into focus. They were dope, but no different from just looking at the real deal. I still didn't see where this was going.

"Grams gave me this camera, and brought me here to take pictures of the flowers. I would walk around, and whenever I saw one I really, really liked, she would tell me to snap a picture of it so that I would always remember it in case it went away. I know it sounds kinda corny now, but it was her way of making sure I held on to things I loved—things that were living—since when my mom died we only had that one picture of her. At least as a grown-up. Grams had pictures of her as a little girl, but those aren't the same—to me, at any rate."

We kept walking and Lovey kept stopping to take flicks of other plants: Ivy, and something called Anemone. She would get right up on the flower and then snap the shot, again and again, pulling the pictures from the mouth of the camera and waving them around in the air. When she liked the way they came out, she'd show them to me.

"You wanna try?" she asked. At this point, she had probably shot about ten different flowers.

"Do I have a choice?"

"Of course not," she said, changing the film cartridge. "Just aim and hit the button on the side"—she handed me the camera—"but only when you see something you really, really like."

"Got it," I said sarcastically, holding the camera down by my side. I wasn't going to take pictures of plants. But I played along and pretended like I was looking for my "special" flower because, at the end of the day, I didn't want to blow this date.

We kept on walking through the maze of green, brown, and orange, the weird shapes and smells, sprinklers misting over the flowers, people in green suits spraying and trimming. There were tons of old people, arms wrapped around each other for protection from the nippy wind, probably on their hundredth date. The women would lean over and sniff the flowers, and the men would smile and pretend they weren't bored to death. I let myself imagine that that might end up being me and Lovey one day. Then there were a bunch of kids just running around, happy to be in a place where there were no cars or noise except for their own laughter. For them this was paradise. But there weren't too many people our age there. And it dawned on me, the reason why—because people our age go on dates at the movies. Chris would've been right again.

After a bunch of walking and me pretending to look for a flower that I *really, really liked,* Lovey stopped. We were by the biggest heads of cabbage I've ever seen, but that didn't really impress me, probably because, well, it was cabbage! I mean, seriously, cabbage isn't a flower! Cabbage is . . . *cabbage!*

"You're not even trying," she said, frustrated now and, I could tell, a little disappointed in me.

"I am!" I yelped.

"No, you're not," she said, tucking her hair back behind her ears. She looked at me and just shook her head, and for a second it seemed like she regretted bringing me to the garden. Damn.

"Okay, okay," I said, rubbing my hand along her arm. "You said the rule was to take a picture only when I saw a flower I really liked."

"Exactly," Lovey said, turning toward the massive cabbages.

"Well . . ." I spun her back toward me and held the camera to my face. "Smile."

I hit the button once. Then again, and again, backing away, coming in closer, dropping to one knee, pretending I knew how to get good angles.

Lovey stood there obviously embarrassed as people walked by

watching me act ridiculous. I knew it was working though, because she was laughing. I stood to my feet and checked the photos.

"Oh, God, this flower is unbelievable! Oh, I'm so moved! The most beautiful flower I've ever seen! I mean, you should see this!" I fanned the photos out like a deck of cards, so she could see all the pictures of herself.

"Okay, okay," she said, pushing the camera away. Her cheeks were lit up, red as roses. And then, the moment happened. You know the moment when everything fades to black and the soft music comes out of nowhere—violins and romantic instruments, and everything starts moving in slow motion, except for your hearts, which pound faster than ever, and each of you can somehow hear them thumping in your brain, and all you have to do is take one step and meet each other for that first awkward, electric kiss? That moment.

Lovey, still buzzing from the flower joke, stood there gazing at me like I wasn't some screwed-up dude, but instead the coolest guy she knew. And for me, I looked at her as the only thing, as far as I could see, that could keep me from being more screwed up than I already was. I stepped forward. She leaned in closer, her eyes slowly opening and closing, and opening, and closing. My eyes were wide open, of course. I wanted to see this. And feel it. And taste it. And then:

A peck.

Record scratch.

Yep, just a peck, followed by, "I want to show you my all-time favorite flower," and that sweet smile. Not exactly what I was expecting. But still, a peck was still technically considered a kiss, right? It was better than nothing.

Lovey held my hand tight now, weaving her fingers in between mine. We walked along a rock path of what she called succulents, a word that for some reason I couldn't stop laughing at. Sometimes I feel like I'm so mature. Other times I know I'm as ridiculous as everyone else my age.

"Here it is," Lovey said, pointing at her favorite plant, having her ta-da moment. "It's called Sempervivum."

The plant wasn't like those pretty, dainty little flowers that we were looking at before, thank God. It was way better than those. It looked like a mix between a brussel sprout and some kind of weird star plant.

"Simple what?" I said, caught off guard by another crazy name.

Lovey sounded out the word like I was a little kid learning to read.

"Sim-per-VIV-um," she said. "Means live forever."

I squatted down. The plant's petals looked more like pointy green fingers with red tips, different from the petals I was used to seeing.

"Does it?" I said, looking up at her. "Does it live forever?"

"Of course not." She shrugged. "But it definitely survives longer than most plants. All through the winter and everything. You barely even have to water it. It's like toughest of all the plants. The survivor."

I looked back down at the Sempervivum, touching it, squeezing the layers of odd juicy finger-leaves. They felt sort of human, which was a little freaky, but I couldn't front like I wasn't fascinated by it. It was pretty cool for a plant. I can't even believe I'm saying this, but it was. So I pulled the camera up, got in close, and snapped a photo.

The cab ride home was just as crazy as the cab ride to the garden was. Instead of the constant slamming on brakes, this cabbie was just speeding, whipping around corners, swerving in and out of traffic, doing his best not to hit the brakes at all!

"We gotta start taking the bus," I said to Lovey as we walked up her stoop.

"Hell yeah," she replied, turning to me once we got to the top. She shuffled through all the pictures we took and pulled out the one I shot of the Sempervivum. She slipped it into my jacket pocket, then tugged on my coat like she was about to button it, but instead pulled me close.

"Thank you for being open," she said, her voice smooth as she leaned in and kissed me. This was *not* a peck.

"Thank you for taking me," I said, returning the kiss.

"Did you learn anything?" she asked, her eyes closing as she kissed me again.

"Yep." I smirked. "I learned that you're a good kisser." I pressed my lips against hers again, this time kissing her longer and pulling her as close as possible. I wrapped my arms around her, and I could feel her hands gripping my back. After a few seconds she pulled away.

"Damn right," she said, moving toward the door.

I waited to go in, but before she actually opened the door, she turned back toward me, gave me one last kiss, and said good night. *Wahhhh!* I couldn't believe it. But it was cool, I just bounced down the steps like I wasn't trippin', even though I was. I felt good. Better than good.

When I got to the bottom, I heard the robotic sound of the camera snapping. I looked up and there was Lovey, standing at the top of the stoop, kneeling and being overdramatic like I was in the Botanic Garden, this time taking tons of pictures of me. I'm glad no one was walking down the street and saw her, because they would've thought we were doing a photo shoot or something. Totally embarrassing. She laughed.

"Real funny," I said.

And she shouted out, "It's called payback!" while blowing me a kiss.

CHAPTER 16
FORWARD

"Simple what?"

"SemperVIVum, man. It's like this flower that's hard to kill. It kinda looked like a star inside a star inside a star." I was on the stoop with Chris trying to explain this crazy plant. I could've pulled out the picture and showed him, but for some reason I didn't want to. I know that sounds stupid, but I kinda wanted to keep the photo to myself. Like a me-and-Lovey thing.

I had stopped by Chris's building when I left Lovey's because I was way too gassed up to just go be alone, but he wanted to get out of there because his mom was frying fish. And just like he didn't want that fishy smell all in his clothes, he also didn't want his mom all in our business, which she was always trying to be in. So we walked up the block to my house. It was actually better that we didn't hang at Chris's house anyway. I wouldn't have been able to just sit in there without thinking about everything that went down with Lovey's mom. Talking about it with her made it all so fresh again, and to be honest, it was the last thing I wanted to think about. Not after such an amazing date.

"Man, that don't sound like no fun date to me. But then again, you ain't really no fun type of dude these days," he said, texting somebody. He had been saying that for a few days now, ever since I told him what Lovey told me about her mother. It really messed with Chris, partly because, like me, he was there, but also because he felt like it was too heavy to put out there so early. But I tried to explain to him, Lovey and I just sort of have a thing. I guess it's trust.

"Yeah, whatever. Fun enough to make out with her," I bragged. I know, I know. I kissed and told, but what can I say? I was excited!

He snapped his head toward me, bug-eyed. "What?"

I couldn't hold back the smile. And it was a big one.

"You heard me."

He put his hand out for a grown man handshake, and after we shook, he leaned back like a proud dad again.

"My boy is all grown up."

"Man, whatever."

Across the street Mr. Ray was sitting outside too, talking to everyone who walked by. Brownie, whose real name was John Brown, stopped to yap to him. He was probably around six, and just knew that he was going to grow up to be a famous singer. He'd be outside dancing and singing his heart out all day, so whenever Mr. Ray saw him, he would ask Brownie to perform something old-school.

"The Temptations? Sam Cooke? What, you don't know no Sam Cooke?" Mr. Ray would tease, and Brownie would laugh and laugh.

Mr. Whitaker also stopped to talk to Mr. Ray. Mr. Whitaker (all the old guys called him Whit) was a minister who preached at a church around the corner. He wasn't a young guy, but not as old as Mr. Ray either. Just old enough to have a little bit of gray hair in his beard, but nowhere else. He always wore sharp suits, and my mom would always talk about how nice his shoes were. But the most important thing about Mr. Whitaker is that he was always in the street trying to bust up gangs and keep police from doing crazy stuff around here. He wasn't afraid of nobody, and that's why everyone liked him.

Mr. Whitaker had both hands in his pockets and rocked back and forth on his heels as he stood at the bottom of Mr. Ray's stoop, talking. Chris and I wasn't saying too much at this point, just because Chris was way too occupied with all the texting he was doing to talk to me. But it was cool. I knew it was a girl—it always was—and I was used to it. The dude had game.

"So how was it?" Chris said, still staring down at his phone, his thumbs moving crazy fast.

I tried to be cool. "It was just kissing, man. Chill."

Chris looked up from his phone. "Just kissing?" He slipped his phone in his pocket. "It's never just kissing, man."

Here we go again with Chris's theories on girls, even though I have to admit, he was usually right.

Chris started grilling. "Was her eyes open or closed?"

"What?"

"Look, man," he said, "if a girl keeps her eyes open when she kisses you, then she's not sure about you yet, in that way. But if she closes them, then she likes you. Simple."

Made sense.

"Okay, well, how am I supposed to know if her eyes were open or not. Mine were closed."

"WHAT! You closed your eyes?" Chris barked. "You know what that means? Means you love her!"

"Man, you crazy. I like her, but I don't *love* her."

The streetlights started flickering and Chris stood to his feet almost at the exact same time. Like clockwork. It wasn't even really dark yet, but I knew he was about to roll.

"Oh, yes you do. You love her. You just don't know it yet." Chris stood on the step in front of me and shook his head like he was disappointed. "I thought you and me was gonna grow up and be old playas like the Ray brothers, but you closing your eyes every time you kiss a girl!"

We both busted out laughing and he gave me dap before heading back down the block to his crazy building. Building 516. I sat there on the stoop and thought about the nonsense Chris was talking. If you close your eyes, you love her. *Yeah, right.* Closing your eyes don't mean nothing. Maybe I just closed my eyes because I didn't want her to open her eyes and catch me looking. Then she might not think I was into it or something, like I didn't like her. Maybe that's why I closed my eyes. I wish I would've thought of this when Chris was standing there spazzing on me. But even if I did tell him this, all he would've done was tell me I'm lying. And that might've been true.

When Mr. Whitaker finally left, Mr. Ray waved me over.

"Mr. Miller," Mr. Ray called, holding his hand out for a shake. "Had a good day?" He gripped my hand tight.

"Pretty good," I replied, zipping my jacket. The temperature was dropping and it was getting pretty chilly out. "What about you?"

"Not bad. Just been sitting out here, watching life and trying to learn something from it."

"Yeah, I guess you can say I kinda been doing the same thing."

"Oh yeah? I figured you spent your day watching Lovey, trying to learn something from her!" Mr. Ray knocked me on the arm. I never should've told him we were going out.

"Well, that too. She took me to the Botanic Garden, the one over there off Eastern Parkway."

Mr. Ray looked surprised. "What the? The homeless shelter, the garden, these are some, uh"—he searched for the right word—"peculiar dates y'all going on."

I took a seat. "That's where she wanted to go. It's a whole thing," I started, but then I caught myself. Some things shouldn't be told. If anyone understood that, it was Mr. Ray. "It's a long story," I said simply.

"Ah. Gotcha. Well, did you learn something?"

I thought for a moment about the day. The taxi. The kiss. The Polaroid in my pocket. "I think so."

"Good." Mr. Ray was obviously all out of cigarettes, because this was definitely one of those times he would've been sparking one, taking a drag, and blowing the smoke high into the air. "Tomorrow we've got a funeral. Whit came over here to tell me that one of the boys he was trying to help clean up his act got killed a few nights ago, and that his mother wants a simple memorial service." Mr. Ray paused for a second, and I could tell by how tight his face was that he was disappointed by the news. You would think he'd be used to this by now, but it was kind of cool that it still bothered him. He continued. "His mother said even though Whit was like her son's mentor, she didn't want to have it in his church because she was scared her boy's friends wouldn't be comfortable there. So it'll be at the funeral home. We'll just be carrying the casket, and maybe we'll provide a little food afterward, but nothing major. Whit said the boy's mother wants this to be smooth and quick. So come straight here after school so we can be ready by two."

"Got it." I stepped off the stoop, then paused. "Before I leave, you never told me if *you* learned something today."

Mr. Ray stood up, brushed his pants off, and stretched his long body, which had to be stiff from all the sitting. "Matt, I been sitting here looking at all the kids playing in the street. The people walking down the block, some friends, some strangers, some I've known since they were the same age as those kids, stopping to talk to me or share a joke. And I realized that it's not that death is bad. It's not. It's just that life is so good. So damn good that you just wanna hold on to it, and everybody in it. But we can't. But what we can do, is appreciate it more. Y'know, smell the flowers."

Mr. Ray gave me the old-man finger-gun and headed up the steps. "Have a good night, son."

As I walked across the street to my house, I heard Brownie, who definitely shouldn't have still been outside, running down the block yelling Mr. Ray's name, begging him not to go inside because he finally learned an oldie—"My Girl." By the time I reached my door, Brownie's little voice was belting out the words, some right, some wrong, and Mr. Ray's deep, raspy voice began singing right along with him.

When I got home I noticed that there was a message on the house phone's answering machine. It was my father, just rambling on and on about how Dr. Fisher was trying to kill him, and that all she was doing was breaking his legs more every day because she didn't want him to ever leave. His exact words were, "She got it bad for your daddy, boy. I can tell. And you better be careful, because you got my genes. Next thing you know, that girl, Love, be done broke your legs too." He laughed hard enough to cough, then ended the message with, "Bring me some real food next time you come, okay? Love you, knucklehead."

End of new messages.

Then it was straight to bed. It had been a while since I came home and went right to my room, took my suit off, brushed my teeth, washed my face, turned the lights off, and went straight to bed. No TV. No Tupac. The only thing I made sure to remember (after listening to my father's ridiculous message) was to open the notebook, THE SECRET TO GETTING GIRLS, FOR MATTY, to the page where mom laid out how to make the OMG Omelette. I was planning to cook breakfast in the morning. It had been forever since I had done it, but I felt like I was ready; plus, I was tired of eating burned bodega bagels. And also, I made sure to take the Polaroid picture out of my jacket pocket. I had a place for it on my dresser, right next to the old photo of me, Mom, and Dad at the beach. But when I pulled out the Polaroid, it wasn't of the Sempervivum. Lovey had tricked me! She'd slipped a photo of me smiling into my pocket. I don't even remember her taking it. Shoot, I don't even remember smiling! I wrote FIRST DATE WITH LOVE on the white part at the bottom and stared at my face. It wasn't like I had a big cheese or nothing, but it was definitely a grin, and no joke, it wasn't bad. Maybe I had been smiling and didn't even know it.

I put the photo in its spot, next to the old one of me crying. I looked at the pair and could feel a little bit of laughter tingling inside me. Then I hit the light and got in bed. I pulled the covers over me, and when I yawned, it felt like the first time I had ever done it. Like I just let months of tired out of me. At the end of that yawn I was back in the church again. At my mother's funeral. But this time no one else was there. No preacher. No crying people. My dad wasn't there, and there wasn't even a casket. Just me and Mom, sitting in the front row. We hugged and she held my hand, and somehow we were talking, though neither one of us was actually saying anything. It was weird. I couldn't figure out where everyone else was, though. Maybe the funeral hadn't started yet. Or maybe the funeral was over.

CHAPTER 17
ONE STEP AT A TIME

His name was Andre Watson, and I knew him. Well, not really, but I had seen him once. As a matter of fact, the one time I saw him was the day I met Lovey at Cluck Bucket. He was the dude in line trying to get her phone number. The one that she hit with the snapshot joke and embarrassed in front of everybody. He deserved that, but even though I didn't know anything else about him, I'm sure he did *not* deserve to be killed.

My job was to set up the chairs and tables as usual, and of course help carry the superlight casket in. Me and Mr. Ray probably could've carried it by ourselves, but it happened to be the windiest day of the year and Mr. Ray didn't want to take no chances. So the usual pallbearer team came. Benny, Robbie Ray, and even Cork, sober, which was definitely a surprise. I hadn't seen him since everything had happened with my dad. He was on the opposite side of me, so it was a little bit awkward as we carried the casket in, being forced to look each other in the face. Of course he did everything he could to avoid it, and in some weird way, that's all I needed to let it go. I knew he felt bad. I knew he was sorry, so there was no reason to hate him, especially at somebody else's funeral. If it was my dad's funeral, maybe it would've been a different story.

Inside the funeral home were maybe fifteen people. Mr. Whitaker stood at the podium, Andre's mother sat up front, and just about everyone else stood in the back, along the wall. Most of the people there had to be eighteen or nineteen, even though a lot of them looked much older. A lot of hard lives and young faces. I could bet this wasn't their first funeral, and it wouldn't be their last, and that Andre's was the next face painted on a neighborhood wall, or the next RIP tattoo.

Mr. Whitaker tapped the mic to make sure it was on.

"Good morning, everyone," he said softly. "First let me say to Janine Watson, Andre's mother, that no one here feels the way you feel . . ." I swallowed hard hearing those words again. The same words that the minister said to me at my mother's funeral. The words that started this whole funeral-crashing thing. The preacher continued: "but we will do whatever we can to support you. Second, to all of you out there"—he nodded to the back of the room where we all were standing—"I have a few words, and they come on behalf of Janine, Andre's mother. She wants me to tell you that she knows you all loved Dre, but you have to let him go without trying to get revenge on anyone."

I looked at Ms. Watson, and as usual, I counted the seconds before the breakdown. I knew there would be an explosion of tears coming, and I stood along the back wall with everyone else, waiting for it, watching her tremble and struggle to keep the pain down. It had been a few days since my last funeral, and even though I was doing okay—I mean, I had a girl, and my dad was making it—I couldn't help but slip back into my normal groove of being weirdly anxious to see the meltdown, to be comforted again by someone else's pain.

But before Ms. Watson crumbled, my phone buzzed. I slipped it out of my pocket and peeked at the screen.

1 NEW MESSAGE

Where are u?

I thumbed quickly.

Funeral home

Mr. Whitaker, meanwhile, noticing that no one seemed to care about what he was saying, decided to try a new approach.

"As a matter of fact, Janine, I think it would mean more if you came up and said it yourself." He reached out his hand to her.

Ms. Watson walked up to the microphone. She was a young woman. She wore a black top and black pants and had a nose ring. She had dark circles around her eyes, a mix of runny makeup and no sleep. She looked out at everyone for a moment before saying anything. It was almost as if she was purposely meeting eyes with every single person there, the whole crew. She even locked eyes with me for a second, and I didn't even know Andre.

"Good morning." Her voice was sweet, but shaky. "I just want y'all to know that I don't blame none of y'all for this, but I need y'all to end it. No more of this mess. He was nineteen years old," she said, her eyes filling quickly. She repeated, "Nineteen years old!" I felt itchy. Like, anxious. I knew it was coming, and it was going to be a big one. Maybe even the biggest one I had seen yet. Ms. Watson looked down at the casket and clinched the podium tight to try to keep herself from shaking.

My phone buzzed.

I NEW MESSAGE

It was Lovey again.

Headed to work. I'm close. Come outside

Come outside? But Ms. Watson was so close! I tried to wait a few more minutes before I typed anything back, but Lovey texted again.

I got something for u ;-)

??? I texted, trying to stall.

Matt just come out! she texted back.

I couldn't believe what I was missing, but I also couldn't not go outside to see what Lovey had for me. What can I say, the girl had me. I tried to slip out the door as quietly as possible, but the stupid breeze pulled the door open hard, slamming it against the wall, making a loud bang.

The entire funeral whipped toward me. I mean the preacher, the mother, and the twelve or thirteen hard-looking dudes in the back. Some of them turned with their hands on their waists, and at that point I threw my hands in the air, went straight into robot face, and slowly backed out of the door before something bad happened.

"Everything okay?" Lovey asked, as I closed the door softly.

She had her hair down and it was flying all over the place. She was wearing her grease-stained Cluck Bucket uniform, but to me she was all cute. Her hands were behind her back, obviously hiding something.

"Yeah, everything is cool," I replied, still feeling dumb about the door, and anxious about what I was missing inside. "Wassup? What you got for me?"

Lovey pulled her hands from behind her back. "This," she said, proudly holding a small flower pot. "A Sempervivum."

She moved closer and placed the plant in the palm of my hands. I looked down at it, a star inside a star inside a star. It's funny, I didn't really notice until right then that I'm as awkward when I receive a gift as I am when I take a picture. Some people are really good at it. They can jump up and down and light their faces up whenever somebody gives them something. But not me. I didn't know what to say or do but look dumb.

"Um. Wow," I said, staring into the pot. I gotta say, I never thought getting a flower as a gift would be cool. But for some reason, it was. "Thanks," I said, reaching out with one arm to give her a half hug. Lame! I wanted a do-over so I could do a better job expressing how thankful I was.

We sat down on the steps.

"Are there any kind of instructions I need to take care of this? I mean, I've never had plants or anything."

Lovey pressed her hand against my chest softly, just for a second, then said, "Just water it sometimes. Think you can handle that?"

I smirked. "Hmmm. I don't know. How about you come over every now and then and water it for me. I mean, you're already such a flower master."

"Hmmm. I'll see what I can do, if you promise to make me more cookies. Y'know, a trade." I knew she had a thing about my block, so the fact that she was even entertaining this idea of coming over was good enough for me.

"Ah," I said, fully aware that I was smiling now. "Just cookies? I think I can work that out." She had no idea what she was getting herself into. I was gonna cook her into a coma!

She leaned in for a kiss, but before I could meet her in the middle, the funeral home door flew open again, banging against the wall, scaring us both half to death. This time it was Mr. Ray.

"Matthew, what you doing? We gotta get the casket outta here." Then he noticed Lovey. "Oh," he said, surprised. "Hey, Love, didn't know you were out here. Um, Matt, you know what, I think we got it. Just take these for me," he said, holding out a handful of leftover funeral programs mixed in with some cancer pamphlets. I ran up the steps and grabbed the folded papers. "Ya'll make sure to get out the way, we're coming out in a second," he added.

Lovey got up, and the both of us stood on the side of the steps, waiting for the casket to be marched out. She grabbed one of the programs.

"Andre Watson," she said to herself, staring at his picture, trying to figure out where she knew him.

"You remember him?" I asked.

Lovey looked and looked but couldn't figure it out.

"Remember that day in Cluck Bucket when I asked for a job and that guy was trying to get at you?"

Lovey's eyes got big.

"Oh my . . ." She put her hand over her mouth. "Jesus."

The door slammed open again, and Robbie, Benny, Cork, and Mr. Ray came stepping out the double doors of the funeral home, carrying the casket, two on each side. It was a silent march down the steps, into the car. Behind them was Ms. Watson walking arm and arm with Mr. Whitaker. Her face was now covered in black streaks from her makeup, and the preacher was practically holding her up so she wouldn't fall down the steps. I had missed the explosion. I wasn't in the room when she shattered, sending me into some kind of warm trance that normally made me feel better about my life. This time I only got to see the aftermath of it all. The wobbly legs and the melted face.

She stumbled down the first few steps, clinching Mr. Whitaker's arm tight. Then she stopped and whispered something to him. He nodded and she took a deep breath and let go of his arm, and with the wind roaring and blowing hard, she slowly walked the rest of the way by herself. She wiped her eyes, but the tears kept coming as she went step by step, alone, to the car.

I looked at Lovey's face—plain, but still pretty. Her eyes filling with water because of both the wind and the funeral. Then I looked at the gift she got me. The Sempervivum, still small, just barely sprouting (if sprouting is what you call it), with so much life ahead of it. I thought of my mother, and felt the warm feeling again. Like the one I normally feel at the funerals, but it was different this time. It was for a different reason. I reached for Lovey's hand as we watched the cars start, smoke blowing from the exhaust pipes, kicking brown and orange and yellow leaves up. Robbie Ray was in the front car, and Mr. Ray was driving Ms. Watson in the second, both men hanging their neon FUNERAL tags on the rearview mirrors at the same time. Teenagers stood on the steps and watched, some lighting cigarettes, others slipping fingers behind their sunglasses to wipe hidden tears. And Lovey wrapped her fingers around mine, and we both squeezed tight.

ACKNOWLEDGMENTS

This is going to sound weird, but the only reason this book could be written at all is because my mother took me to a lot of funerals at a very young age. So . . . uh . . . thanks, Ma. And thank you to my Aunt Bud and Uncle Calvin, whose constant jokes (oftentimes about really hard things) flooded me with inspiration. This one is definitely for you both. My older sister, Dhimitri Gross, and my college homeboy, Christopher Smith, I appreciate you responding to the random calls and text messages about all the medical stuff. I mean, seriously, I totally get why you have to go to school to be a doctor. Nekeya O'Connor, thanks for the help with patois. Kia Dyson, thanks for pretty much being the muse for the character Love. And last, but surely not least, thank you to my awesome agent, Elena Giovanazzo (E Money), and my insanely talented editor, Caitlyn Dlouhy, for once again believing in me and my crazy tales.

THE BOY IN THE BLACK SUIT

BY JASON REYNOLDS

Discussion Questions

1. What happens to Matt in the exposition of the novel? Does this set the tone for the rest of the book? How are the students at school treating Matt? Are they treating him differently?

2. How do Matt's thoughts and actions demonstrate he is a conflicted character? How does the author let the reader know what he is thinking versus what he actually says?

3. How does Matt first meet Renee? What type of girl is Renee and how do you know?

4. Who is Mr. Ray? Discuss Mr. Ray's character. What conclusions can be drawn about Mr. Ray from the first few chapters in the novel?

5. The author specifically mentions the funerals for the elderly, as well as the funerals for teenagers that have passed through Willie Ray's doors. Discuss why the author would mention teenagers' funerals.

6. How does the use of slang words affect each character? Why would the author use slang from two different time periods?

7. Discuss when Mouse gets up to talk at the funeral. What is ironic about Mouse's character? What elements of his character make the irony comical?

8. Consider why Matt attends the funerals. What satisfaction does he receive from the funerals? What does his reaction indicate about his coping skills?

9. Why couldn't Matt make an omelet? How do you know? What is Matt struggling with?

10. What happened at Chris's house that made Matt and Chris go from good friends to best friends? How does disobeying Chris's mom affect them at the end of this chapter?

11. What happens in Chapter 3 that adds to the conflict in the novel? How will this episode affect Matt's character?

12. In Chapter 5, Chris says, "Because you were blowing me up like

something was wrong." What does he mean by this phrase? How do you know?

13. How does Matt feel toward Renee? How do you know? Why do you think Matt cares about what Chris thinks of her?

14. Matt has to decide whether or not he wants to go to school after his dad's accident. Would you go to school? What are the benefits of staying home versus going to school?

15. What effect does Mr. Ray's character have on the novel, overall? What is his role throughout the book?

16. Discuss why you think Mr. Ray takes Matt to his house. What is unexpected about Mr. Ray's house?

17. How are the men in the novel handling the pain of loss? What does this say about how society expects men to handle loss?

18. What does Mr. Ray compare the game of chess to? What reasons does he give? Do you agree?

19. Evaluate Matt and Chris's friendship. How do their characters defy the media's perspective of young black males? How are Chris and Matt alike? How are they different? How are they different from other kids in the hood?

20. Explain the ways in which Renee surprises Matt. Why couldn't Matt find what he was looking for with her?

21. Consider what impact the Cluck Bucket has on the neighborhood. What role does it play in the novel?

22. Discuss why you think Matt hates flowers? What could the flowers be symbolic of? What is ironic about the names of the two women Matt cares about: Love and Daisy?

23. Take a position on why Matt finally decides to go see his mother. Why does he go? How can Matt's visit help to build a resolution?

24. What does Matt decide to bring to Love's Thanksgiving? How does his decision make him feel closer to his mom? What does this gesture show about how Matt feels about Love?

25. Where does Love take Matt for Thanksgiving? How is this place very different from where he thought they were going to go? What does this say about Love's character?

26. Who is Candy Man? What game do Matt and Candy Man play when they meet? What does Matt find out about Candy Man? What type of irony is the author using in this scenario?

27. What makes Love mad on the car ride home? How does her

reaction affect Matt? What may happen to their relationship if they do not communicate again?

28. What connection does Matt have with Martin Gandry? How do you think Mr. Ray feels when Matt tells him he met Martin Gandry? Discuss whether or not Matt did the right thing by telling him.

29. Discuss Matt's relationship with Mr. Ray. How does the relationship they share bring a little closure into their lives for both of them?

30. Where do Love and Matt go on their first "real" date? What is ironic about their destination? What gift does Love give Matt? How does the gift help him? Is the gift symbolic?

This guide has been provided by Simon & Schuster for classroom, library, and reading group use. It may be reproduced in its entirety or excerpted for these purposes.

TURN THE PAGE
FOR A SNEAK PEEK AT
ALL AMERICAN BOYS

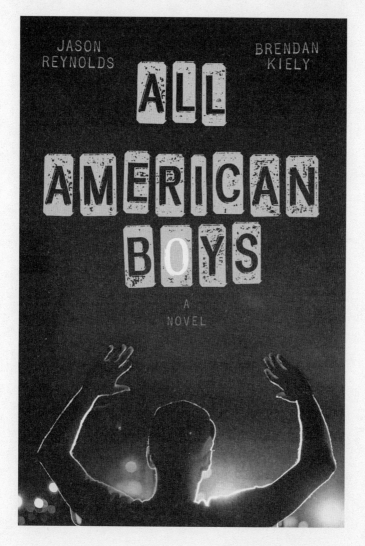

Your left! Your left! Your left-right-left! Your left! Your left! Your left-right-left!

Yeah, yeah, yeah.

I left. I left. I left-left-left that wack school and that even more wack ROTC drill team because it was Friday, which to me, and basically every other person on Earth, meant it was time to party. Okay, maybe not everybody on Earth. I'm sure there was a monk somewhere on a mountain who might've been thinking of something else. But I wasn't no monk. Thank God. So for me and my friends, Friday was just another word for party. Monday, Tuesday, Hump Day (because who can resist the word "hump"?), Thursday, and Party. Or as my brother, Spoony, used to say, "Poorty." And that's all I was thinking about as I crammed into a bathroom stall after school—partying, and how I wasn't wanting to be in that stiff-ass uniform another minute.

Thankfully, we didn't have to wear it every day. Only on Fridays, which was what they called "uniform days." Fridays. Of all days. Whose dumb idea was that? Anyway, I'd been wearing it since that morning—first bell is at 8:50 a.m.—for drill practice, which is pretty much just a whole bunch of yelling and marching, which is always a great experience right before sitting in class with thirty other students and a teacher either on the verge of tears or yelling for some other kid to head down to the principal's office. Fun.

Let me make something clear: I didn't need ROTC. I didn't want to be part of no military club. Not like it was terrible or anything. As a matter of fact, it was actually just like any other class, except it was Chief Killabrew—funniest last name ever—teaching us all about life skills and being a good person and stuff like that. Better than math, and if it wasn't for the drill crap and the uniform, it really would've just been an easy *A* to offset some of my *C*s, even though I know my pop was trying to use it as some sort of gateway into the military. Not gonna happen. I didn't need ROTC. But I did it, and I did it good, because my dad was pretty much making me. He's one of those dudes who feels like there's no better opportunity for a black boy in this country than to join the army. That's literally how he always put it. Word for word.

"Let me tell you something, son," he'd say, leaning in the doorway of my room. I'd be lying on my bed, doodling in my sketch pad, doing everything physically possible to not just stop drawing and jam the pencils into my ears. He'd continue, "Two weeks after I graduated from high school, my father came to me and said, 'The only people who are going to live in this house are people I'm making love to.'"

"I know, Dad," I'd moan, fully aware of what was coming next because he said it at least once a month. My father was the president of predictability, probably something he learned when he was in the army. Or a police officer. Yep, the old man went from a green uniform, which he wore only for four years—though he talks about the military like he put in twenty—to a blue uniform, which he also only wore for four years before quitting the force to work in an office doing whatever people do in offices: get paid to be bored.

"And I knew what he was trying to tell me: to get out," Dad would drone. "But I didn't know where I was going to go or what I was going to do. I didn't really do that well in school, and well, college just wasn't in the cards."

"And so you joined the army, and it saved your life," I'd finish the story for him, trying to water down my voice, take some of the sting out of it.

"Don't be smart," he'd say, pointing at me with the finger of fury. I never managed to take enough bite out of my tone.

And trust me, I knew not to push it too far. I was just so tired of hearing the same thing over and over again.

"I'm not trying to be smart," I'd reply, calming him down. "I'm just saying."

"Just saying what? You don't need discipline? You don't need to travel the world?"

"Dad—" I'd start, but he would shut me down and barrel on.

"You don't need a free education? You don't need to fight for your country? Huh?"

"Dad, I—" Again, he'd cut me off.

"What is it, Rashad? You don't wanna take after your father? Look around." His voice would lift way higher than necessary and he'd fling his arms all over the place temper-tantrum style, pointing to the walls and windows and pretty much everything else in my room. "I don't think I've done that bad. You and your brother have never had a care in the world!" Then came his favorite saying; it wouldn't have surprised me if he had it tattooed across his chest. "Listen to me. There's no better opportunity for a black boy in this country than to join the army."

"David." My mother's voice would come sweeping down the hallway with just enough spice in it to let the old man know that once again, he'd pushed too hard. "Leave him alone. He stays out of trouble and he's a decent student." *A decent student.* I could've had straight *A*s if I wasn't always so busy sketching and doodling. Some call it a distraction. I call it dedication. But hey, decent was . . . decent.

Then my father's face would soften, made mush by my mother's tone. "Look, can you just try it for me, Rashad? Just in high school. That's all I ask. I begged your brother to do it, and he needed it even more than you do. But he wouldn't listen, and now he's stuck working down at UPS." The way he said it was as if the lack of ROTC had a direct connection to why my older brother worked at UPS. As if only green and blue uniforms were okay, but brown ones meant failure.

"That's a good job. The boy takes care of himself, and him and his girlfriend have their own apartment. Plus he's got all that volunteer work he does with the boys at the rec center. So Spoony's fine," my mother argued. She pushed my father out of the way so she could share the space in the doorway. So I could see her. "And Rashad will be too." Dad shook his head and left the room.

That exact same conversation happened at least twenty times, just like that. So when I got to high school, I just did it. I joined ROTC. Really it's called JROTC, but nobody says the *J*. It stands for the Junior Reserve Officer Training Corps. I joined to get my dad off my back. To make him happy. Whatever.

The point is, it was Friday, "uniform day," and right after

the final bell rang I ran to the bathroom with my duffel bag full of clothes to change out of everything green.

Springfield Central High School bathrooms were never empty. There was always somebody in there at the mirror studying whatever facial hair was finally coming in, or sitting on a sink checking their cell phone, skipping class. And after school, especially on a Friday, everybody popped in to make sure plans hadn't been made without them knowing. The bathroom was pretty much like an extension of the locker room, where even the students like me, the ones with no athletic skill whatsoever, could come and talk about the same thing athletes talked about, without all the ass slapping—which, to me, made it an even better place to be.

"Whaddup, 'Shad?" said English Jones, making a way-too-romantic face in the mirror. Model face to the left. Model face to the right. Brush hairline with hand, then come down the face and trace the space where hopefully, one day, a mustache and beard will be. That's how you do it. Mirror-Looking 101, and English was a master at it. English was pretty much a master at everything. He was the stereotypical green-eyed pretty boy with parents who spoiled him, so he had fly clothes and tattoos. Plus his name—his real name—was English, so he pretty much had his pick when it came to the girls. It was like he was born to be the man. Like his parents planned it that way. But, unstereotypically, he wasn't cocky about it like you would think, which of course made the ladies and the teachers and the principal and the parents and even the basketball coach even more crazy about him. That's right, English was also on the basketball team. The captain. The best player. Because why the hell wouldn't he be?

"What's good, E?" I said, giving him the chin-up nod while pushing my way into a stall. English and I have been close since we were kids, even though he was a year older than me. We were two pieces of a three-piece meal. Shannon Pushcart was the third wing, and the fries—the extra-salty add-on—was Carlos Greene. Carlos and Shannon were also in the bathroom, both leaning into the urinals but looking back at me, which, by the way, is a weird thing to do. Don't ever look at someone else while you're taking a piss. Doesn't matter how well you know a person, it gets weird.

"You partying tonight at Jill's, soldier-boy?" Carlos asked, clowning me about the ROTC thing.

"Of course I'm going. What about you? Or you got basketball practice?" I asked from inside the stall. Then I quickly followed with, "Oh, that's right. You ain't make the team. Again."

"Ohhhhhhhhhhhh!" Shannon gassed the joke up like he always did whenever it wasn't about him. A urinal flushed and I knew it was him who flushed it, because Shannon was the only person who ever flushed the urinals. "I swear that's never gonna get old," Shannon said, laughter in his voice.

I unbuttoned my jacket—a polyester Christmas tree covered in ornaments—and threw it over the stall door.

"Whatever," Carlos said.

"Yeah, whatever," I shot back.

"Don't y'all ever get tired of cracking the same jokes on each other every day?" English's voice cut in.

"Don't you ever get tired of stroking your own face in the mirror, English?" Carlos clapped back.

Shannon spit-laughed. "Got 'im!"

"Shut up, Shan," English snapped. "And anyway, it's called 'stimulating the follicles.' But y'all wouldn't know nothin' about that."

"But E, seriously, it ain't workin'!" from Shannon.

"Yeah, maybe your follicles just ain't that into you!" Carlos came right behind him. By this point I was doubled over in the stall, laughing.

"But your girlfriend is," English said, with impeccable timing. A snuff shot, straight to the gut.

"Ohhhhhhhh!" Of course, from Shannon again.

"I don't even have no girlfriend," Carlos said. But that didn't matter. Cracking a joke about somebody's girlfriend— real or imaginary—is just a great comeback. At all times. It's just classic, like "your mother" jokes. Carlos sucked his teeth, then shook the joke off like a champ and continued, "That's why we gotta get to this party, so I can see what these ladies lookin' like."

"I'm with you on that one," English agreed. "Smartest thing you've said all day."

Off went the greenish-blue, short-sleeved, button-up shirt, which I also flung across the top of the door.

"Exactly. That's what I'm talkin' 'bout," Shannon said, way too eager. "'See what these ladies lookin' like,'" he mimicked Carlos, the slightest bit of sarcasm still in his voice. If I picked up on it, I knew Carlos did too.

"I can't tell you what they'll be lookin' like, but I can tell you who they won't be lookin' at . . . you!" Carlos razzed, still on get-back from Shannon being slick and for laughing at my basketball crack. It had been at least three minutes since I made that joke, and he was still holding on to it. So petty.

"Shut up, 'Los. Everybody in here know I got more game than you. In every way," Shannon replied, totally serious.

I kicked my foot up onto the toilet to untie my patent leather shoes. Just so you know, patent leather shoes should only be for men who are getting married. Nothing about patent leather says "war."

"Argue about all this at the party. Just make sure y'all there. It's supposed to be live," English said, the sound of his footsteps moving toward the door. He and Shannon didn't have mandatory basketball practice like usual, but were still going to the gym to shoot around because, well, that's what they did every day. For those guys, especially English, basketball was life. English knocked on my stall twice. "Look for me when you get there, dude."

"Bet."

"Later, 'Shad," from Shannon.

"Aight, 'Shad, hit me when you on your way over," Carlos called as the door closed behind them. Carlos grew up right down the street from me, and, like English, was a senior and therefore could drive, and therefore (again) was always my ride to the party. We smoked him with the jokes all the time because he'd tried out for the basketball team every single year, and got cut every single year, because he just wasn't very good. But if you asked him, he was the *nicest* dude to ever touch a ball. What he actually *was* good at, though, was art, which is also why he and I got along. He wasn't into drawing or painting, at least not in the traditional sense. He was into graffiti. A "writer." His tag was LOS(T), and they were all over the school, and our neighborhood, and even the East Side. Whenever we were heading to a party, for him it was just another opportunity to speed around the city in his clunker, the backseat covered in paint markers and spray cans, while he pointed out some of his masterpieces.

Really they were more like *our* masterpieces, because I was the one who gave him some of the concepts for where and how to write his tag. For instance, on the side of the neighborhood bank, I told him he should bomb it in money-green block letters. And on the door of the homeless shelter I suggested gold regal letters. And on the backboard of a basketball hoop at the West Side court, I suggested he write it in gang script. I never had the heart to do any actual tagging. I mentioned how my father was, right? Right. Plus Carlos was a pro at it. He knew how to control the nozzle and minimize the drip to get clean tags. Like, perfect. I never really told him, just because that wasn't something we did, but I loved them. All of them.

When I walked out of that stall a few minutes later, I was a different person. It was like the reverse of Clark Kent running into the phone booth and becoming Superman, and instead was like Superman running into the booth and becoming a hopefully much cooler Clark Kent, even though I guess Superman might've been more comfortable in the cape and tight-ass red underwear than an ROTC uniform. But not me. No cape (and for the record, no tight-ass red underwear). I stepped out as regular Rashad Butler: T-shirt, sneakers that I had to perform a quick spit-clean on, and jeans that I pulled up, then sagged down just low enough to complete the look.

My brother had given me this sweet leather jacket that he had outgrown, so I threw that on, and *bam!* I was ready for whatever Friday had in store for me. Hopefully, a little rub-a-dub on Tiffany Watts, the baddest girl in the eleventh grade. At least to me. Carlos always said she looked like a cartoon character. Like he could ever get her. A *cartoon character?* Really? Please. A cartoon character from my *dreams.*

But before I could get to Jill's and get all up on Tiffany, I had a few stops to make. It was still early, and I had a couple bucks, so I could get me some chips and a pack of gum to kill the chip-breath. Can't get girls with the dragon in your mouth. But other than that I was flat broke, and it was never cool to party without cash, just because you always had to have something for the pizza spot—Mother's Pizza—which everyone went to either after the party was over or when the party got shut down early, which happened most of the time. Plus, you had to have money to chip in for whoever's gas tank was going to be getting you to and from the party, like, for instance, Carlos. So I caught a bus over to the West Side to first pick up my snacks, then meet Spoony at UPS, just a few blocks from home, so he could spot me a twenty.

The bus took forever, like it always did on Fridays. Forever. So at Fourth Street, I got off and walked the last few blocks toward Jerry's Corner Mart, the day darkening around me—crazy how early it gets dark in the fall. Jerry's was pretty much the everything store. They sold it all. Incense, bomber jackets, beanies, snacks, beer, umbrellas, and whatever else you needed. It was named after some dude named Jerry, even though nobody named Jerry ever worked there. Jerry was probably some rich old white dude, chillin' on the East Side, doing his thing with some young supermodel with fake everything on a mattress made of real money. Lotto-ticket money. Cheap-forty-ounce money. Bootleg-DVD money. My money.

I pushed the door to Jerry's open. It chimed like it always did, and the guy behind the counter looked up like he always did, then stepped out from behind the counter, like he always did.

"Wassup, man," I said. He nodded suspiciously. Like he always did. There were only two other people in the store. A policeman and one other customer, back by the beer fridge. The cop wasn't a security guard, the weaponless kind with the iron-on badges. The kind my dad tried to get my brother to apply for because they pay decent money. Nah. This cop was a cop. A real cop. And that wasn't weird because Jerry's was pretty much known for being an easy come-up for a lot of people. You walk in, grab what you want, and walk out. No money spent. But I never stole nothing from anywhere. Again, too scared of what my pops would do to me. Knowing him, he'd probably send me right to military school or some kind of boot camp, like Scared Straight. He'd probably say something to my mother about how my problem is that I need more push-ups in my life. Luckily, I'm just not the stealing type. But I know a lot of people who are, and there was no better playground for a thief than Jerry's. I guess, though, after a string of hits, Jerry (whoever he is) finally decided to keep a cop on deck.

I bopped down the magazine aisle toward the back of the store, where the chips were. Right by the drinks. Grab your chips, then turn around and hit the fridge for a soda or a beer. Boom. I looked at the chip selection. Like I said, Jerry's had everything. All the stank-breath flavors. Barbecue, sour cream and onion, salt and vinegar, cheddar ranch, flaming hot, and I tried to figure out which would be the one that could be most easily beaten by a stick of gum. But plain wasn't an option. Seriously, who eats plain chips?

While I was trying to figure this out—decisions, decisions— the other person in the store, a white lady who looked like she'd left her office job early—navy-blue skirt, matching blazer, white sneakers—seemed to be dealing with the same dilemma, but with the beer right behind me. And I couldn't blame her. Jerry's had every kind of beer you could think of. At least it seemed that way to me. I didn't really pay her too much mind, though. I figured she was just somebody who probably had a long week at work, and wanted to crack a cold brew to get her weekend started. My mother did that sometimes. She'd pop the cap off a beer and pour it in a wineglass so she could feel better about all the burping, as if there's a classy way to belch. This lady looked like the type who would do something like that. The type of lady who would treat herself to beer and nachos when her kids were gone to their father's for the weekend.

Now, here's what happened. Pay attention.

I finally picked out my bag of chips—barbecue, tasty, and easily beatable by mint. That settled, I reached in my back pocket for my cell phone to let Spoony know I was on my way. Damn. Left it in my ROTC uniform. So I set my duffel bag on the floor, squatted down to unzip it, the bag of chips tucked under my arm. At the moment the duffel was open, the lady with the beer stepped backward, accidentally bumping me, knocking me off balance. Actually, she didn't really bump me. She tripped over me. I thrust one hand down on the floor to save myself from a nasty face-plant, sending the bag of chips up the aisle, while she toppled over, slowly, trying to catch her balance, but failing and falling half on me and half on the floor. The bottle she was holding shattered, sudsy beer splattering everywhere.

"Oh my God, I'm so sorry!" the lady cried.

And before I could get myself together, and tell her that it was okay and that I was okay, and to make sure she was okay, the guy who worked at Jerry's who everyone knew wasn't Jerry, shouted, "Hey!" making it clear things were not okay. At first, I thought he was yelling at the lady on some you-broke-it-you-bought-it mess, and I was about to tell him to chill out, but then I realized that he was looking at my open duffel and the bag of chips lying in the aisle. "Hey, what are you doing?"

"Me?" I put my finger to my chest, confused.

The cop perked up, slipping between me and the clerk to get a better look. But he wasn't looking at me at all. Not at first. He was looking at the lady, who was now on one knee dusting off her hands.

"Ma'am, are you okay?" the officer asked, concerned.

"Yes, yes, I'm—"

And before she could finish her sentence, the sentence that would've explained that she had tripped and fell over me, the cop cut her off. "Did he do something to you?"

Again, "Me?" What the hell was he talking about? I zipped my duffel bag halfway because I knew that I would have to leave the store very soon.

"No, no, I—" The lady was now standing, clearly perplexed by the question.

"Yeah, he was trying to steal those chips!" the clerk interrupted, shouting over the cop's shoulder. Then, fixing his scowl back on me, he said, "Isn't that right? Isn't that what you were trying to do? Isn't that what you put in your bag?"

Whaaaaa? What was going on? He was accusing me of things that hadn't even happened! Like, he couldn't have been talking to *me*. I wanted to turn around to check and make sure there wasn't some other kid standing behind me, stuffing chips in his backpack or something, but I knew there wasn't. I knew this asshole was talking to . . . at . . . about . . . me. It felt like some kind of bad prank.

"In my bag? Man, ain't nobody stealing nothing," I explained, getting back to my feet. My hands were already up, a reflex from seeing a cop coming toward me. I glanced over at the lady, who was now slowly moving away, toward the cookies and snack cake aisle. "I was just trying to get my phone out my bag when she fell over me—" I tried to explain, but the policeman shut me down quick.

"Shut up," he barked, coming closer.

"Wait, wait, I—"

"I said shut up!" he roared, now rushing me, grabbing me by the arm. "Did you not hear me? You deaf or something?" He led me toward the door while walkie-talkie-ing that he needed backup. Backup? For what? For who?

"No, you don't understand," I pleaded, unsure of what was

happening. "I have money right here!" With my free hand, I reached into my pocket to grab the dollar I had designated to pay for those stupid chips. But before I could even get my fingers on the money, the cop had me knotted up in a submission hold, my arms twisted behind me, pain searing up to my shoulders. He shoved me through the door and slammed me to the ground. Face-first. Hurt so bad the pain was a color—white, a crunching sound in my ear as bones in my nose cracked. After he slapped the cuffs on me, the metal cutting into my wrists, he yanked at my shirt and pants, searching me. I let out a wail, a sound that came from somewhere deep inside. One I had never made before, coming from a feeling I had never felt before.

My initial reaction to the terrible pain was to move. Not to try to escape, or resist, but just . . . move. It's like when you stub your toe. The first thing you do is throw yourself on the bed or jump around. It was that same reflex. I just needed to move to hopefully calm the pain. But moving wasn't a good idea because every time I flipped and flapped on the pavement, with every natural jerk, the cuffs seemed to tighten, and worse, I caught another blow. A fist in the kidney. A knee in the back. A forearm to the back of the neck.

"Oh, you wanna resist? *You wanna resist?*" the cop kept saying, pounding me. He asked as if he expected me to answer. But I couldn't. And if I could've, I would've told him that I didn't want to resist. Plus, I was already in cuffs. I was already . . . stuck. The people on the street watching, their faint murmurs of "Leave him alone" becoming white noise— they knew I didn't want to resist. I really, really didn't. I just wanted him to stop beating me. I just wanted to live. Each blow earthquaked my insides, crushing parts of me I had never seen, parts of me I never knew were there. "Fuckin' thugs can't just do what you're told. Need to learn how to respect authority. And I'm gonna teach you," he taunted, almost whispering in my ear.

There was blood pooling in my mouth—tasted like metal. There were tears pooling in my eyes. I could see someone looking at me, quickly fading into a watery blur. Everything was sideways. Wrong. My ears were clogged, plugged by the pressure. All I could make out was the washed-out grunts of the man leaning over me, hurting me, telling me to stop fighting, even though I wasn't fighting, and then the piercing sound of sirens pulling up.

My brain exploded into a million thoughts and only one thought at the same time—

please

don't

kill me.

Discover the gritty world of acclaimed author
E. R. FRANK.

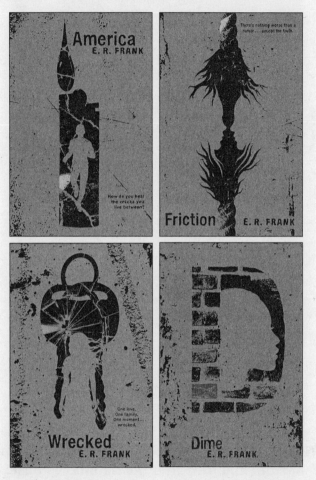

★"AN IMPORTANT WORK."—*School Library Journal* on ***Dime***, STARRED REVIEW

★"A WRENCHING TOUR DE FORCE."—*Kirkus Reviews* on ***America***, STARRED REVIEW

★"GRIPPING . . . UNSETTLING."—*Booklist* on ***Friction***, STARRED REVIEW

"COMPULSIVELY READABLE."—*School Library Journal* on ***Wrecked***

THE
GOSPEL
OF
WINTER

A NOVEL BY

BRENDAN
KIELY

**A fearless debut novel about the restorative power
of truth and love after the trauma of abuse.**

"Unflinching and redemptive."—Colum McCann,
New York Times bestselling author of the National
Book Award winner *Let the Great World Spin*

PRINT AND EBOOK EDITIONS AVAILABLE
From Margaret K. McElderry Books
TEEN.SimonandSchuster.com